Also by Steven Parlato
The Namesake

The Precious Dreadful

STEVEN PARLATO

Simon Pulse

New York London Toronto Sydney New Delhi

SIMON PULSE

An imprint of Simon & Schuster Children's Publishing Division
1230 Avenue of the Americas, New York, New York 10020
First Simon Pulse hardcover edition February 2018
Text copyright © 2018 by Steven Parlato
Jacket illustration copyright © 2018 by Getty Images/majivecka, Aerial3, malven57
For information about special discounts for bulk purchases, please contact Simon & Schuster
Special Sales at 1-866-506-1949 or business@simonandschuster.com.
The Simon & Schuster Speakers Bureau can bring authors to your live event.
For more information or to book an event contact the Simon & Schuster Speakers Bureau
at 1-866-248-3049 or visit our website at www.simonspeakers.com.
Jacket designed by Stephanie Hannus and Mike Rosamilia
Interior designed by Mike Rosamilia
The text of this book was set in Bell MT Std.
Manufactured in the United States of America
2 4 6 8 10 9 7 5 3 1
Library of Congress Cataloging-in-Publication Data
Names: Parlato, Steven, author.
Title: The Precious Dreadful / Steven Parlato.
Description: First Simon Pulse hardcover edition. | New York : Simon Pulse, 2018. |
Summary: A writing group triggers fifteen-year-old Teddi Adler's memories of her
lost childhood friend, Corey, causing her to question everything about her life, including
her feelings about two boys and the ghost-girl who will not leave her alone.
Identifiers: LCCN 2017024507 (print) | LCCN 2017038659 (eBook) |
ISBN 9781507202777 (hardcover) | ISBN 9781507202784 (eBook)
Subjects: | CYAC: Supernatural—Fiction. | Memory—Fiction. | Dating (Social customs)—
Fiction. | Loss (Psychology)—Fiction. | Alcoholism—Fiction. | Authorship—Fiction.
Classification: LCC PZ7.P24125 (eBook) | LCC PZ7.P24125 Pre 2018 (print) |
DDC [Fic]—dc23
LC record available at https://lccn.loc.gov/2017024507

*To Benjamin and Jillian,
for your strength, your insight,
your humor*

"There is a crack, a crack in everything.
That's how the light gets in."
—Leonard Cohen, "Anthem"

∿

"You have been my friend," replied Charlotte.
"That in itself is a tremendous thing."
—E. B. White, *Charlotte's Web*

1

I don't know if this is even my story to tell. Corey and I swore all those years ago we wouldn't ever. But it's starting to come out on its own now in all sorts of ways. So I'm kind of like, "F promises."

Besides, it's not as if we're friends anymore. I haven't even seen him since that summer we were seven.

And what's a childhood vow worth at practically sixteen? Nothing? Everything?

My brain does this warp-speed thing, especially when I think about telling. But I should start at the start. I'm Teddi Alder. Ordinary.

Everything about me is halfway. Five six, I'm stalled between jockey-little and catwalk-tall. Sophomore year ended yesterday, so I'm officially midway through the obstacle course called high school. I'm also half a virgin. So.

About the story, I could say it's a riddle wrapped in a mystery, some creature lurk-deep in the swamp of memory, but that's a little too Stephen King. A little too *Friday the 13th*, and it's not quite like that. Nope, not a horror story, not exactly. But horrible enough.

Shoot! My alarm's about to bleat. Not sure why I even bother to set the freaking thing anymore. I haven't slept a full night since I was about seven.

I slide through the curtains strung up in the doorway of my room. Polyester panels offer zero privacy, but at least they don't creak the way a door would. Silence helps me slip undetected through my mother's room to downstairs. No real challenge there. The woman slumbers deep as a dead thing.

I head to the bathroom for a quick whiz and parts-washing, drag a brush through my hair, swipe on deodorant, veto mascara. Snagging clothes draped on the bathroom door hook, I dress.

In the kitchen, Binks eyes me from stoveside. Tail beating half speed, he noses his squeak bone, gears up for a morning howl. Administering a preemptive ear scratch, I select a container from the cabinet. "Why can't you eat the dry stuff?" Peeling back the lid, I hold my breath, dump moist chunkage into his bowl, and say, "Filet mignon, my ass."

As he goes to town, I grab an apple from the basket on the counter. Bruised and a little mealy, but it'll do.

One hand on the broad, metal handle of the front door, I pick with my fingernail for the millionth time at the PLEASE COME AGAIN! sticker, a vestige—like the heavy glass door itself—of our apartment's former life as Mike's Mart, the Alder family store. Leaning back against the door, satchel shoulder-slung, I scan the kitchen, extra shabby in the slatted morning light.

"I hate it here."

Parting the ancient venetians, I peer across the driveway. The pool won't open for hours, so all's quiet; just Jimmy the Park Guy, spearing chip bags and assorted crap from the grass.

I step out, relishing the blast-furnace pulse on my face. Summer vacation has begun.

2

Today's slated to be another 90-plusser. God must be going for a record. I can't recall it being this hot as a kid. Then again, when I reflect on kidhood, I remember every summer the same: scorch-sticky, alive with insects. Limitless. At fif-nearly-sixteen, it's different. Now all I see are limits. But I thrive on heat.

Summer's my favorite. Partly because I have a late July birthday, but I also love the heaviness, that sense you could bite the air. The dusk-whirr of insects. Sparklers. And I'm not the type to moan about humidity frizzing my hair (that's why God invented bucket hats), especially since there's currently no particular boy to impress. So, my status as a demi-virgin appears secure. Which should make Brenda heave a brew-infused sigh of relief.

Brenda's my mother. Her greatest unspoken fear—though she speaks it loud and often—is that I'll follow her footsteps to the maternity ward before I hit eighteen. Bio-Dad was some stoner with a hyperactive groin.

I was almost one—right after Mom's high school

graduation—when he took off. Along with a lifelong habit and a memento named Teddi, Papa left a Dear Brenda card containing 200 bucks. Mom handed most of it over to Daddy's dealer, spent the next couple of months in a haze.

When the paternal grands booted us from their basement rec room, we landed in this apartment in the partially reno-ed Mike's Mart. Mom's folks let us live here, though they considered me proof of their daughter's failure. We never quite bonded. When they kicked it a few years back, we weren't exactly broken up. Always seemed like us against them.

When I was tiny, Mom taught me to call her Brenda, so people would think we were sisters. Now I mostly do it to annoy her, my not-too-subtle challenge to her authority. I've also given multiple assurances her life trajectory is not one I wish to emulate. But my very existence is a reminder of her questionable choices, so these declarations have little impact.

She now follows this unswerving schedule: Work. Drink. Snooze. Drink. Work. No illegal substances, at least. Booze is now her mood-altering agent of choice.

I opt for coffee.

I'm at Java Jill's, my town's chuckle in the face of corporate takeover. Those pink-and-orange coffee huts sprout like crabgrass on every corner, but JJ's continues to do a jamming business, in spite of the caffeine-homogenization of Everytown, USA. Willa and I have a dramatic personal impact on Jill's financial solvency; we subsist on their "Rockin' Shockin' Turbo Brew."

Solo today, I sip my jumbo iced, with amaretto syrup and double espresso shot, a frosted brownie on the side. Tastier than a caffeine drip.

Surprising there aren't more kids here, this being our first day on academic parole. Median customer age has to be about eighty. Dentures castanet-clack as the elders slurp hot coffee and gossip-swap.

I'm trying to decide what the day holds. The thing about summer freedom is the inertia. Given a span of unscheduled days and infinite possibility—small-town infinite—I'll end up lying in bed 'til noon, baking in the sun, doing nothing. And though summer is the season to veg, I've vowed this year will be different.

I'm craving change, and for once, I've decided to do something about it. The challenge is choosing. Downtown Players is holding auditions; this summer's classical, some Shakespeare romp. But the library's hosting SUMMERTEENS: A Youth Writing Intensive. I'm officially torn.

I'm not exactly aching for a summer stage return. I was a Lullaby Leaguer in a production of *The Wizard of Oz* when I was five; Corey was one of those Lollipop kids. But that was a lifetime ago.

Still, writing's too much work, especially after an essay-heavy school year. Sadly, these appear to be my best options. This town's no cultural cornucopia, and I've got to get occupied, if only to keep my mind from racing.

I've vowed not to waste summer crashed in bed. My default

setting—scoff and roll over—nearly kicked in this morning, so I've landed at JJ's first thing, hoping caffeine plus change of scene might equal motivation.

There is also the ARG Factor.

As I said before, there's "no particular boy," but that's no reason not to dream. Aidan Robert Graham just finished junior year at my school. Generously muscled, he's intense, but with a swoony, white grin and precise stubble dispersal—a dusting across the chin, a shadow above his upper lip. Best to forget those lips. He is, after all, mere feet away, wearing a mug-shaped button that reads TRY ME!

Aidan and I have a passing acquaintance. Translation: I'm fine with the fact that he just called me "Terry" while serving my beverage.

All right, I'll admit to a level of interest beyond passing. We've small-talked here and in study hall. And we shared a bleacher—and meaningful eye rolls—during spring assembly. Though not soul baring, these interactions prove Aidan *is* aware of my existence.

But it's decision time. Theater or writing? Library or community center? I'm about to choose the way I make all important decisions, with a coin toss, when I'm interrupted by the arrival of brooding muscle. Mr. Delicious stands beside me.

Determined to appear unruffled, I study Washington's profile, eyes affixed to the quarter in my palm.

Aidan knuckle-taps my tabletop. Treating me to that blinding smile, he says, "Hey. I'd ask if you come here often, but we both know you're here practically as much as me. Mind if I sit, Terr?"

He's getting warmer. If he'd shave a couple more letters, he'd be set. I could learn to answer to "Te."

Not waiting for my reply, he slides onto a chair, planting elbows on the table.

"Where's your friend?"

"Willa? I'm guessing in bed. I'll tell her you asked."

"God, no. Don't encourage her." He tilts back his chair. "This way we can talk without her gawking."

I swish my coffee, suppressing a blush.

"Summer plans?"

"Funny. I was just having a passionate internal debate on that exact topic."

"What do your folks say?"

"That'd be folk. Singular. Just my mom, Brenda."

"Lucky you."

"Lucky?"

"Yeah, half the surveillance, half the expectations. My parents demand nothing short of perfection."

"Well . . . that shouldn't be a problem for you."

His chair legs drop. Eyes clouding, he drums the table and says, "My father's quick to point out I'm far from perfect."

Unsure how to respond, I feel guilty noticing he even frets handsomely.

Finally, he says, "So, your parents are split?"

"Not exactly. It's been just Brenda and me as long as I can remember. My bio-dad was sort of perma-fried, took off when I was a baby. But I did have a pseudo-dad for a while."

"Pseudo?"

"Peter was rehearsal pianist for this production of *The Wizard of Oz* when I was a kid. Not sure what he saw in Brenda, but they were happy for a while."

Aidan thumbs through the sugar packets.

"Sorry. I don't know why I'm telling you this."

"Maybe you need to."

"Maybe . . . They were even engaged, 'til Brenda botched it. Papa Sperm returned when I was six. The allure of 'true love' proved too strong for my mother. She broke Peter's heart. And mine. He moved out of state. I hear from him at Christmas."

"That's rough."

"Worst of all, when Mister Soulmate left after a week, he took my Dora DVD player, my state quarter collection, and Mom's engagement ring. He also pocketed whatever self-esteem she had socked away."

"Wow."

"Oh, God. Did I seriously just spew childhood humiliation all over you?"

Nodding, Aidan says, "Clean up at table three."

"Okay, quick change of subject."

"You working?"

"No." I blush—*Damn!*

"How're you going to afford a new DVD player?"

"Very funny. I won't be sixteen 'til the end of July, so . . ."

"A baby, huh?"

"Hardly. But with no summer job, I'm trying to decide whether to try out for the play. Or join a writing group at the library."

"Writing in summer? No way. You should definitely audition. It's a cool group. I used to be involved. Kissed a few leading ladies in my day."

"I'll bet. So are you auditioning?"

"Nah, too busy. No time to memorize all those lines. But I could totally picture you in that play. I heard they're doing *Twelfth Night*. You'd kill as Miranda."

I almost correct him—Miranda's from *The Tempest*—decide it doesn't matter when he's not even certain of *my* name. "Seriously?"

"Yeah, you should audition with that Papa Sperm story. It'd be memorable, for sure."

"Oh."

"And Miranda goes undercover as a guy, doesn't she? With the right lighting, you could be a convincing dude."

"Excuse me?"

"Wait. I just meant . . . it's . . . you're not into the whole hair and makeup thing. Most girls would get all iced before coming to see me. But not you. That's . . . gutsy. Real, y'know?"

Heat rising in my cheeks, I regret my careless morning

prep. "Wait. You thought I came to see *you*? I'm just here for coffee."

"If you say so." His wink is less than charming. "In that case, can I get you a refill?"

"No. Thank you. And, Aidan?"

"Yeah?"

"My name is Teddi. NOT Terri. T-E-D-D-I. TEH-dee!"

He shrugs. "Anyway, I'd definitely cast you. You should audition. TEH-dee."

"Awesome, thanks."

"No prob. Sure you won't take a refill?" With the marker from his apron pocket, he crosses out TERRY, writes TEDDI on my cup, and says, "My treat. For luck."

"I'm all set." Snatching the cup, I dump it in the trash. Then, as he heads behind the counter, I say, "Viola!"

An old lady in the next booth drops her bear claw and stammers, "Y-Yes?"

Striding toward Aidan, I repeat, "Viola. The character in *Twelfth Night* is Viola. Not Miranda." Enunciating, I finger-jab his left pec on each syllable: "Vi!"—poke—"Oh!"—poke— "La!"—poke. I won't lie; I can't help admiring how his chest stands up to the pressure.

Without another word, I tromp out of JJ's. Decision made, I hook a hard left toward the library. SUMMERTEENS, here I come.

3

Honestly, this place has always skeeved me. Head down, I cross Literate Green, the park that rings the library. Bordered by overgrown azaleas, it might've been charming last century; now, it's Drug & Thug Central. On warm evenings, you can stroll at your own risk through a field of discarded panties, liquor bottles, and syringes. Brenda probably hung here, back when.

Downtown Players offers a free matinee at the library band shell every August. Willa and I went once. The audience rewarded their labors with swearing and periodic cigar-butt flinging. Yet another reason not to audition.

An adjective reverbs in my head as I pass through the automatic door: *grim*. Sure, cozy spaces abound: cubby-style workstations; a large oak table with brass lamps; cushy, threadbare chairs for reading. The kid's department flaunts colorful cutouts—beach balls, suns—courtesy of the slave labor of Hopeville Elementary.

Plus, if this paper-plastered community arts board is for

real, they've got a lively roster on tap: poets, local actors. According to one flyer, a Scandinavian crochet master's scheduled. The accompanying headshot—mongo cleavage—borders on lingerie catalog photo. Kid art and alluring speaker pic aside, the overall effect remains cheerless.

Sure, I'm an avid reader, but I don't come here unless it's a necessity. I tend toward Hale's, the indie bookstore across the street, with their gluten-free, vegan cupcakes and Live Jazz Saturdays. Occasionally, I'll hit the mega-chain bookstore/café/office supply/music/toy and hobby/literary-licensed trinket hub next to Foundry Hill Commons, our mall.

According to the SUMMERTEENS flyer, the writers' group meets in L718, but there's no indication where that is. Nice way to perpetuate info desk job security. I walk over and "Ahem" to the least bookish library employee ever.

He springs up, a spooked herd animal, his camouflage an eclectic style fusion: Urban Care Bear T-shirt, pierced eyebrow, pea-green asymmetrical buzz. Demeanor more jarring than ensemble, he's no docile grazer. He leaches aggression. As he rears to full height, I notice his name tag. Unsettling, it says JOY.

I think better of calling him that, or of drawing attention to the tag. Maybe Joy's short for something super manly, maybe it's a mix-up. Ironic commentary on his disposition? Whatever. Not my business. I squelch the urge to chew my thumbnail—my go-to tension habit. Instead, I take a deep breath and, feeling like a billy goat addressing the bridge troll, I begin.

"Hi. I need some information."

He scowls. Not my day for meaningful intergender communication.

"So. I guess you get that a lot." I fake laugh.

Cricket. Cricket.

"Oh. Was that supposed to be a joke?" He yawns, covers his mouth with a tattooed paw.

"No, not really. I . . . I'm here for the teen writing program."

Fully disregarding me, the troll pretend-examines some papers. I wait. He organizes the pens in the Snoopy mug on his desk. I wait. Completing a respectable 200-count as he thumbs a copy of *Library Today!*, I repeat, "Yup, SUMMERTEENS Writers. That's what I'm here for."

With a constipated smile, he says, "Well, you're about thirty-two hours early."

Glancing at the big clock above him—it's 10:04—I do some quick head-math. "Okay, so tomorrow at . . . six p.m. Got it. But you haven't told me where. And before you say 'L718,' I've got the room number. Your job is to tell me where the room is."

"Oh, so you really *are* using me for my information. I thought we were more than that."

The guy's brutally deadpan, but I detect a smile behind the challenge. Deciding turnabout aggression is fair play, I half-cheek it on his desk and say, "We so could be."

He does a reflexive *You-shitting-me?* double take. Then he stutters, "Uh, s-sorry, I'm spoken for."

"Your loss. But for reals, Joy, where the heck is L718?"

He looks puzzled; then, glancing at the name tag, he says, "Ha, Joy! That's not my name. I wear whatever tag's handy. It's a privacy thing. With our lineup of unpleasant patrons, I never use my actual name. Yesterday I was Wendell."

I don't mention that so far *he's* the most unpleasant person I've encountered in the library. Instead, I say, "Well, you'll always be Joy to me." Then I risk asking, "But what is your real name? Or do I qualify as one of the Unpleasants?"

He says, "Look, you seem nice, but I really do have a girl-friend. Her name's Glade."

"And I really do just want to find L718."

"Follow me."

Standing again, he's less imposing, actually pretty skinny. Sans hostility, he seems younger, too, a bit older than me. And this time, his smile's not constipated at all. It lights his hazel eyes.

Still, I hang back 'til he stage-whispers, "Come on," and trots down the steps. Following, I avoid touching the railing, which looks as if its last wipe-down was pre-Clinton era.

He says, "Watch your step," pointing toward loose vinyl stair covers. Sliding the last length of rail, he lands, high-tops thudding. I join him in the dim, fluorescent-jittery hallway.

Trailing, I ask, "How long you worked here? Or am I get-ting too personal?"

"I started volunteering freshman year for community ser-vice credit, decided it was cool. They hired me when I turned sixteen. This'll be my final stint before heading to school in the fall. Not a bad summer gig. Pays better than drive-thru duty, and they have great events."

"Scandinavian crochet?"

"Uh, no way. Not that one." He smirks. "I'm more into Bolivian tatting."

At a loss for a textile-based comeback, I watch as he slips into a room marked EMPLOYEES ONLY. Ignoring exclusivity— the lounge is as grimy as the rest of this place—I follow.

Bank of smeary cabinets above a far-past-stainless sink. Counter piled with books, vinyl records. Heaped dish rack: mugs, plastic utensils, Tupperware. Alongside, a goldenrod fridge crowned with *National Geographics.* A Formica table and castoff chairs waiting dead center.

Joy roots briefly in a sink-side drawer. "Crap. No keys. Ah well, best laid plans."

Heading to the hallway, he leads me past a towering oak-and-glass bookcase. Just beyond, he points toward a metal door with a brass plaque. Bingo: L718. SUMMERTEENS HQ.

"It's locked, but you can take a peek."

I lean past him; disregarding the musty smell, I press my cheek to narrow glass, surveying shadows. The room fits the rest of the library, shabby minus chic. More mismatched seating, of the folding variety, plus basement-rec-room-quality uphol-stered chairs. A lopsided plaid sofa. Decrepit school desks.

"Inviting."

"It's not five-star, but creative mojo's what counts, and they say this place oozes mojo."

"It's oozing more than that." I gesture to a vaguely human-shaped ceiling stain.

We "eeeewww" in unison.

Ending a prolonged pause, I say, "So, you never did tell me your real name."

"Why don't we wait 'til tomorrow, introduce ourselves officially in group?"

"Um . . . what?"

"The writers' group, remember? The reason we're down here."

"I get it. I just didn't expect you'd be part of it."

"Is that a problem?"

"Course not. Just a surprise."

"Well, I hope it's not an unpleasant one."

"We'll see."

With that, I follow Joy the Troll upstairs to register for my SUMMERTEENS adventure.

4

Sylvan Park is a rainforest tonight, temp hovering mid-80s, the air alive with night sounds: frogsong, crickets, intermittent yowls from some distant cat tryst. Binks snuffles maniacally through damp grass as we crest the hill on midnight poop maneuvers.

Brenda may not be home for hours. On night maintenance at the community college—mopping, wiping whiteboards—she generally hits Spanky's for a few brews with her coworkers, Mandy and Dev, after clocking out.

Plagued with reluctant rectum, Binks does his "urgency dance," trotting, whirling. Mid-squat, he stops—I swear, he shrugs—and drags me several yards for another attempt.

I don't mind. I love roaming on nights like this. Admittedly, not the safest pastime, but I've got my mace-blaster flashlight and my cell in case any weirdoes emerge from the leafy dark.

Sylvan sprawls a mile-plus long, at least a half-mile wide, with a ball field, playground, and a wooded section with a series of ponds, in addition to the pool. Dense trees frame the park on three sides, and our street, with the rather obvious name, Parkview, borders the fourth.

We live just past the pool house, the perfect locale back when our building was a store. There was a snack bar with umbrella-ed tables in the driveway. Brenda remembers working there as a kid, spending summers reeking of fryer oil.

The store and snack bar are long gone, but swimmers still mob the pool from Memorial to Labor Day. Corey and I swam there when we were little. Until he moved. It was no fun going alone. These days if the lifeguards are especially chiseled, I'll take a book, pretend-read, and scope them out. Rarely do I dip more than ankle-deep, even on the hottest days.

Not a big swimmer. It's not fear, exactly, but ever since I slept over at Willa's at nine and her older brother forced us to watch *Jaws*, well, sometimes, even in a pool, I end up searching the water, scouting fins. Never underestimate the effect of a giant neoprene fish on an impressionable, young mind.

Pool season changes our neighborhood. It's normally dull, a commercial/residential mix, but hot weather brings an influx, rowdy pool-goers who park in our driveway and parade their oiled flesh. June through August, the calliope tunes of Mister Melty's truck are inescapable.

Every summer we call the cops about a hundred times. There are constant daytime fights; at night, kids climb the chain link, or savage it with bolt cutters, and sneak in to swim.

Nothing tonight. Cops did a sweep earlier, loaded a noisy

bunch into their patrol van. An arrest usually translates to a peaceful night or two.

"Any luck, buddy?"

Binks plants himself in the grass, glowers like I've insulted him. Then he rolls belly up for a scratch. The damp delivers a welcome chill as I sit and strum his wooly ribs. Stretching, I squint at weak city stars, just visible through humid haze.

My mind spins through thoughts of Aidan's Miranda remark, Joy smiling. Why am I nervous about this writing group? Just a dumb summer activity. To stay busy.

Rolling onto my side, I gaze down the bank at the pool.

The spotlight paints the surface, illuminating each ripple. The filter purrs. Water like undulating glass, so clean I can read depth marks on the bottom even from this distance. Almost looks inviting, makes me wish for my own bolt cutters. Then, several years of sleepless nights crashing down, I close my eyes. Picturing Aidan with Joy's green hair, I smile.

Binks nudges me alert, his nose to my chin.

"Ah, Binksy, what am I going to do with you?"

He stares intently, sad cockapoo eyes seeming to reply, *Keep me.* Then, sitting at attention, he growls low and bolts for the woods, leash snapping free.

"Shit, Binks! Get back here!" Last time he ran off, we suffered skunk stink for a week.

As I jump up to chase him, my sneaker skids. I yelp, airborne. Slamming flat, my head whiplashes, whams against a grass-sunk stone. Teeth clacking, the wind *oofs* out of me. Lying stunned, I try to find my breath.

Whether from the damp ground, or my shock at falling, I shudder. Goose bumps rise. The frog symphony abruptly cuts off. Noiseless, the one sound's internal, this seashell shush in my ears. How hard did I whomp my head? Slipping my hand up under my nape, I run fingers through the waves there. No blood. Small favors.

I breathe deep to shake this peculiar dread.

When I hear it—*Splishoosh*—I sit up quick, suffer a dizzy disconnect. Sparks flick the edge of my vision. Squinting, I face the pool. Nothing. Then . . .

A small figure, thigh-deep on the stairs. I don't consider how a child got in the pool, but the kid's too young to be there alone. In the middle of the night. When I call, "Hey!" the kid turns toward me. Though I can't see features, I sense a smile, the slope of the head somehow familiar.

"Corey?" *Can't be.*

Rushing the fence, I yell, "You shouldn't be in there! Where's your mom?"

No answer, just a tinkling laugh.

Remembering my flashlight, I push it through the fence gap, catch the tiny form in its beam. Hands lift, shielding the face. Flimsy sundress, tangled hair, a daisy pendant draped against her chest. Giggling again, she slips beneath the surface.

The spotlight doesn't reach this end. I can just trace the

trickle trail as small feet flutter-kick to the far side. Minutes lumber. I pace the fence. Then, wedging my sneaker through the taut grid, I raise my body a few feet to see into the water. No sign of her. Rattled, I drop to the grass and race along the fence, yelling "Little girl!"

No response. No head breaking the surface. Yanking off my sneakers, I mount the fence. Halfway up, I hear my name. Tightening my hold on the chain link, I swing my head around to find Aidan on the grass.

Grasping my calf, he looks like he's spotted some exotic animal, perhaps an alien—rather than an everyday crazy person—dangling above. Extra reasonable, he asks, "What are you doing?"

Jerking my leg free, I strain toward the top rail, and shout, "There's a kid in the water!"

"Seriously? Shit!"

The fence sways, nearly jolting me off, as Aidan rises. Joining him, I'm unsure how to make it past the barbs. Jamming the toe of his left sneaker through the fence, he steadies, swings his right leg over. Straddling the top, he stands, as if riding a unicycle. Gripping the top bar, he does a shaky handstand and vaults over. He hangs for a moment before dropping to the deck, sneakers slapping cement.

I follow his lead, swinging one leg over the fence, but, attempting to clear the points, I slip. Screeching, I lose balance, spiked metal jabbing my thigh as I fall. Luckily, my cutoffs snag on the barbs, and I'm suspended—upside down. Hearing my squeal, Aidan turns to help, but I shout, "I'm okay! Find her!"

Depositing wallet and phone on the deck, doing a quick visual sweep, he dives. I track his underwater progress, his body eerily elongated against glowing turquoise.

I do a mid-air crunch. Clutching the fence again, I wrench free, tearing a strip from my shorts. Hardly aware of the pain as my bare feet smack the deck, I run, training my flashlight on the shallows.

Beam skimming the murk, I search for signs of a submerged child. Nothing. Thinking she may have slipped from the pool during our frenzied climb, I sprint the perimeter, beam bouncing. There'd be tracks if she'd left the water, so I fan my light across the deck. Dry. Except for a small puddle from Aidan's splash.

Surfacing mid-pool, he strokes to the ladder, hoists onto the deck. Doglike, shaking water from his hair, he bounces, unblocking his ears. Striding from the pool edge, he says, "There's no one in the water."

"But . . . I saw her."

On the edge of anger, he asks, "Was this some frigging joke?"

When I don't answer, he stomps past me, pissed. Bending to retrieve his phone and wallet, he grumbles about losing his contacts in the pool. Then, without looking at me, he says, "Can you make it back over on your own?"

I stay silent, and he turns toward me.

He can tell from how I stand, tears filling my eyes, this is no prank. Tension in his jaw easing, he approaches.

Taking my hands, he asks, "Teddi, are you all right?"

"I'm sorry about your contacts. But I saw something, Aidan." Inhaling deeply, I add, "Honest to God, I did."

"Right."

Shivering despite the muggy night, I step toward the pool. Unsure why my next question feels so important, I ask, "Do you believe me?"

"Well," he hedges, "I believe *you believe* you saw something."

"Which translates roughly to 'let's not upset the crazy girl.' Right?"

"Not exactly."

"Well, what then?"

"Isn't it possible you just *thought* you saw someone? Like a . . . mirage. It was pretty dark."

"Great theory, but we're not in the desert, it wasn't a palm tree, and I'm not in the habit of hallucinating mischievous children in peril."

"Look, I won't pretend to have a better explanation. But if a kid *was* in the pool, she must've dissolved."

"We should call 911."

"And say what? We saw an evil night creature?"

"I never said she was evil."

"What then, an apparition? A mergirl? We'd just score a ride in the back of a cruiser."

He's probably right, but I know what I saw.

"So that's it?"

"For now. Look, Teddi, all I'm saying is tomorrow, in the bright of day, things might make better sense."

It's already starting to seem unreal. Could I have imagined it? Could the little girl be some kind of insomniac delusion? A result of the bump to my head?

"You must think I'm a total nut."

He shakes his head no.

"What then?"

"You're brave, Teddi. The way you went over that fence—"

"I don't feel brave. I feel stupid."

One hand on my shoulder, he brushes the hair from my eyes and says, "Don't."

"What?"

"Put yourself down."

"Why not?"

"You're pretty fierce, Teddi."

"Aidan, what were you doing in the park, anyway?"

He doesn't answer. Instead, leaning closer, he cups my chin with his right hand, lifts my mouth toward his.

I barely have a chance to process the kiss—soft, mildly chlorinated—when I hear a familiar, low jingle, a license plus vet tag *ting-ting*, followed by harsh panting. Binks skids, stopping short of the fence. Black lips rippling, he launches against chain link.

"Yikes! Talk about evil creatures! Who do you suppose owns this little fucker?"

"Um, that'd be me."

"Oops."

Laughing, I kneel and, fingers through the fence, tousle Binks's fluffy bangs. He calms. I'm about to stand when I notice it: a painted daisy pendant dangles, clinking gently against chain link. Afraid to touch it, I force myself to twist it free and slip it into my pocket. Somehow, I'm sure it's best not to show it to Aidan.

As he walks me home, I say, "You never did tell me what you were doing in the park."

He hesitates. "Just taking a shortcut home."

"From?"

"My girlfriend's house." Breaking into a grin, he says, "I'm busting you, Teddi. I was just out wandering. Thinking."

We cross my driveway in silence. It's shattered by Binks's wailing when I shove him inside. As we move toward a genuine lip link beneath my outside light, a moth invades Aidan's ear.

He fidgets like a little boy as I remove the fluttering intruder. Then, smiling, he says, "Well, this was . . . unusual."

"But nice?"

Leaning against my building, he says, "I don't suppose you'd invite me in? You know, for a closer look at my ear."

"Bad idea. Enticing as I find your ear, my mother will be home soon, and—"

"It's okay, Teddi." Wrapping me in a quick hug, he says, "It's pretty late, anyhow."

When I say, "See you around?" he makes an X over his heart and answers, "Count on it."

5

I've barely made it inside, can still see Aidan heading down Cedar, when a single headlight plays across the multi-bay garage behind our place.

Spying through the blinds, I watch Dev's cycloptic Saturn rumble up the drive, burping smoke from tailpipe and passenger window. God, I hate when Brenda smokes! Of course, she denies it, claims I'm smelling Mandy's secondhand.

I debate dashing to my room, playing possum, but it's not as if I'm a kid caught past curfew. Instead, I open the fridge, grab the nine-grain, some ham and Swiss, the mayo jar. It's a given she hasn't eaten anything beyond stale popcorn, a couple hot wings, and it's my job to keep some meat on her bones.

Binks stands sentinel by the door. You'd expect he'd arf himself silly, but he's used to the noisy drop-off signaling Brenda's arrival. Dashing past me, he snags a favorite squeak toy, Cinnamon Girl, and flies back to his post. In quizzical pup mode—head cocked, eyes twinkling—he chomps his plush girlfriend with anticipation.

I can gauge Brenda's condition based on her struggle inserting key into lock. Tonight it takes three instances of key-chain hitting asphalt, and a stream of PG-13 language, before she gains entry.

I make no move to intervene. She gets pissed if I offer help, says the implication is she's incompetent. I'd go beyond implying. Besides, the correct term is *shitfaced.*

Once she's in and sunk into the living room chair, I approach, sandwich in hand. I always lead with food. Though she initially balks, I can usually get her to eat at least half a sandwich. As she does, I unlace her sneakers and ask about her night.

Her mood is decent, sadly owing to the fact that she got "those elevator doors gleaming." But who am I to judge her accomplishments? I mean, what have I done lately—other than possibly hallucinate a child in peril and, oh yeah, potentially score a hunk? Hmm, not bad.

Speaking of hunks, I commit to sharing my Aidan news. I doubt Brenda will greet my proclamation with enthusiasm, but coming clean is preferable to creeping around. Besides, the whole boy talk thing is supposedly crucial to the mother/daughter dynamic.

Sitting next to her on the chair arm, I adjust my mental posture, straightening inwardly, preparing for her reaction. I just get out the words, "So, I've got someth—" when Brenda's features do this stuttery jig, her eyes spilling tears.

It'd be alarming except I'm used to her moods. She can go from chuckle to despair in a wink; life with her is a nonstop ride on the Emo-Go-Round.

"Oh, Brenda." I pat her shoulder in a "there, there" gesture that succeeds in making her bawl harder. Binks huffs; appalled by sloppy melodrama, he slouches kitchenward.

Contributing a huff of my own, I ask, "What is it?"

"Oh, Teddi." She mashes my cheeks in a fish-face squinch. "You deserve better than this!"

Banking on sarcasm as mood enhancer, I reply, "Well, duh. You're not just figuring that out?"

Her eyes puddle again, the tears joined by a thin drizzle from her left nostril. My humor's a total fail. Momma has officially entered the Cave of Sorrows.

"I'm so lonely, Teddi. It's obvious Dev's not interested in me, beyond work buddy. I caught him kissing Mandy in the adjunct copy room tonight." She cracks her knuckles. "I've been thinking a lot about Peter."

I strive to formulate a response that's not blatantly unkind. Failing to produce one, I zip it, letting her slip neck-deep into regret. Part of me—I'm ashamed to admit it's a large one—thinks she deserves it.

Still, she's my mother, so, priming my sympathy pump, I eke out a cupful of compassion. Hand on her back, I say, "It'll be okay, Mom. I'm here."

Stifling a teary burp, Brenda snatches a fist of tissues from the coffee table, honks into it, wipes her eyes. Then, announcing how "freaking pointless all this is," she unleashes a lament over the details of her cursed love life. I stop her when she strays onto sexual frustration terrain. Sex is a topic best left untackled by Brenda and me.

She eventually settles down/sobers up sufficiently to recognize me as more than a giant ear. Finishing her sandwich, she smiles, blots her mouth, and says, "That hit the spot, Teddi. So. Sorry for steamrolling you. How was your day?"

I toy with "Good" or "Nothing new," but stick with the plan to share my romantic dispatch. Foolish choice, especially when she's spent the last forty minutes bemoaning her own relationship woes.

"I met a guy."

The minute I say it, I wish I hadn't. Before I can continue, Brenda cuts in with a four-word interrogative: "Are you shitting me?"

"Technically we didn't just meet. I know him a little from school."

Ratcheting up the hostility, she repeats, "Teddi, I said, 'Are you *fucking* shitting me?'"

Delicate flower, my mom.

Though impossible to laugh it off at this point, I can never forego a last shot at humor. I say, "Oh, Mother, you're making Binks blush."

"I'll tell you one thing! I forbid you to see this boy, whoever he is!" Standing, she wings her sneakers toward the front closet. Binks springs up from his bed and yips.

Screaming, "Shut up, Binks!" she storms into the bathroom, slams the door, runs the exhaust fan.

I may not have inherited her lack of discernment or affinity for mind-altering substances, but Brenda and I share a more-than-passing resemblance when it comes to temper. Pounding the door, I yell, "His name is Aidan. He works at JJ's, but I find it pretty frickin' hilarious, you even imagining you have a say in this!"

Barely muffled by the buzzing fan, she shouts, "I'm trying to protect you, you dumbass!"

"I don't need your protection. I have better judgment than you ever will, with or without your perpetual beer fog. And Aidan happens to be amazing. He vaulted over the pool fence tonight to save a little girl!"

After a protracted pause, during which I hear her pee and brush her teeth, she emerges. She's also managed to morph her features into those of a reasonable human. She regards me with mild eyes, no hint of anger.

Considering her mood shift an invitation, I risk continuing. "He's a good guy, Mom."

"I don't care if he took a bullet for you, Teddi. I am your mother, and I say you're not ready to date. Case closed."

I watch in disbelief as she heads upstairs. When she hits the top step, I shout, "I'm nearly sixteen! You're okay granting me adult status when it comes to managing things around here. I've been running this place since I was twelve. But any time I mention boys, you go ballistic. Can we just have a normal conversation for once?"

"Well, if I'm recalling correctly, the last time you were interested in a boy, things didn't go so smoothly."

"Oh. My. God. Are you kidding me? We were just talking, Mom. And Ryan barely touched me. For the millionth time, it was not necessary to call the cops."

"He was five years older than you, Teddi. And since when is it necessary to remove clothing to have a conversation? You realize I could have pressed charges, right?"

Since she's rolled out the heavy artillery, I follow suit. "What you've conveniently forgotten is I never would have met Ryan Hecht if not for you."

Even from the bottom of the stairs, I see her swallow hard, as if I've backhanded her. This is treacherous territory, but I'm past caring.

"Teddi, don't." It's plea more than command; the weakness in her voice makes me go for the kill.

"I'd have had no reason to be at an Alateen meeting if not for your lousy parenting."

Curious fact about the Alder women and deliberate cruelty: rather than deflating, it has the power to inflame us. Brenda's on me before I can blink. She blows down those stairs like something out of a Japanese horror flick.

But then—due to latent maternal instinct, or Binks's frantic yapping—she stops short of cuffing me. Instead, smoothing the hair from my forehead, voice flat, she says, "My issues may have led you to that meeting, but it wasn't me who got you in the backseat of that boy's car. That was your choice, Teddi. And it makes me question whether you'll ever be anything but a worthless slut like your mother."

With that, she turns and heads back up to her room. Binks glowers as if to say, *That last bit was totally uncalled for.*

6

I had no desire to sneak through Brenda's room after our verbal throw down, so I parked it here on the couch. Insomnia's a given. Between Phantom Swimmer, Moth Invader, and Brenda Battle—not to mention Boyfriend?—my mind's spent the last two hours sprinting, a hamster on a jet-fueled wheel.

Binks, however, dove straight into the snuggle zone. Muzzle glued to my hip, he was promptly snoring, but after absorbing my anxiety via chin osmosis, he shot me an irritated glance and opted for his own bed. I'm fine being ditched; it gives me a chance to screen chat.

Willa's groggy face is a lit bulb in the center of my screen. Yawning, she says, "Hey girl, why you calling so late?"

"Is it too cliché to blame Brenda-Fight Insomnia?"

"What else is new?"

"Well, there is one thing."

My Aidan glow must be apparent, even on her 7-inch

screen, because she pops awake, squealing, "Ooooh! Teddi's got a boyfriend! Teddi's got a boyfriend!"

"God, I hate your innate ability to spoil every surprise by always anticipating what I'm about to say."

"Perk of a lifelong friendship. I've memorized all your quirks, the anxious way you gnaw your thumb. The chronic pigheadedness. Your customary postdairy gassiness."

"Don't make me sound so glamorous."

"Seriously, you should look into lactose pills."

"Remind me. Why are we friends?"

"Because no one else will put up with us. So . . . are you going to spill the deets, or do I have to come over there?"

"Not a great idea for two reasons. One: it's three forty-five, and two: Brenda."

"Compelling arguments. So, fill me in! What's Lucky Boy's name?"

"Brace yourself."

She stretches back her top and bottom lips to expose ample orthodontia. "Braced."

"Funny, but you know what I meant. By the way, your bite looks kind of off. Been wearing your elastics?"

"Well now, in light of your sad, little effort at suspense, it must be somebody major. Who is it, Teddi? Don't tell me. Aidan Graham."

"You literally suck. You got that?"

"Sweet Baby Jesus! Are you serious? You're dating Mister Coffee?"

"Nothing as concrete as dating, but we did have a stimulating poolside interlude tonight."

"No. Way."

"Way."

"Damn! All my hours of coffee shop ogling—I could've bankrolled a London vacay with the cash I've dropped there—and you've taken the leap! Broken the counter barrier! Not to mention shattered the Jefferson High caste system. A soon-to-be-senior asked you out?"

"Not quite, but we did kiss."

"EEEEEEEEEEEEEEEEEEEEE!!!!!!!"

I rapid-tap my laptop's decrease-volume button. Last thing I need is Brenda coming downstairs for round two.

"Tell me everything!"

I fill Willa in on the hostile morning meeting with Aidan, my trip to the library. Impatient as ever, she says, "Get to the good stuff, the poolside interview!"

"Inter*lude*."

"Interlude, schminterlude! Just tell me about the kiss!"

I relate how Aidan and I met up in the park. Rather than describing the girl in the pool, I tell her I *thought* I saw someone. And I don't bother mentioning the daisy charm. Really, what's the point? Willa's interest lies exclusively in the romantic angle.

When I describe our kiss, she gushes, "Oh, lordy! *Chlorine Kisses!* That would be the greatest poem title! If you don't write it, so help me, I will!"

"Go for it, Wills. Sappy love poems have never been my thing. In fact, I'm rethinking the writing group idea. With Aidan and me possibly on the cusp of . . . well, something, do I honestly want to tie up my summer with a bunch of writers?"

Willa tsks in tandem with her patented eye roll. "Teddi, promise you're not getting all extreme, building a life plan on the basis of one poolside smooch. A guy of Aidan's caliber, ultra-scorch and buffly? I bet he has condoms home-delivered in bulk. A little liptime probably means zero to him."

"Shit, Willa. You been hanging with Brenda behind my back?"

"Sorry. I just don't want you getting hurt. And I don't want to end up being known as 'That Psycho Girl Who Neutered Aidan Graham,' but let's not forget, I've pledged to de-nut any bastard who messes with you."

"God! What happened to 'EEEEEEEEEEEEEEEEEE'?"

"I'm happy for you, honest. And more than a tad jealous. Those lips, those abs—sadly, the abs are a product of imagination. You need to fill me in on those. Video preferred."

"I wonder how Nic would feel about you requesting footage of another guy."

"You know Nicky's the easygoing type, but we're not really discussing my boyfriend. Listen, Teddi, I'm sorry I went all

Brenda on you. Your Aidan news is stellar." Behind the "stellar," her smile's dollar store—booklight dim.

"I'm sensing a 'but.'"

"I just . . . it's premature sacrificing for 'your relationship.' Who knows if you even have one? My two cents: Do that writers' thing. It sounds cool."

Since she's not my mother, I'm willing to admit she's got a point. "Wills, I get it. I'm not exactly choosing wedding colors. But I'd be crazy not to take a chance. Aidan and I could end up being for real."

"That makes sense."

"And Willa, it's sweet of you to offer your vigilante castration services. But let's wait 'til Aidan actually breaks my heart before plotting revenge, all right? I'd like to dwell in the prospect of new romance before going worst-case scenario."

"Gotcha. So, when are you seeing him again?"

"Not sure. But he works across the street, and I'm a pretty major caffeine addict, so I suspect soon."

"And what if your best friend just happens to accompany you?"

"That could be tolerable. In fact, I was going to ask you to join me at the library tomorrow."

"For the writing workshop?"

"Could be the ideal chance for you to write that poem."

"No thanks. Other plans. Nic and I are auditioning for Downtown Players."

"I had no idea Nic was interested in Shakespeare. Or the theater."

"Neither does Nic. I signed us up. Should be an excellent opportunity to grow as a couple. Unless he kills me."

"I would."

"Well then, Backup Plan, I'd better scratch your name off the audition sheet."

"Only if you enjoy breathing."

She raspberries so forcefully, I'm compelled to swipe spit off my forehead. "Love you, Willa Manila. Night-night."

"Love you more, T Bear. Blissful dreams."

Blissful is highly unlikely. I'll be lucky to dream anything, my mind's so overwound.

Prowling downstairs, I replay the day's highlights. Wish I had the power to freeze-frame our kiss; I'd dwell there 'til sunup. Instead, I ricochet from park to library to coffee shop to home, moments auto-unreeling. It's nearly five before my eyelids sag.

7

Sitting on the steps to L718—an hour early—I'm sweating; my feet jitterbug from countless java shots. My brain ultimately powered off near dawn. Dreams all sensory overload: Strange cicada buzz. Heat on my face. Wet earth smell.

Tossing, I kept hearing this tickly laugh. Even dream-caught, I knew it was Pool Girl. Able to shut her out by calling Aidan into the dream, I still wasn't comforted. His smell was off, dank. Boggy.

Just before 9:00 a.m. I gave up, rolled off the couch with this knot in my gut, my neck and shoulders workout-sore.

Willa was eager for breakfast at JJ's, but the Aidan Special wasn't on the menu. Norah said he'd called out, claimed he's been "a regular ass-dragger" lately. I took her remark as a personal insult, but Willa shot me a serious "Down, girl" look before I could respond.

Wasting the morning over coffee refills and choc-aroons, we hit the mall. It was a classic boredom wander, roaming for an hour or so, stopping to gab with kids from school.

Nic met us mid-afternoon. I provided backup as Willa broke the news of their audition. We braced for "Hell no," but he was surprisingly intrigued. That's how we ended up trolling the classics at Hale's.

We spent an hour parked on the worn leather couch at the rear of the bookstore, drinking iced mochas, reciting passages from *Twelfth Night.* Though I doubt they have a prayer of being cast, I assured Willa they'd do Shakespeare proud.

They invited me for a quick supper before the audition, but I decided to hang at Hale's. After a while, sensing I'd slid into loiterer territory, I secured my couch spot with the purchase of a cool blank book, green leather with Celtic-knot cover, and a special pencil, hand-carved, giraffe-patterned.

So I'm set for writers' group. At least, supplywise.

"Hey!"

I nearly leap from my skin, an apparent caffeine-based reaction. Journal and pencil falling, I spin to find Joy—though today's name tag says CARLOS—a few stairs above.

"God, you scared me!" I bend to pick up my stuff. "Did you ever consider announcing yourself before sneaking up on a person?"

"An announcement would defeat the purpose of sneaking up." He slides down the railing, lands next to me.

"Look, I'm not quite up to a round of your trademark, semi-hostile banter today."

He starts with "Color me bummed"; then, legit concerned, he asks, "Something wrong?"

"Not sure. Guess I'm having second thoughts about being," I scrawl an air signature with my new pencil, pinky extended, "A WRITER."

"So who expects you to be? Think of it as a diversion. A fun summer activity, sponsored by the friendly folks at your local library. No one's wagering on you to win a freaking Pulitzer."

Rather than the intended comfort, his remark thwacks a dollop of disappointment atop my plate of unease. "Thanks, Carlos."

Taking a step back, he says, "Don't get me wrong. I'm not saying your writing *won't* be prize-worthy. Just that it's not a requirement."

"No, I get it. Relax. Go with the flow. Have fun. Et cetera. Et cetera."

"Exactly. So why are you here so early? Don't you have someplace better to be?"

"If I had someplace better, I wouldn't have enrolled in SUMMERTEENS in the first place." Catching his expression, I add, "Oops. That sounded snottier than I intended."

"True enough. Look, I have to get the room set up. I'll see you later." He strides down the hall, swinging a ring full of keys.

I follow.

"Um, maybe I could help?"

Without slowing, he says, "There you go again, trying to get cozy with me. I told you, I have a girlfriend."

He's kidding. I get that, but it's irritating regardless. I reply, "Right, Meadow."

"Glade."

"I knew it was something woodland; almost went with *Thicket*. Well, *Glade's* got nothing to fear; I couldn't be less interested in you."

"Whoa, who's semi-hostile now?"

"No, it's just . . . I'm sort of seeing someone, too. His name's Aidan. He's a barista, and he's hotter than the beverages he serves."

He laughs. Then, pushing open the door, he says, "Well, in that case, what are you waiting for? Give me a hand!"

Following him into L718, I judge it seriously in need of a scrub. At the far end's a low, carpeted stage with a beat-up podium. One corner overflows with sub-tag-sale-quality toys: cash register, dulled chalkboard, dress-up costumes that practically shriek "Dust mites!" Familiar, somehow. I picture Corey in a Pikachu mask, me with tattered fairy wings.

Stifling a germ-cringe, I ask, "How many are signed up?"

"Right now, ten; not bad for summer. Eleanor likes to split into groups, so she'll probably go with three teams, two threes and a four. You'll be able to do some good work."

"But not Pulitzer quality."

"Never can tell. Give me a hand, would you?" He rolls this round plywood table into the center of the room. As he steadies it, I unfold the metal legs.

"Let's set this up for four. One group of three can take the school desks; the other can have the couch and chairs. Of course, once you get started, folks'll be free to roam."

"That's reassuring. So, tell me about Eleanor. Is she nice?"

He just smirks. Then he says, "It'd be a stretch for me to describe her as *nice*. *Colorful* may be a more appropriate word."

"Oh, great."

"What?"

"*Colorful* is generally a polite way of saying abnormal. Oddball. Nutjob."

He grins.

"Am I getting warm?"

"Oh, you're hotter than that barista boyfriend of yours. Eleanor is undeniably odd. But she's a talented writer and a great teacher. She's not a bad sister, either."

"You're kidding."

"No, she's had a couple stories published; her chapbook, *Mulberry Bush*, won honorable mention in a national contest, and her college students give her high marks on rankyourprof.com. I mostly steer clear; it feels wrong knowing her sexiness quotient."

"Because she's your sister."

"Wouldn't you be grossed-out by folks proclaiming your sister's 'boner-worthiness'?"

"Ick. Makes me glad I don't have siblings."

"So you're an only?"

"More like an anomaly. I'm the one mistake my mother didn't make repeatedly."

"Ouch."

"Sorry. Too heavy on the self-loathing?"

"A tad. But you should write that down. It's a killer line."

"Uh . . . thanks."

We smile stiffly; then he scopes out the room, making a few furniture adjustments, and says, "Guess we're good to go. I need to head upstairs for a few. Feel free to chill. Folks should be arriving soon."

Flopping into a dusty armchair—mites be damned—I glance at the owl clock behind the podium: 5:35. I hate being first to arrive. Of course, I also hate walking into a full room. This is better, a head start. That gets me thinking. Spotting a sharpener mounted inside the door, I christen my giraffe pencil with a fresh point. Then, returning to the armchair, I close my eyes, attempting to beckon creative thoughts.

Cracking open the blank book, I write my name inside the cover, turn the page, scribble the date. Then, per Joy-los's suggestion, I carefully print: *I'm the one mistake my mother didn't make repeatedly.*

"No head starts!"

Evidently conditioned to sudden exclamations, I don't jump this time. Closing my journal, I say, "Sorry?"

"You've started without me. Hardly fair to the rest of the group."

"You must be Eleanor." This is obvious not merely because of her surprise entrance, an uncanny echo of Joy's, but also because she plainly shares his ironic, teasing nature. Must run in the family.

I stand.

As she extends her hand, I notice two things. First, though her brother described her as a writer and teacher, Eleanor also moonlights as a Scandinavian crochet master. She's the woman on the flyer. Second—and I can't believe I'm saying this—she is, indeed, boner-worthy.

I suppose I expected a physical resemblance, and, though lacking green hair or piercings, they are similar, the freckly complexion, those hazel eyes. But, where her brother has this guarded quality, Eleanor's face is wide open. Her cheekbones are skiable; she's a couple inches taller than Joy, and while his green hair's choppy, Eleanor's—would it sound too fan-girly to say her brown hair "cascades"?

She breaks my reverie with "And you are?"

"Oh! I'm Teddi, Teddi Alder."

"Alder? Like the tree?"

"Um, yeah. I guess."

Scanning her clipboard, checkmarking my name, she says, "Alder, the Goddess Tree, *c'est fascinant.*"

"Goddess?"

"Yes, let's bear that in mind. Just remember, even a goddess needs to know her place." She taps her chest. "Eleanor is in charge here."

"No worries."

"But qualities of the alder: Strength. Resilience. These are aspects to explore in your writing. Absolutely. Did you have any idea, for example, when submerged in water, alder wood hardens to the toughness of stone?"

"Can't say I did."

"Names are significant, Miss Alder. They shape—to some degree, they even dictate—the people we become. It's a shame about *Teddi*, though."

"Wait, what?"

"Is it short for something?"

"Not that I'm aware of."

Barely audible, she says, "Pity."

"I'm sorry?"

"Oh, just thinking aloud."

My first impression of Joy was "Bridge Troll," but his sister must be a sorceress, because I freeze as if enchanted, devoid of a smart-ass comeback.

She retrieves her bag—needlepoint, monstrous—from the floor and crosses to the table.

Welcoming the interruption of voices and feet on the stairs, I turn to greet my rescue squad.

If these are my heroes, I'm in for it.

Two life-sized Barbies saunter past. Unmistakable self-tan fans, they resemble human/carrot hybrids in painted-on booty shorts and sky-high wedge sandals. Perched side-by-side on the plaid couch, Left Blonde says, "Wow, couldn't they have *tried* to de-scum this place? Seriously, I recognize that couch from my days in pre-K reading group."

Right Blonde says, "Seriously."

Trailing the Barbies is a trio arranged in descending order of attractive. The first guy's chunky, cute in a forest creature way, with a shag of reddish hair and giant glasses.

Pumping Eleanor's hand, he announces, "I'm Ken."

I almost steer him toward the couch, to plant him between the Mattel twins.

Guy number two is skele-slim, with fearful brown eyes and a Superman tee. He scurries to the back of the room alongside Ken, and they hunker on the edge of the stage.

Guy three, so pale he seems to glow in the hallway gloom, wears a cropped muscle shirt and board shorts. Stepping in, he scans the room, chimp-sneers at the Barbies; then, with an exaggerated eye roll, he proclaims, "I'm out." Leaving, he nearly collides with a sixth arrival, this tiny girl with thick, black braids.

I recognize Marisol from school. She's in my grade, but we've never said much beyond hello. She lives with her aunt, I think. Last year, rumors spread about them being witches.

She smiles, apparently relieved to see a somewhat familiar face.

Sidling over, she says, "Hey. Teddi, right?"

"Yep, and you're Marisol?"

Three more kids wander in. I barely have a chance to notice them—two girls, a guy, tall/short/tall—before Eleanor chirps, "Greetings, all! Welcome to SUMMERTEENS Intensive! Let's get to work!"

Unsure of Intensive decorum, I wave, to get her attention. Oblivious, she uncaps a marker, scrawls *Eleanor Edlenson* in foot-high letters on the whiteboard. I briefly picture Brenda tailing Eleanor with squirt bottle and ink-tainted towel.

"Um, Eleanor, shouldn't we wait for . . . uh . . ." I almost say "Joy," then "Carlos." Ultimately, I finish with "your brother?"

I guess decorum prohibits speaking out. Eleanor confirms this; eyes narrowed, glaring, she says, "I'll thank you to refrain from speaking over me, Teddi."

"Well, you weren't actually talking, and I had a question. Sorry."

"Accepted. Yes, my brother. I'm not sure how you got the idea he'd be joining us."

"Oh. He said—"

"Edwin says a lot of things, Miss Alder."

Edwin? Edwin Edlenson? So. I've uncovered the real reason he swaps name tags.

"He will be around. To help set up, to offer an occasional thought on someone's work, to facilitate activities, but Eddie's

50

not really part of the group. Is that an issue?" Her brow hitches.

"No, ma'am."

"Good. Then, if there are no further questions, shall we continue? I'm sure your comrades are eager to leap into the creative process. And we frankly cannot afford to waste writing time. This is, you'll recall, an *Intensive.*"

I glance at my "comrades." No eager leapers evident. The Barbies fix on their phones. Ken and Superslim examine their footwear. The three late arrivals paw through musty costumes, and Marisol stares straight ahead, trying not to laugh.

I make a "speak no evil" motion. Then, through laced fingers, I say, "Let the writing brilliance begin."

Eleanor prints three words—COLOR, ANIMAL, GARMENT— on the board, instructing us to choose one item for each category. She calls this a getting-to-know-all-about-you exercise. As we prepare to read our lists, she tells us to "imprint these identifiers."

I go over details, memorizing folks by color, animal, garment. Surprisingly, the Barbies don't claim eye-poking pink as their favored hue, and woodland Ken chooses neither chipmunk nor vole, but "the genus *Gymnogyps*, species *californianus.* The endangered California condor."

Once we share our lists, Eleanor divides us into three equal groups. The Tardies disregard her attempt to split them, and, plainly lacking energy to insist, Eleanor lets them remain clustered. She demands, however, that the Barbies part. This leads to Marisol and me being assigned to different factions. Mine includes Ken and Left Barbie—not her given name. Eleanor says we'll mostly stick with these groups, occasionally sharing among the whole gang.

She gives us thirty minutes to build our lists into "spontaneous script," cautioning us not to feel pressured, not to self-edit. Assuring us if we "trust the magic percolation of ideas, words will intuitively emerge," she places an egg timer on the table, probably to reinforce the no pressure thing. When the timer buzzes, she says, "Pencils down." Then she asks for volunteers.

Met with silence, she approaches our group. "How about it, Teddi?"

I duck my head, pretend not to hear her.

Left B's no more eager, but agrees to read. Her pages detail her cosmetic process, a haunting account, narrated by her bedroom mirror. Honestly, it's informative. I never knew, for instance, such diversity exists in the world of makeup brushes.

According to Eleanor, Left Barbie's created a "rumination on reality versus reflection." Left appears insulted by the word *rumination*. It's tempting to question her grasp of complex vocabulary, but I won't perpetuate the dumb blonde stereotype. For one thing, I'm blond. Plus, she correctly used *disingenuous* in her piece. No flies on her, vocabwise.

When Ken points out her lack of an animal, she hisses, "There are no animals at the makeup table."

52

Eleanor soothes, "Prompts are meant to inspire, never to limit. Petra is simply following her muse."

It's funny, but now that I've learned her true name—Petra Rio—I have a feeling we're going to be very good friends. Not really.

Ken reads next. After a promising start, "I am a sweatshirt, black as a breast feather," his condor obsession surfaces. His piece, though fact-filled—wingspan/diet/pesticides/habitat— is hardly engaging. Plus, he somehow manages to recite nearly three pages on a single breath.

When Eleanor abruptly stops him, he beams, clearly antici- pating praise, but all she says is "That was . . . uh . . . thorough, Kenneth. One word: *edit.*"

Up next, I scan my piece. COLOR: Green. ANIMAL: A lonely giraffe roaming the savannah. I've gone nontraditional with GARMENT. Rather than a piece of clothing, I've draped a daisy charm around the giraffe's neck.

The pendant just makes sense, given that I haven't taken off the real one since the other night. I'm used to it; barely notice it beneath my top. It may seem wonky, but I believe it's some kind of talisman connecting me to Pool Girl.

As I mentally prepare to read, Eleanor frowns and says, "Teddi, would you mind terribly if we skipped you? We're a mite short on time."

Badly concealing relief, I say, "Wow, really? That's a disap- pointment."

"I promise you can read first tomorrow. And I'd love to make copies of your pages for each of us to take home. If that's all right with you."

I'm not wild over the idea. It's not as if they're classified documents, but it's embarrassing, the idea of Left—okay, Petra—and Ken spending the evening poring over "Ballad of the Sad Giraffe."

Since she's given me the option, I say, "Would you mind making just one copy? For yourself? No offense, guys."

Ken does look offended, but Petra barely listens, newly engrossed in her lip liner.

Eleanor agrees. Moving on to Marisol's group, she gives our threesome a chance to further bond. Amazingly, this does not happen.

8

Marisol and I exit the 'brary, and I hear, "Teddi, wait up!"

As Aidan jogs toward us from behind the building, Marisol fans herself and says, "Super Fuego!" before jumping into a waiting VW. Its bumper sticker reads 100% SPIRIT-FUELED.

After a quick kiss, Aidan asks, "How was writers' club?"

"Interesting." I touch his forehead. "All better?"

He looks puzzled, 'til I say, "I stopped at JJ's this morning. Norah said you were sick."

"I'm fine. Just couldn't deal with customers today, opted for a sleep-in. Don't worry, Norah will forgive me."

"I don't know. She was pissed; she called you an ass-dragger. I almost felt obliged to defend your honor."

Eyes darkening, he says, "Let me handle Norah! It's no big deal."

"Sorry, didn't mean to upset you."

"No, it's . . . no harm, no foul." His smile returns, and all is right with the world. "So tell me about the group. Anybody cool?"

"Depends on your definition of cool. There are some characters." Just then, the last emerge.

Ken shouts, "Good night, Teddi. Nice work!" Then, he lopes over, trailed by Skinny Guy, a.k.a. Todd. Fist-bumping Aidan, he announces, "I'm Ken, Teddi's writing partner. This is Todd."

Aidan says, "Partner, huh?" causing Todd to snicker. Ken turns bright red.

I poke Aid in the ribs and say, "This is my friend, Aidan."

Eyes on the sidewalk, Todd speaks above a whisper for the first time. "We'd better mosey." His voice is Mufasa low.

Trudging toward the bus stop, Ken calls back, "Pleasure to meet you, Aidan."

Aidan yells, "Back at you!" Then, faux-scowling, says, "Should I be threatened?"

"Well, I don't know. Ken and I have a real spark, don't you think?"

My phone peeps. A Willa text: **we rocked it!** ☺

I text back: **hoopla!**

She replies: **meet @ sprinkles??**

Aidan asks, "What's up?"

"My friend Willa and her boyfriend, Nic, nailed their *Twelfth Night* auditions. She wants to meet for ice cream. You up for it?"

He frowns. "Wait, she's the one with the hair—and the x-ray vision, right?"

"Um, yes."

"I'm shocked to hear she has a boyfriend, honestly."

"Meaning?"

"The way she's always checking me out."

"Oh, that's just Willa. She and Nic have been a couple for practically ever. Besides, you, my friend, are highly check-able."

"Why thank you. And a big back atcha." He leans in, lips puckering.

Stopping him pre-kiss, I say, "Hold up. I thought you were attracted by my refreshing lack of physical appeal."

"Shit, I was hoping you'd forgotten my accidental douchery. Y'know, that came out all wrong. You just made me sort of nervous."

"Wait, *I* made *you* nervous?"

"Well, yeah. You're just so . . . there. Sort of uber real. I've never met anyone like you.

And you're remembering it wrong. It was a reference to your incredible natural beauty."

"Well, in that case, you may kiss me." He does. "So, want to hang with my friends, Mr. Graham?"

"Well, if they're as cool as Kevin and Tom, how can I resist?"

"Ken and Todd. Be nice. Those guys aren't bad, once you get past the halting speech and cut-it-with-a-knife awkwardness."

"I'll take your word."

I text Willa back: **we'll c u there**

She immediately replies: **WE???**

I text back: **ARG & I**, to which she responds: **EEEEEEE!!!!**

I fear that girl's going to use up all the *E*s one day.

Aidan puts his arm around me, but as we're about to step onto the path toward Morris Street, I hear "Ahem." It's that Edlenson Boy.

"Oh, hey."

"Sorry to bother you, Teddi." He locks eyes with Aidan. For a moment, I sense this zing of recognition between them. Then he extends his hand. "Hi, I'm Ed."

Aidan freezes for a beat; then he squeezes Edwin's hand and says, "Aidan."

It starts to seem like they're stuck, joined à la Harry and Voldemort with wands fused, so I add my hand to theirs and say, "So. Ed. Good to be able to call you by your legit name at last. Though there's something to be said for Joy. It suits you."

Aidan drops Ed's hand, wraps his arm back around my shoulder. Then he says, "Can we help you with something?"

Ed's jaw twitches as he says, "No, just . . . you forgot this." Pulling my giraffe pencil from his backpack pocket, he hands it to me.

"Oh, thanks." I slide the pencil into my satchel with the leather book. "Would've sucked to lose that the first night. Cost me nearly four bucks."

The three of us stand, stalled, unsure what else to say.

Just then, a red Honda pulls up, punching a hole in the tension. The tinted window lowers to reveal Eleanor. Smiling and—really?—blatantly eyeing Aidan, she says, "Nice to have you aboard, Teddi. I look forward to reading your piece." Then, snapping fingers at Ed, she says, "Step lively, *Petit Frère*. Time's a-wasting."

Shooting her a disgusted look, Ed says, "*Little Brother* lost its charm around the time I sprouted body hair." Waving in our direction, he says, "See you," and hops into the passenger seat. They drive off, Eleanor blowing through the red at the corner of Morris and Bank.

We watch them, momentary mutes, until Aidan says, "Nice hair."

"His or hers?"

"Well, she's smokin'—if you're into that type. But I meant his. Are those idiotic green spikes supposed to be a statement?"

"Oh. I don't know, it kind of suits him."

"Really? As much as the name Joy?"

Funny he remembered that name.

"Since we're debating green, you're not going all green-eyed monster, are you?"

"Wow," he shakes his head, "my eyes aren't *green*, Teddi." Shutting them, he asks, "Have you even noticed what color they are?"

"Frosted-berry blue with the tiniest gold flecks around your pupils."

"But you just said—"

"The term *green-eyed monster* is from—"

"Shakespeare, I know, I took sophomore English. What's *Othello* got to do with anything?"

"It refers to jealousy."

"And?"

"If I didn't know better, I'd think you are."

"Jealous. Of him? You've got to be kidding!"

"Well, you acted pretty hostile, Aid. And for no good reason. I barely know the guy, but he's been very clear about the fact that he has a girlfriend."

"Whatever. Look, we best get moving. It's almost dark, and this isn't the safest place at night."

We cross Morris like polite strangers. But, stepping onto the opposite curb, Aidan takes my hand. "You noticed the gold flecks, huh?"

"Yeah, I . . . I've pretty much memorized you—you idiot."

He smiles, this sad-sweet grin I don't recognize and says, "That's what I was talking about before. You being uber real. Who else would admit that?"

"Sorry, I suppose it is kind of pathetic, huh?" I look away.

Touching my cheek, he says, "Not pathetic. More like kind of incredible."

I stare back into those cloudless eyes 'til he says, "Where did you say we're meeting Willow and Rick?"

I don't bother correcting him. So he's got short-term

memory issues. And a jealous streak. Big deal. Sensitivity paired with physical perfection is a fair trade-off.

As we approach Sprinkles, Willa calls, "Hey, lovebirds!" from beneath a flowered umbrella.

Torn between cartwheeling and prying up the nearest manhole cover to disappear under, I choose option three. Flashing Willa a quick birdie, I yell, "Control your woman, Nicholas!" Aidan looks as if he might opt for the manhole.

Nic acts super serious. Shaking Aidan's hand, he says, "Nice grip." Then, nodding soberly, he adds, "It's good to finally meet my girlfriend's ideal man. You *are* pretty spectacular. Go ahead, make a muscle."

After an uneasy glance in my direction, Aidan guffaws, obliges by flexing. Willa and I compose ourselves, memorizing the ice cream menu. Trying to out-gallant each other, Aidan and Nic insist on ordering for us.

At the mini picnic table, Willa says, "This is so awesome!"

"I'm still pinching myself."

"You should be!"

I opt not to be insulted.

Squeaking, "Almost forgot!" she slips me a blister pack, imprinted with DAI-RE-LIEF CHEWABLE, and whispers, "Take one. For all our sakes."

I say, "Bite me," but, figuring it can't hurt, I pop a chalky caplet. "Mmm, vanilla school paste." Digging in my satchel, I chase the chewable with a root beer candy, offering Willa one.

Just then, Aidan and Nic return. Laughing, Aid says, "Belch? Seriously?"

"Sir Toby Belch. They had me read the part four times. Could be fun playing a drunk."

"Might also call for some research."

Nic laughs.

Digging into my ice cream, secure in the protection of Dai-Re-lief, I ask, "How 'bout you, Wills? Lead role in your future?"

"Doubtful. But lots of little parts are open. Nicky was the real star."

"Thanks, babe. So, Teddi, tell us about writing class."

As I lick peanut butter topping off my pinky, Aidan says, "From what I saw, it's a total stud factory."

Willa says, "Knew I should've joined," and Nic plops a cloud of whipped cream on the end of her nose. Painting him a fudge mustache, she continues, "So did you write it, that poem we discussed?"

Mouthing "Shut up!" I say, "We did do some writing. Tonight's exercise was a basic icebreaker, introducing ourselves using a color, an animal, and an article of clothing. Then she had us write, stream-of-consciousness style. It was sort of—"

Willa interrupts. "Well, your color had to be green, and the animal's a given. Giraffe! But the clothing's way tougher. Face it. You're no fashionista."

I cover Willa's mouth with my hand, which she immediately

licks. Wiping my palm on my shorts, I say, "Who invited her?"

"Actually, *she* invited *us*."

"Thanks for leaping to my defense, Aidan. Teddi's notoriously mean to me. You must think of some way to improve her mood." She bats her eyes, and Aidan's cheeks redden. Somehow, this makes him even more appealing. Who knew such a thing was possible?

Eager to change topics, Aidan asks, "When do you find out if you got parts?"

"Callbacks are tomorrow. Not that we'll get one."

"Of course we will, Nicky. You were brilliant! And they'll have to accept the fact that they can't have *you* without *me*." Her eyes widen. "You guys have got to come see us!" She taps her phone furiously. "I'm texting you the box office number. Reserve early!"

Nic and I share a conspiratorial *Freakin' Willa* moment.

I almost warn her not to get ahead of herself—at least 'til they're sure they've been cast—but Willa has a way of converting enthusiasm into outcome. She may be magic.

It's a feat I've never quite managed, willing dreams into reality. Although, gazing across the table into Aidan's blueberry eyes, I realize I may have succeeded in doing exactly that.

9

I'd anticipated alone time after Sprinkles, but Aidan says, "I'll need some major dozage to be bright and bushy for Norah in the a.m."

Following a leisurely good night, I peer through the blinds, track his progress across the park 'til he dissolves into blackness.

Tonight's poop walk is brief; I steer Binks away from the pool. He's miffed to be hauled in immediately postbusiness, but I have no wish to encounter Pool Girl, figment or not.

Scrubbed and snug, I retreat to my room. Sure, I absconded this morning before Brenda achieved consciousness—left her a note about SUMMERTEENS—but she has this gift for resuming an argument mid-thought, even days later. And I won't wreck my mood by engaging tonight. When she slogs in around 1:30, I kill the lamp, clinch my lids, and hope she spares me an Aidan rehash.

But the hamster wheel inside my skull, coupled with Binks's

scrabbling as he paces outside the bathroom door, foil any attempts at sleep.

Eyeing the clock—2:17—I click the bedside lamp and slide the journal from my nightstand, dubious about my ability to assemble words anybody'd want to read.

I try picturing Eleanor enthralled, riveted by my story, but instead, I envision an ink attack, my pages doused in red. She hates my name. Hard to imagine she'd savor my writing.

Although, she did warn us not to fixate on quality. Her advice was "Write reckless—from the gut—if you wish to generate rich, creative fodder." She also said the most prized writer traits are "fearlessness and fertility."

I may never master fearless, but fertile just means cranking out lots of words. That I can handle. I scan my draft. Seriously, a lonely giraffe? Ugh.

Channeling Eleanor, I say, "At this stage, any writing is good."

Closing the no-longer blank book, I slide the workshop packet and pencil from my satchel and scan tomorrow's assignment. Brief, but intriguing.

Old Friend: Recount a scene in which you interact with a childhood friend, preferably one with whom you're no longer in touch. Place the scene in an actual location, grounded in memory. Use rich, descriptive language to engage multiple senses. Note: Memory is tricky. Focus on emotive rather than literal truth.

* * *

"Corey."

I'm startled at my own voice. Closing my eyes, I see him, sharp as if he were beside my bed. He's wearing red high-tops, his favorite tee, the one with Gordy, that dopey, big-eyed cereal box spokesfrog he loves. His brown forehead's flecked with beads of sweat. Grinning, he pokes a sliver of sour apple candy through his used-to-have-front-teeth gap and signals for me to follow, starting up the path to—

"Teddi?" Brenda taps the wall outside my room.

Groaning, I open my eyes. "Yeah?"

"Just making sure you're home safe."

"Where else would I be?"

Poking her head through the curtains, she says, "Truce?"

I put my pencil down.

"Can I come in?"

With every fiber, I want to say no. "Sure."

"So," she sinks into my beanbag, "how was the workshop?"

"Fine. I was actually about to do some homework for tomorrow, so—"

"So I should get out?"

"Not what I said."

"But you wouldn't stop me, would you?"

"God, Brenda, can we *not* do this right now? I really do want to get some work done."

Rooting beneath my bed, she scores a stray sock, slips it on, hand puppet–style. Then, in a familiar dopey voice, she asks, "What you writing, Teddi?"

Surrendering a smile, I answer, "Really not sure, Sockie. I just now read the assignment. We're supposed to write about a childhood friend." For some reason, I continue. "I was thinking of Corey."

She attempts a smile, falls short. Sliding Sockie back under the bed, she crosses to my bureau. "Wow. Corey. Haven't heard that name in . . . What's it been? Five years?" Her back to me, she tracks my reaction in the mirror.

"Closer to nine. We were both seven when they moved away."

"Well, life happens . . ."

"Yeah, but we were like twins. You used to call us Ebony and Ivory. Remember?"

She doesn't answer.

"We were *supposed* to stay in touch."

"And it's my fault you didn't."

"Didn't say that."

"Didn't have to."

It's comforting, this communication shorthand we've developed after years of just us. Reflecting back a sad smile, I ask, "How was work? Dev treat you different?"

Sighing at the change of subject, she flops back on the beanbag. "Because of Mandy? I doubt he has any idea, Teddi. And I really didn't come in here to talk about *my* love life." The way she stresses *my* makes me cringe. "We covered that topic last night."

"So, instead you want to discuss mine."

"If I'm being honest, yes."

"Tremendous."

"I just need to make sure you understand."

"That men are crud? I get it, Bren. You've drilled that particular lesson into my head since . . . always."

"No . . . I—"

"Aidan is different, Mom. I need you to trust me. I don't intend to sneak around, and I really don't want to fight about this. But I will. It's important to me."

"Teddi, look. You think you know."

I fold my arms into a shield.

She takes a second to gear up before saying, "You're so sure this Aidan is *the one*. But you're *fifteen*, Teddi." Her eyes flash— fear, not anger—as she says, "I was—"

"I know. The same age when you met *him*." We never use his name, and I certainly don't refer to him as "Dad," but she knows.

"Yes. And it wasn't long before—"

"God! I'm familiar with the biology, Mother. And the timetable. The proud family history. But none of it has anything to do with me and Aidan. Honest. I'm in no hurry to become somebody's baby mama. The idea nauseates me. It's a little too trailer park."

"Tell me how you really feel."

"Augh! Mom, you know I didn't mean it like that." When she doesn't respond, I venture back into desperate-humor realm. "Actually, trailer park might be a step up from this dump."

She strains to hoist out of the bean seat; failing, she reaches, and I tug her to her feet. Steadying, she says, "So apparently you're going to continue saying hurtful stuff until I'm forced to slug you." Instead, she smoothes my eyebrow with her thumb.

I feel a hint of relief 'til, in this unnatural sitcom-mom lilt, she says, "I was actually thinking it might be a good idea if . . ."

Wincing, I lift a pillow, raise it in front of my face. From behind it, I say, "Cripes, Brenda, you're starting to frighten me."

Exhaling through her teeth, she says, "Hear me out."

"I'm listening."

"It might be a good idea for me to meet this boyfriend of yours."

"Oh, shit."

"Teddi."

"Sorry, I just . . . that's just . . ." I make this medicine-taste face. "Ack."

"Not the response a mother dreams of."

"I honestly don't know *how* to respond. Aidan and I aren't even officially *going out* yet. It would be epically bizarre to introduce him to my family. Such as it is."

"Nice."

"You know what I meant."

"I suppose I do."

"Obviously, you guys'll have to meet at some point, just not yet. How about . . . around Christmas? Or . . . to commemorate our silver anniversary or something. If you're still interested."

"Wait, can I at least come to the wedding?"

Pretending to mull it over, I answer, "Rehearsal dinner."

"Deal." She shakes my hand like we've just sealed some business contract. "Look, I'm willing to be a slightly less rabid mama lion. If you promise not to do anything foolish."

"Brenda, when have I ever been foolish?" Before she can open her mouth, I clap hands to ears and yell, "Ryan Hecht doesn't count!"

Prying my fingers away, she says, "Yes, Ryan Hecht certainly does count. He is, in fact, the sexual barometer by which your foolishness will forever be measured. But if you honestly learned something from that experience—"

I go out on a limb. "I assume you mean something beyond what it feels like to have a boy's hand on my—"

"Enough!" She actually laughs; whacking me with the pillow, she plops it on the bed. "On that note, darling daughter, good night."

As she pushes the curtains aside, I jump off my bed. Catching her arm, I spin her into a clumsy embrace and, in a decent Sockie voice, I say, "Wuv you, Mums."

She delivers a quick squeeze. "Wuv you, too, Little Only. Wuv you, too."

After she leaves, I lie motionless, trying to reclaim that Corey moment. No luck. Why is this so hard? The prompt was made for Corey.

I say it aloud, "Old Friend."

Then, in the margins of the assignment sheet, I scribble COREY COREY COREY repeatedly. Lids drooping, I pencil-scratch a list of special spots:

Pool
school
schoolPool
Park park Dark
Path pathpon—Pond
POND

Eyes flying open, I snap to attention. "The pond."

Yawning in the desk-lamp dim, I crack my neck. How close was I skating toward the edge of sleep? Hopping from bed, I do a few lunges, some toe-touches.

My head feels fogged-in, but I need to write now that I have a sense of where to go with this. Shit, though! The pond?

Giraffe pencil ready, I crack the leather book open to a clean page. Concentrating, I will Corey to materialize. For a second he hovers, just beyond reach, and I panic, afraid I've forgotten him. Then, clear as a finger snap, he flashes into focus.

Corey smiles, but his eyes are flat. Button-black, like stones. Across his left cheek, an orange smear: pollen. He holds a fistful of black-eyed Susans.

With a monster breath, I touch pencil to page, hand shaking. In bold capitals, I print four short words.

10

COREY AT THE POND

Harsh buzz in my ears. Metallic insect whine. We pick through heavy branches rimming the path. Corey points to tri-clustered greens, reminds me, "Leaves of three . . ."

"I know."

It should be cooler here under the branches, but even in shade, heat hugs me tight as a long lost aunt. Sweat pastes my Scooby tank to my back, sunburn pinching my shoulder blades.

Corey leads. We're explorers some days, sometimes the last of a secret tribe. Today he chooses: Croc Hunter and Terri. I go along, even though Terri mostly stands to the side cheering Steve on.

"Corey, we should play Croc Hunter back in the Cretaceous."

He grins agreement. "Great idea, Terri."

Prehistoric fits; the path's bordered by neck-high ferns, cones of skunk cabbage. Hiking farther, past evil red berries, humongous webs, everything looks primeval, except the ground litter. Aluminum flip-top rings, cigarette butts. Chip bags.

Other things I pretend not to see. Corey calls them "hypes and condos." *He says hypes are for drugs, and the other . . . he's not sure. But his cousin told him those have something to do with S-E-X. He laughs at me for calling them "little nasties, milk balloons," warns me I'll catch a disease if I dare touch one.*

I follow him, road noise shrinking, shrinking as we go deeper. We pass Stone Loop, this patch of ground-down, burnt grass. Rocks, some furniture-big, form a lopsided circle. They're sprayed with initials, swear words, dirty pictures. In the middle a jumble of smaller stones, blackened chunks of wood, melted plastic bottles.

"Crikey, we've stumbled on a camp, Terri! Must be a family of Cro-Magnons."

Corey nails the Croc Hunter accent, so I don't bother correcting him. We both know there were no cavemen in the Cretaceous.

"Look, Steve. What do you make of this?"

It's a picnic table; someone's lugged it from the grove. Coated in spray paint, same as the rocks, it's scorched, carved with crude symbols. Climbing on top, I wonder how Corey will explain this.

"Never mind that, Terri. Look over here! A nesting area! I'll bet there are some huge crocs around here."

We've made it. Dragonflies sew patterns into the surface; dashed stitches appear briefly, dissolving into scum-green skin.

Drawn by ripples, Corey spots a pair of eyes; a mini snout rises and dips below slime. "It's a baby Archelon, Terri. Isn't she a beauty?" Moving closer, he lifts a thick sheet of bark, testing its weight like a baseball bat. "If I can stun her with this, I'll bet we can catch her."

"I'm not sure that's a good idea, Steve. You don't want to hurt her."

"It's all right, Terri. I know what I'm doing."

Raising the slab above his head, he inches across the mushy bank, close to the water.

"NO!"

Ignoring my cry, Corey swings. The turtle sinks from sight before the weapon can connect—THWACK!—with the mucky surface. Knocked off balance, Corey falls, legs splatting, head and torso briefly sunk in ooze.

Frozen, lump-in-throat, sweat slicks my forehead and armpits.

Spluttering, Corey struggles to right himself, manages to sit up, swipes his face clean of green scum.

Seeing he's not hurt, I bust out laughing.

"Dang it, Teddi!" He's mad for just a second, eyebrows knitting. Then he joins me on the bank, coughing laughter and spitting "turtle juice."

I put my pencil down.

In a case of life imitates prewriting—this is hardly art—I swipe sweat from my forehead. Exhaling slowly into the dim, I shiver. "Enough remembering for tonight."

Just as I close the journal, my phone rings. I quick-check caller ID. Aidan.

"Hey! I thought you'd be comatose by now. Weren't you supposed to turn in early?"

Sounding bleary, words soggy, he says, "Did. Kept dreaming. 'Bout being with you. Took it as a sign. Figured I'd call, say hey."

"Hey."

"What you up to?"

"About five six."

"Ha. Come out to play?"

I hesitate. "What? Now?"

"'S not like you have school tomorrow. Summer, Teddi. Let's make the most of it. Carpe me um."

"Yeah, right. Try running that by Warden Alder. She's less than thrilled about the mere idea of you. She'd piss a bullet if she caught us meeting up in the wee hours."

"Who says she'd catch us? Stealth is practically my middle name."

"Your middle name is Robert. And if you don't want it to be *Deceased*, you won't tempt fate."

He sighs. "But I miss you."

"You're cute. But you don't know Brenda. It's better if I play by the rules, at least 'til she gets used to the boyfriend concept."

He's quiet. I'm sure he's hung up. "Aidan?"

His only reply is a deeper sigh.

"I suppose I shouldn't be presumptuous. About the boyfriend status, that is."

After an agonizing fourteen-second lag, he says, "Kind of an outdated term, but I'm good with it if you are."

"Oh, I'm beyond good."

"So come meet me."

"God, you are a persistent chap, aren't you!"

"Ha, *chap*! You really are playing it retro, aren't you? Should I throw a pebble at your window or something?"

"Absolutely not." Now it's my turn to sigh. "Aid, I'm serious. It's a bad idea. Besides, I look like roadkill, all blotched and bed-heady."

"Prove it."

"How?"

"Come to your window."

Slipping from bed, I tiptoe, sidestepping the creaky floorboard. Though it's not likely to rouse Brenda, this is no time to get cocky. Brushing aside a paisley panel, I peer out, momentarily blinded by the streetlight. Then, a streak of movement: Aidan's waving hand.

He's across my street, phone to ear. As he steps into the aluminum pole's arc, I see he's barefoot, in cutoffs, shirt artfully unbuttoned. Even in low light, those are major league abs.

"Very tempting."

He smooches into the phone; then, turning, he drops his shirt mid-back, does a little butt shake.

"I'm sure the neighbors are enjoying this. Did you know seven sex offenders live on Parkview? Brenda's got the registry taped to the freezer door, updates it every Tuesday."

"Is this an attempt at sexy talk?"

"Is that an attempt at sexy dancing? Because you might want to invest in lessons."

"Whoa, now you've hurt my feelings."

"Sorry, tiger."

"Come outside."

I stall. No way would I risk sneaking through Brenda's room for a night rendezvous. But I could go the Narnia route.

"Give me five minutes."

Crossing from the window, I flip on my bureau lamp. Freeing my hair of its ponytail, I run fingers through. Yielding to girly vanity, I dab on strawberry lip stain, retrieve my flashlight from the bureau, head to the closet.

Inching the slider open, confident Brenda won't hear it squeak on its track, I shove clothes aside and step into the closet. Shining the flashlight, I study the door at the back.

Locked with a simple hook and eye, it's smaller than average, a Wonderland-size entry. It opens to a staircase leading to the never renovated portion of the store. When I was little, this setup was horrifying, like having a gaping hell mouth inside my closet. I'd lie in bed imagining every sort of monster—vampire, demon, plain old axe murderer—pressed to the other side, sniffing the dark.

Even now it sometimes freaks me out imagining the generations of spiders—and tribes of mice—that have lived and dreamed and died there.

But tonight it's my risk-free passage to freedom. And

beyond it waits Aidan. So it's a tunnel of . . . well, if not yet love, at least good old-fashioned teengal lust.

Unlatching the hook, I push the door open, admitting it's improbable an evil clown lurks in the gloom.

I point the flashlight downstairs, illuminating a million vague, threatening shapes. It's been years since I've been down there, but I'm fairly sure no torture devices or human remains are present. Just forgotten store equipment: shelving, a standup fan, twin coolers. Along with a decade's worth of junk we haven't thrown away: baby toys, bicycles, mounds of clothes we'll never wear. Harmless stuff, thick with dust and webs.

I will my feet to the edge of the first step. Left arm tight across my torso, I grip the flashlight in my right hand. About to descend, I hear a whisper behind me.

"Teddi, you there?"

I barely keep from shrieking, recognizing Aidan's voice coming from my cell. I left it on my bureau. Stupid! Racing back through the closet, I retrieve the phone.

"Sorry! On my way. Just a little creeped."

Taking the steps sloth-slow, I inch along, toes clinging to each stair edge before I slide my foot out into darkness.

"Creeped by what? Zombie? Boogeyman?" He laughs. "Don't tell me Malevolent Pool Child has returned!"

"You're not helping."

"Sorry. What can I do?"

"Talk to me."

"About what?"

"Anything. No! Something nice."

I shuffle across the floor, cursing as I bump a shelf edge, send a stack of boxes sliding.

"Teddi! You okay?"

"Fine. I'm fine. Just knocked something over." Faking composure, I ask, "So. What's your favorite color?"

His answer comes out a question. "Orange?"

"Fave food?"

"Baklava."

"All-time favorite movie?"

He doesn't respond immediately. "Promise you won't laugh?"

"Of course."

"Milo and Otis."

"Wow. Really?"

"You promised."

"I'm not laughing. Just . . . incredulous."

"C'mon, the comic mishaps of a kitten and pug pup. What's not to love?"

"Well, I've never actually seen it, so I'll take your word. I'd just pegged you for an action/adventure type."

"Oh, *M&O*'s packed with action *and* adventure: rushing river, angry bear. I could go on."

Now I do laugh, surprising, considering my flashlight's begun to sputter, and I'm less than halfway across the pitch-dark store.

"Aid, I'm sort of freaking. I'm coming through the sealed-off part of the store and it's really dark and it's super creepy and my flashlight's about to crap out!"

"It's okay, Teddi. I'm right outside."

"Where exactly?"

"Across the street. Why?"

"Do me a favor. Come to the back of my building. There's a glass door across from the garages. That's where I'm headed."

"On my way."

"And, Aidan?"

"Yeah?"

"Keep talking."

My flashlight dies. I can barely see by the glow of my cell display. Every time I speed up, I collide with something, a tarp-draped cooler, a stack of picnic umbrellas.

Fortunately, Aidan's memorized the plot of *Milo and Otis*; he relates it in detail that, under other circumstances, would be excruciating. In this case, absorbed in his retelling, I make it across the room without losing it.

Running my hand along exposed plywood, I find the electric box, debate whether to hit the overheads. There's no way Brenda can see them, and the windows are draped with old quilts, so it's unlikely anyone outside will notice.

I thumb the switch. Nothing. Then, a low hum. Wading in blackness, I'm blinded as my half of the room goes fluorescent bright. I rub my eyes. As details come into focus, I'm embarrassed how ordinary—if skanky—it is in here. Turning, I review my path, a shuffle trail across the dusty tile.

I note the giant fan, not particularly threatening, except for the hopefully vacant wasp nest inside its wire cage. Judging by the constellations of mouse poop, the umbrella pile doubles as a rodent timeshare.

Along one wall a heap: black garbage bags marked TEDDI SUMMER and TEDDI WINTER, my ancient bouncy horse—his name was Pharaoh—and loads more I haven't seen in years. An Alder Time Capsule. I make a mental note to research HAZMAT suit rentals; might want to wade through this mess one day.

I briefly consider restacking toppled boxes—drinking straws and French fry containers—when Aidan raps on the glass behind me. His voice plays in stereo, from my phone and outside.

"Teddi, let me in! It's mad buggy."

"One second!"

I stop short at movement in the shadows by the ice cream cooler. Bracing for a herd of mice, or worse bats, I stiffen. There are footprints, smaller than mine, oozing up from the dust, muddy. They lead behind the cooler.

Head voice practically screeching *NO!*, I glide toward the prints. Forgetting Aidan, and everything else, I slide my phone into my PJ pocket. On my knees, I inspect the tracks. Smudges of dried mud. Whoever made them had to be small—and walking on tiptoe.

Sniffing, I note a faint chlorine smell.

The temperature drops.

I expect to see my breath.

I hear my name again.

This time, it's not Aidan, but a whisper from behind the freezer. Followed by this eerie giggle.

Crawling toward the cooler, I jiggle the dead flashlight, squeeze the battery compartment. The beam appears, weak, wavering. Training it on the tarp, I edge closer, reaching with my other hand. When I yank the fabric free, a form swims into focus through the dusty glass cooler lid.

"Who are you?" My voice is a pinched rasp.

No answer.

A word passes my lips, "Fawn?" then thins like mist. "You can't be her."

Hair hangs, a matted net, her features obscured. But I sense her gaze, can make out one eye, round as an owl's. Her skin's translucent, milky-quavering.

As I reach forward, her hand lifts. Bone-pale fingers clutch toward me from behind freezer glass.

Her mouth opens slightly. I hear a low hiss, catch this damp scent again, not chlorine. Vegetal, murky.

Lips moving, she points to the lump beneath my tank top.

Lifting the daisy charm, I raise my trembling hand. "You want your flower back?" I slip the chain from my neck and whisper, "Take it."

Pounding on the door behind me, Aidan shouts, "Teddi!"

I yell over my shoulder, "Coming!"

As my head snaps back, the flashlight dies. I hear frantic scuffling behind the cooler. Ripping the tarp aside, I plunge into the gloom, just register the gray rush as a mouse flattens, slips through a crack in the wall.

Surprise. No sign of a child—or anything besides cobwebs—back there.

Stunned to tears, frustration bolting me in place, I stare at the pendant in my shaking hand. "She was here. I know it!"

Inspecting the floor, it's impossible to spot any tracks, even my own. If hers were there, I've obliterated them crawling across filthy linoleum.

Shoving the charm in my pocket, I stand dead still—no idea how long—willing her back.

Aidan's voice slaps me back to reality. "If you're not coming out, I'll head home. I'm getting eaten alive out here!"

Blinking, I taste blood. My thumb's gnawed raw, cuticle ripped away. "God, sorry, Aid! Be right there."

I lunge for the door, toward Aidan's arms, away from this craziness. Shivering, I grasp the dead bolt. His expression stops me. His eyes—*vicious*. Clearly, he does not enjoy waiting.

When I mouth "Sorry" through the smeary glass, his eyes lighten. Pressing his face to the outside pane, no longer menacing, he's little-boyish, with his pig-squashed nose.

Wrestling the bolt, I twist left. It unlocks with a *snick*, and

Aidan pushes in, shoving me off balance with the heavy glass door.

"Thank God, you're here! I almost—"

"What took you so long?" His eyes flash anger, but—swiping a hand across his face—he produces a smile.

"I . . . I got scared, Aid. There was . . ."

He's not listening. Pushing the door shut, he rebolts it.

"I missed you, Teddi."

His eyes make me hesitate, but he advances, stride shaky.

"Aidan, are you drunk?"

He doesn't answer. Opening his arms, he repeats, "I missed you."

I back up a step.

"I asked you a question."

"What? No, I'm not *drunk*. Shit! Why are you being such a bitch?"

Now I step toward him, past him actually, to swing the door open. "This was a bad idea. You need to go."

"Make me."

I just glare at him, fists rammed deep in PJ pockets, trying to look tougher than I am.

Stepping back, Aidan squints as if trying to focus. Pouting, he's a little boy again, disappointed to leave the playground.

I have this urge to embrace him. Make everything better. Allow him ten more minutes on the jungle gym. Instead, I say, "I'll call you tomorrow."

Hands raised in an I-surrender stance, he backs toward the door, head hanging. I recognize this shame face from years of Brenda regret.

"I'm sorry."

"For what exactly, Aid?"

"Um . . . the bitch comment. Being a major dick. You didn't deserve that. I just, I really wanted to see you, and I . . . it felt like you were trying to get rid of me."

"Why would I do that?"

"I don't know. But why'd you take so long to let me in? I thought you changed your mind."

"About what? Coming out with you?"

"More than that. About me. Us."

"Oh, God."

"What?"

"You're not trying to convince me you of all people have low self-esteem. Because honestly, I'm not buying it." Pulling his shirttails, I lead him to this antique soda machine. Standing him in front, I brush the hair from his eyes and say, "Look."

He studies his dusty reflection, offering a tentative smile. "Not bad."

"No, no. Not 'not bad.' Very good indeed."

Peering into my eyes, he says, "Teddi, I really am. Sorry, I mean. Sometimes I just . . . I have these," he speaks to his feet, "moods."

"Moods?"

"Attic-black moods. The last thing I ever wanted was to be like my father." A single tear trails his cheek. "The way he treats her."

"Your mom?"

He seems not to hear. "We almost left once when I was small. She said she was done. But . . ." He shudders.

"What happened?"

"I was in my car seat when he broke the windshield." He smiles remembering it, the corners of his mouth lifting, eyes overcast. "Glass everywhere. Her forehead bleeding."

"My God."

He coughs. "But we went for counseling. And things got a little better. We learned to duck when the rage-clouds rolled in, and he mostly quit breaking shit. So we stayed."

"Aidan, I'm so sor—"

Pressing a finger softly to my lips, he says, "Anger's cost me girlfriends in the past, but I'll prove I'm more than my father's son. You, Teddi Alder, deserve nothing but my very best."

As we kiss, the tension of the last few minutes drains away. It probably had more to do with Pool Girl's visit than with anything Aidan said or did.

"What is it, Teddi?"

Now it's my turn to study my little piggies. "A couple days ago I barely felt worthy of ordering coffee from you, and now—"

"You shouldn't ever think that way. You're amazing."

"Me?"

He leans toward me, lips slightly parted. As I close my eyes to kiss him, an image seeps in: bone-pale fingers reaching toward me, lips moving. A chill creeping through me, I break Aidan's embrace, rush for the door.

"Teddi, where are you going?"

"Out of here! Come on!"

Yanking the door handle, I squeeze Aidan's hand, drag him into night.

11

After escaping the store, I'm full-tilt shaking, stuttery. Aidan looks worried, but I refuse to tell what happened. We roam the neighborhood. When he mentions skunks, I quickly agree to skip the park, but I'm actually thinking of her.

In search of snackage, we hit Round-the-Clock, at the corner of Baldwin and Welles. Trolling the aisles, we seek that perfectly balanced sugar-salt-grease ratio. At the counter, Aidan rummages in his pocket, producing a Ziploc stuffed with dollar bills and coins. Forking over $12.83 for our booty, he says, "You're officially a cheap date. But I have two whole bucks left. How 'bout an Italian ice?"

"Any lemon?"

Fishing in the case, he says, "Sure is."

"Then I'm in."

"It's good to see you smile."

Resisting the immediate urge to stop smiling, I answer, "It's good to have a reason to."

He beams. "Well, bringing smiles to female faces is kind of my trademark."

"I meant the Italian ice."

Passing Aidan's change, the clerk says, "Hold on to this one. She's something special."

We demolish a sack of peanut butter pretzels, a four-pack of cupcakes, and a bag of Twisted Fish candies as we wander anywhere but home.

Eventually we settle on Aidan's house. Afraid to wake his folks, we spread our salty-sweet remnants—a bag of cheesy puffs, half a raspberry soda, the lemon ice—on a table in his backyard gazebo.

We listen to the crickets and distant cars, our contribution to the night chorus the papery scrape of wood spoons against ice. The stillness feels perfect, sacred even.

Brushing DayGlo cheese powder from my chin, Aidan presses his lips to mine. Then, winding a strand of my hair in his fingers, he asks, "Tell me?"

I'm not sure whether it's the distance from my place, or the multitude of carbs I've ingested. It could be how Aidan studies me by the citronella candle glow. For whatever reason, I'm brave. Pulling the slim chain, I lift the daisy free from my collar and say, "So, I found this."

Taking the pendant, he lets it swing between his fingers. "Wow, I wonder which Kardashian dropped this."

"I'm not saying it's valuable, but it might be important."

"Important how?"

"It must belong to the girl in the pool. I found it dangling from the fence the other night after she disappeared."

He shakes his head. "Not this again. I thought we agreed there was no girl in the pool."

"Well, no. We didn't agree, actually. You decided. I went along because you're so darn persuasive—not to mention super hot—when you're soaking wet."

We kiss again, lips a perfect fusion of citrus and salt. Then Aidan draws back. "But seriously, you're not still obsessing over the pool incident?"

The way he says "incident" somehow implies there was no incident at all.

"I'm not obsessing. Not exactly. It's just . . . I haven't been able to stop thinking about her. What if she's a runaway or something? Don't we have some responsibility to—"

"I told you that night! We are not getting the cops involved! They'll just want to know what we were doing in the park at two in the morning."

"I never thought of that . . . but if you weren't in the park that night, we wouldn't be sitting here right now." I press my nose to his in an Eskimo kiss. "Funny how fate works."

Eyes crossing slightly at close range, Aidan inches backward on the bench. A thought creases his brow.

"Hey, Aid, what *were* you doing in the park, anyway?"

I can't read him; his expression seems designed to keep me at a distance.

"Shit, Teddi, would you please just drop it?"

Snatching the empty snack containers, he crushes them, pitching the wad into a barrel. Turning to me, arms crossed, he's waiting for some response.

All I can come up with is "Drop what?"

"This Patsy Drew bullshit. It's getting a little old."

I get the distinct impression I'm supposed to say something. That he's expecting me to voice agreement or—is he shitting me?—apologize.

Matching his angry stance, I say, "Are we on the verge of our first real fight? If we are, I want to clarify one thing. Are you comparing me to NANCY Drew, Girl Detective? If so, I'm not sure whether to be insulted or honored."

He scowls.

"Have you read any of those books, Aidan? Have you? Because if you're going to make a literary allusion, you ought to know what it is you're referencing. So, sample titles: *The Secret of the Old Clock. The Haunted Bridge. The Clue of the Dancing Puppet.*"

"What's your point?"

"Well, in spite of the crap dialogue and blatant gender stereotypes, Nancy was always right. But inevitably some Doubting Douchebag questioned her every move."

"What does this have to do with anything?"

"The Douchebag was generally forced to apologize to Nancy at the end of the story."

"So?"

"So do us both a favor, Aidan. Don't be Mister Douche."

Shouting, "Screw this!" he strides toward the porch.

I call after him, "I'm sorry, Aid." Crossing dew-damp grass, I clutch his arm. "You're not a douchebag. I'm just—"

Shaking me off, he says, "Why is this so important, Teddi? You had to be seeing things the other night. If not, it'd be all over the news—or there'd be about a million *Have you seen me?* posters tacked up! Wouldn't there be some sign? If there was an actual missing kid?"

"I guess, but . . ."

"And have you? Gotten a text alert? Seen anything on TV or online? Nothing, right?"

"No . . . but—"

"But what?"

"Sometimes, kids get taken, and . . . no one notices. Or . . . or . . . what if she's out there someplace, hurt, and nobody cares?"

"Do you know how crazy that sounds?"

I take a moment to answer, and probably should take another to reconsider, but instead I say, "I saw her again tonight."

Aidan just gapes like I've sprouted a third boob.

Finally, he says, "What do you mean you *saw* her?"

"In my house. The closed-up-store part. My getaway route.

Where you met me. Mom and I use it for storage; I haven't been in there for years. Anyway, when I was inside. It was pitch-black . . ." I'm shaking again. This time Aidan makes no move to comfort me. "I saw her."

"*Inside* your building?"

"Yes, hiding. Behind an old ice cream cooler."

"How could she get in?"

"I don't know."

"Is she still there?"

"I'm not sure."

"Not sure?" Expression morphing from concern to frustration, he says, "Wait, don't tell me. She disappeared again."

"Yes. My flashlight went out, and then she was gone. And there was just a mouse. I know how impossible it sounds, Aid. But you've got to believe me!"

He pauses to absorb what I've said.

"Did she say anything?"

"It's hard to say."

"Teddi, did she talk to you?"

"She . . . she kind of whispered, 'Give it back.' I think she was asking for the necklace."

I'm preparing for him to put his arms around me. He doesn't. Instead, he laughs. This brief, humorless bark. Then he says, "What the fuck is wrong with you?"

I don't quite know how to answer.

After a minute standing there, Aidan says, "Right. Well, it's late. I'll talk to you."

As I watch him slip through the screen door, my heart shrinks a size. But, vowing not to cry, I activate emotional autopilot. I walk home detached, pondering his question. What *is* wrong with me? I honestly have no answer.

12

Petra perches on the edge of a folding chair. Laptop balanced on tawny knees, she purses her lips. Then, smiling warily, she begins.

"I was ten, it was Sunday. I remember begging to wear my party dress to morning mass. It was lilac with a beaded belt; my mother said it was *too showy* for church.

"But I insisted. Olivia's party was right after, I didn't want to miss a minute, going home to change. I'd helped pick the theme, Unicorn Princess Pageant, and wanted to get there before anyone, so I could check out the decorations. Mrs. Castillo always cut corners; I was nervous we'd end up with Bargain Mart tablecloths and shit."

Pausing to smooth her hair, Petra asks, "It's okay to say 'shit,' right?"

With a soft "Yes," Eleanor gestures for Petra to continue.

An exaggerated throat-clear draws my attention to the corner. Ed slouches there, practicing his eye roll. Coughing to stifle a laugh, I refocus on Petra's story.

"Our Odyssey rolled up Carnival Drive toward Olivia's. First thing I spotted was the balloon arch out front. Hunter green with yellow streamers! All I could think was *That is so anti-princess!* They must've had select colors on clearance.

"Mom shot me a look in the rearview when I said, 'Eeeww!' her lips all pursed, like she was drinking through an invisible straw. She warned, 'Petra, be nice.' When wasn't I? But there's a universe of difference between being nice and lying. I wasn't about to tell Olivia those balloons were anything but embarrassing. She was my best friend!"

Voice cracking, Petra stops reading, slams her laptop. Since we're in large-group-sharing mode, Right Barbie, who's really named Jeanine, sits alongside Petra. She strokes her friend's bare arm and says, "I'm right here, Pet. You're doing great."

Eleanor moves knee-to-knee with Petra. Holding her gaze, she murmurs, the way you'd whisper a skittish dog. "You're teetering on the edge of something, aren't you?"

Petra nods, big-eyed.

"You mustn't run from it, Miss Rio. Please, continue. We're here to support you."

Petra sniffles, a mascara-tear plinking her lap. Gauging our reactions face by face, she exhales and opens her laptop. After entering her password with trembling fingers, she scrolls down, continues reading.

"My mom jolted to a stop, half in the driveway, half in the

street. With the engine running, she jumped out, calling over her shoulder, 'Stay put.'"

Eyes wet, Petra glances up from her screen. I note Jeanine's Honey Cat nail tattoos as she folds her tan hand over Petra's.

"That's when I noticed the flashing lights. An ambulance had pulled right onto the Castillos' lawn, squashed their tulip bed.

"They had one of those wheelie-stretchers; Liv's baby brother, Oscar, was strapped to it, his face puffy, blue-tinged. One ambulance guy pressed a mask over Oscar's mouth and nose. The other pushed this big needle into his chest."

Silence. The circle feels tighter, even though no one but Eleanor has moved a single chair. Ed's joined us, perched on the couch back, completely devoid of smirk.

"I don't remember getting out of the van, but all at once, I was beside the stretcher, close enough to see a string of yellow foam coming from Oscar's mouth. Close enough to catch the dark smell. I tried not to look, but couldn't help seeing the stain spread across his soccer shorts."

I'm plagued by sudden sweat; my stomach burns. I block my nose against the *dark smell* she mentioned. But how can I be smelling it now? In the library? Petra's not that good a writer.

I need her to stop. Now. I almost say so. I could insist, tell Eleanor. Suggest it might be best for Petra if we take a break. But really, it's not Petra I'm worried about. I bite my lip to trap a scream.

Petra continues, but I barely hear. My temples beat. Images

flood my head. The sandal smack of running feet. The tug of thorn and vine. My bloodied palm.

"Teddi? Is everything all right?" Ed's voice, low in my left ear. He's squatting just behind my chair. But I won't open my eyes.

Petra keeps reading.

"Olivia flew from the side yard, a streak of taffeta, her face warped in this horrible clown mask. Holding a big tissue flower, she ripped it, pieces dropping like dead moths at her feet."

My eyes fly open.

"Mrs. Castillo stood mannequin-stiff as Olivia wailed. 'Don't let him die! I didn't mean it! I don't hate him! I'm sorry, Oscar! I'm sorry!'

"That's when my mother grabbed Olivia's shoulders. Shoved her into a sitting position on the grass. Jabbed her finger in Liv's face and yelled, 'STOP IT!'

"At first, Olivia's mom was so calm, but then, when the paramedics loaded Oscar into the ambulance, she totally unraveled. Falling in a heap next to Olivia, she—"

Launching to the center of the circle, I stall, swaying slightly. Their eyes seek explanation, but the words shrivel on my tongue. Ed reaches for me. Shoving him aside, I bolt from the lounge, upstairs, straight to the restroom.

Locked.

I'm about to sprint to the info desk for a key when a little girl steps out of the bathroom. Pushing past, I bolt the door, race to the sink.

Head down, avoiding my reflection, I blast the water, scooping a handful to my face. Rather than help, the warm splash—its familiar sulfur whiff—worsens my nausea.

Ignoring toilet stench, I gulp oxygen, and examine Mirror Teddi. Stress and insomnia have etched mauve crescents below her eyes. I risk offending her and say, "You look awful."

Turning tables, she says, "What the fuck is wrong with you, Teddi?"

"Funny. You're the second person in about twelve hours to ask that."

Eyes glazing, I surrender to glimpses of last night.

I had no reply for Aidan, am no closer to answering my mirror self now. Turning from my reflection, I lean back against the sink. I honestly might be going crazy. Just now, losing it in front of the group . . .

"What *is* wrong with me?"

Breathless, I dry sob. Pacing the cramped space, I grind fists into my eyes, repeating, "Okay, Teddi. You're okay."

I wish it were true.

Minutes pass.

Breathing human-style again, I inspect Mirror Teddi for damage. She looks awful. Puffy, splotched. I risk the water again—no funky smell now—wash my face without inciting queasiness.

A gentle tap and "Ahem" spin me. Wrestling a wad from the paper towel dispenser, I dab my cheeks, blow my nose.

"Who is it?"

"Ed. Are you all right?"

Now there's a trick question. But in true Alder Woman fashion, I reply, "Great, thanks."

"Come out, Teddi."

Twisting the handle with my soggy bouquet, I peek out. "Um, it kind of reeks in here. You might want to stand back."

He inspects me like a seedpod under a microscope, barely allows me to exit the bathroom before repeating, "Are you all right?"

His tone's so comforting—so different from Aidan's last night—my tear ducts kick-start. Ed folds me into a stiff embrace. Snuffling against his chest, I struggle to answer.

Before I can, an elderly totters up. Tapping her cane against the doorframe, she says, "Waiting for the toilet?"

We step aside, and Granny sidles into the tiled cubicle, locking the door.

Eyes shooting sympathy rays, Ed says, "Eleanor sent the group on a descriptive field trip with their journals. They'll be back in twenty minutes. Want to sit?"

"Why not."

We head past the computer workstations, behind Nonfiction. It's empty back here. Ed and I settle into a pair of frayed armchairs facing the window.

Outside, Petra and Jeanine inspect an azalea. In the distance, Todd appears to take notes as Ken interacts with a parking meter.

Picking at loose upholstery threads, I say, "So. You must all think I'm disturbed, the way I ran out. Is Petra pissed?"

Ed grins. "Nah. You made her night. She said she felt 'validated as an artist.'"

"Way to go, Petra. That's some literary killer instinct."

Serious again, Ed inches closer. Concern radiating, he says, "It *was* an intense story, but something else is wrong. Am I right?"

Fearing compassion will reboot my tears, I shift away. But Ed leans forward and says, "Let me help."

"What makes you think you can?"

Eyes boring into mine, he breathes deep before saying, "Is it Ai—" then breaking the gaze, he continues, "your boyfriend?"

"Aidan's the least of my problems right now."

"But you're saying he is one of them."

"Why are you so interested in our relationship, Ed?"

When he doesn't answer, I start to get up.

He stops me. "You're a nice girl, Teddi. And he . . . don't let him mess with your head."

"God. Why would you say that? You don't even know Aidan."

"I know . . . his type. Just," taking my hand, he says, "be careful."

I plan to offer a rote "I'm fine," so my actual answer surprises us both. "I'm scared."

Tightening his grip, he asks, "Of him?"

"No, not Aidan. It's . . . I'm afraid I'm going nuts."

From behind us, Eleanor asks, "Why would you say that?" Eyebrow raised, she shoots a look at Ed.

Letting go of my hand, he springs from his chair, stammering, "I . . . uh . . . should check in at Reference."

Eleanor says, "Splendid idea."

I rise, but she urges—in a tone I've used on Binks—"Stay."

Once I'm back in my chair, she says, "Petra's piece had real emotive heft. It's hardly crazy to react authentically, Miss Alder. You needn't employ the strength of trees in all things. Vulnerability is an asset equal to strength."

Tempted to ask if she also moonlights as a fortune cookie scribe, I restrain my tongue.

"One of my Lit and Comp students said the beauty of literature is its power to provoke emotion. I rather like the use of that word: *provoke*."

"It's not just Petra's story, though. It's the piece I started writing."

"'The Sad Giraffe'?" She tsks, features slipping into a subtle frown.

"Um, no."

"Oh, good! I'd hoped you weren't too attached to that one. I have feedback for you." She fishes in her accordion folder.

"Now, it's fairly pointed. Promise you'll take it in the spirit in which it was intended."

"I'm not in the mood for a critique, Eleanor. No offense."

"Now, let's not be defensive. Writing demands union—creation to self-assessment—and that process, stretching the writerly muscles, becoming an authentic auteur, necessitates discomfort, even pain. You mustn't be upset over one artistic, shall we say, *dud.*"

"I'm not upset over my writing! I couldn't care less about my writerly muscles!"

I expect Eleanor to hit me with a classic librarian shush. Instead, smiling frostily, she squeezes her folder shut. "There's really no call for disrespect of the craft. Whatever struggles you're having."

Lord, the woman's preposterous. Would she give a crap if I told her what's really bothering me?

I decide to test it. "I've been seeing . . . someone."

Her lips purse in a weirdly prim grin. "I met him, remember? Quite the achievement."

"I'm not talking about Aidan. Besides, it's complicated with him. It's not a given we'll be spending any more time together."

"Shame."

"Whatever. Anyway—oh, forget it. You'll just think I'm wacko, too."

Cocking her head, she says, "Try me."

She's the closest thing to a responsible adult in my life, so I give it a shot.

"I'm not sure whether it's more accurate to say I've been seeing some*one* or . . . some*thing*. It started the other night in the park."

I spend the next fifteen minutes describing the pool encounter. How the girl vanished. Her presence inside the store.

Eleanor's spellbound. The way she reacts, I begin to believe I may not be entirely insane.

She asks, "And did she interact? Seem to comprehend you?"

Unsure how to answer, I describe the girl reaching out, lips moving, grasping toward the necklace. Eleanor actually squeals, "How deliciously eerie!"

When I offer the pendant, she scoops it from my hands, examines it like an artifact.

After several moments, I say, "So. Am I?"

Softly, Eleanor asks, "Are you what?"

Dreading her answer, I blurt, "Crazy."

Ken bounds toward us, Todd trailing like a tail, eager to report the observational booty collected on their Literate Green field trip.

I'm relieved when Eleanor says, "Kenneth, be a dear and round up the rest of the group? Miss Alder and I need a moment. We'll be down in two shakes."

Ken mopes toward the stairwell. Todd remains, gawking at

us, like he's on the verge of an important question or declaration. Maybe a sneeze.

Eleanor says, "Todd, a question?"

Muddled, he speckles deep pink; then he spins and sprints after Ken.

Eleanor says, "Crazy? Hardly. There are three more likely possibilities."

"Three. Really?"

Voice a whisper, she says, "Yes. You're either—one: lying in some woeful bid for attention."

"Nope."

"Thought not. Option two: there's a feral child loose, and she's imprinted on you."

"That's unlikely, isn't it?"

"Afraid so."

"Then . . . what's option three?"

Eleanor thrums the edge of her folder. Biting her lip, she regards me seriously. "I fear, Miss Alder, this may be a haunting."

13

Ears covered, Willa shrieks. Like every year, she's missed about 80 percent of the display, ducking beneath a beach towel whenever a firework explodes. Still, she insisted we come. Together. I'm actually okay with it. Our tradition.

This year, I'm extra glad for company. Screw independence! It's nearly two weeks since our disastrous night picnic, and I've yet to get an apology, or hear a word—no call, no text—from Aidan.

Admittedly, I've done my best to avoid contact. After a twelve-day hiatus from Java Jill's, mocha withdrawals have subsided. Aidan pangs? Not so much. And Mister Graham's not alone in having ditched me.

Brenda fled for the holiday weekend, tagging along with Mandy and Dev to his cabin, someplace called Lake Saint Catherine, Vermont. I cannot comprehend her desire to play third wheel with her custodial crush and his girlfriend, but there's no fathoming Mom's questionable choices. Willa floated the possibility of some three-way action afoot, a prospect so reprehensible I refuse to entertain it. More like, Mommy couldn't pass on a four-day, booze-filled/daughter-free holiday. Can't say I blame her.

Ordinarily, I'd appreciate the alone time. This could've been my golden opportunity for a PJ-optional overnight with a certain someone. Course, the timing's all wrong now that we're not speaking. And I suppose it's for the best, in light of my baby free–teens vow.

But since Aidan and I went *poof*, I've been abnormally needy with Brenda. When I told her about our fight, she surprised me, reacted in appropriate maternal fashion. She made a legit stab at seeming disappointed by the demise of my fledgling relationship, even reassured me, saying, "He's not good enough for you, baby." Plus, she stocked the freezer with Forever Fudge ice cream before hitting the road.

Even so, I can't shuck this lame sense of abandonment. I've done my best to dismiss the possibility Binks and I may not be alone. My major concession to Bren's absence—and our possible haunted houseguest—was to leave the lights and TV on all night. But there's been no sign of Miss Phantom since her store appearance. I pray it's over. If there ever was an *it*.

Tonight after fireworks, Willa's sleeping over, so it's unlikely Pool Ghoul will show. It's clear she prefers having me to herself. Besides, despite Eleanor's dramatic reaction, I truly doubt some poltergeist's stalking me. Though a ghost is preferable to the idea I might be losing my freaking mind.

The sky above the ball field is alight with sparks, red and green chrysanthemums fading to smoke in the heavy air. No break in the weather yet. Nine forty-five and the mercury's hardly backed off.

After a month of record temps, this relentless heat's getting to people; cops have broken up three near-brawls. Crowd uproar—peppered with noisy arguments, yowling babies—provides a steady backdrop for the pyrotechnics. I picture Binks in the bathtub, fear-flattened by booms.

Leaning on an elbow, I swig from my water bottle. We're in left field, prime space to survey the crowd, a party mix of ages. Little kids shriek by, toppling lawn chairs of the elderlies. I'm careful not to dwell on the amorazzi, couples our age, leg-twining on the grass. I have this queasy feeling I'll spot Aidan dry humping some Teddi stand-in.

Bad enough we ran into Ed and his girlfriend, Glade. She was this sexed-up, 3D Disney princess, all boobs and glimmer. But ultra-clingy. He practically had to peel her off to say hello. And she was—ack!—super nice. She invited Willa and me to join them for chilled organic fruit cups. I totally wanted to punch her.

Ed looked relieved when I politely declined. Following a brief exchange with Willa, who'd eagerly invaded their cooler, we took our leave.

Later, as we lounge on our quilt, Ed strolls up and says, "Can I talk to you?"

Willa says, "Go for it." Knees cracking, she rises, and we watch as she weaves through the maze of people.

Squatting, Ed says, "Sorry if that was awkward. Glade can be, um, a . . . bit much."

"Why should that matter to me?"

"Oh . . . no reason."

He sputters, on the edge of speaking, until I say, "You going to sit?"

"Sure." Tickling the quilt hem with his finger, he asks, "So, where's the Bean Stud?" When I don't answer, he continues. "Macchiato Man. Lou Latte. Shouldn't he be here?"

I shrug. "Didn't work out."

"That's too bad." Catching himself in a smile, Ed ducks his head like a contrite pony, then says, "All right . . . uh . . . guess I'll see you at the library."

Acting more nonchalant than I feel, I answer, "I guess."

As he strides across the field, this pang occupies my gut. It can't possibly be jealousy, but part of me wants to follow him, and not for the chilled fruit.

Willa reappears. Chin on my shoulder, she says, "So. He's not unattractive."

Rolling onto my back, I say, "Hadn't noticed."

She laughs. Then, swooping her towel in the air, she wafts it down, covering our heads. Beaming, she says, "What do you say we head home? Call it an early night?"

"Sounds good to me. But are you sure you don't mind

bailing on the fireworks? I mean, so far you haven't seen any."

"Nah, I'm good. I do this for your benefit."

"Really?"

"Yuppers."

Slipping free of the towel, I wind it into an enormous turban over Willa's hair.

"So, where's Nic tonight?"

"Probably home practicing lines. I'm starting to regret getting him involved in the play; he's obsessed. He's at rehearsal practically every night, even when he's not on call. Says he enjoys watching the process."

"Well, you've got to be there, too, right?"

"Yeah, but not as much as him." She sighs. "Even when we're not there, it's all he talks about. He's got a Bard fixation or some damn thing. I miss the simpler times. Back when he was into WrestleMania."

"No. You don't."

"You're right."

We gather our junk: sandals, snack bags, a strictly for-show Frisbee. Snapping the quilt in the air, Willa pelts me with sunburnt grass and candy wrappers. Each taking two corners, we fold, Willa humming this skip rope rhyme from when we were kids. With everything stuffed into her big mesh bag, we walk toward my place.

Elbowing through the crowd, I expect to see Aidan. I'd like to believe I'd serve him a helping of cold shoulder. After all,

Willa and I have rehearsed, practicing for that very situation.

Controlling herself for once, she hasn't bombarded me with questions, though she must be dying to. When I described our fight, she accused me of being "crazy and/or nuts" to let him get away.

I overreacted to *crazy*. I'd never hung up on Willa before, a feat when you've known someone since fifth grade. But, in my current state of psychological self-doubt, I suppose heightened sensitivity's not surprising.

Willa called back immediately to apologize. In solidarity, she even promised to boycott Java Jill's. That's true friendship.

Passing home plate, we're arm-in-arm, 'til Willa breaks free. Sprinting ahead, she sings the skipping song again, and I think how much simpler life would be if we'd stayed ten years old. Ten was the perfect age. I was still pre-period. And I'd gotten over Corey moving away after what happened at the pond.

Shit. Why am I thinking about that now?

I watch Willa shrink as she approaches the far-off pool. Suddenly woozy, legs turning to jelly, I falter. Sunstroke's a long shot past 10:00 p.m. Must be this heat.

My eyes are open, but my vision tunnels inward, like I'm seeing the world through a cardboard tube. Straining to focus, reality shimmers, and it's the pond in front of me. Swaying ferns, low-hung branches. The tug of thorn and vine. I bring my hands to my face, study them, expecting—

"T Bear? You okay?" Willa looms over me where I've landed.

"What? Sure. Why?"

"Well, look at you, ass-flat on the grass. Thought you were right behind me."

"I . . . I was."

Eyes narrowing, she says, "Teddi, you seriously look like you just saw a ghost."

A strangled laugh escapes me.

Taking a water bottle from the mesh sack, Willa makes me drink. My head clears, but when I close my eyes, I see him. Corey.

He's laughing, yelling for me to catch up. And he's not alone. This wiry girl, all mangy curls, dirty overalls, stands beside him, arm draped around his shoulder. Corey says, "Come on, Teddi! Fawn knows a secret place!"

My eyes snap open, but my vision's blue-prickly.

Willa's voice. ". . . can't deny it's taking a toll."

"Sure, a toll." I inspect my palms again.

"Teddi, are you even listening?"

"Wait, taking a toll? What is?"

"This whole thing with You-Know-Who."

Locking my eyes on her face helps me focus. "Wills, honestly, you have my permission to say his name. It's not as if we're dealing with the Dark Lord. It's just Aidan."

She repeats the words, "Just Aidan," grimacing as though she's got a raunchy taste on her tongue. Then, eyes going wide, she says, "Holy shit."

I touch her arm. "Wills? What is it?"

Standing, she says, "I've made a shocking mental connection." Her face splits in a grin, but her eyes stay serious. "If it had worked out, someday you might've married that a-hole, and then your name would've been Teddi Graham!"

I can't help smiling back, as I say, "Well, in that case, the death of our relationship is more mercy than catastrophe."

Clicking her water bottle against mine, Willa says, "To breakups!"

I reply, "To ditching d-bags!"

Squealing, she douses me with bottle dregs and shouts, "To crumbling that stale, stinking cracker!" When I'm quiet, she says, "Get it? Graham? Cracker?"

"Good one." Grinning, I reach toward her and say, "Aidan the Flawed."

Clasping my hand, Willa hoists me from the grass, declaring, "Aidan the Bastard!"

"Aidan the Prick!"

We raise fists in triumph, and I yell, "Aidan the Shit-Heel, Dream-Crusher Graham!"

"Hey."

We've practiced repeatedly, but this was never part of the script. I spin, and he's standing there, working his best sheepish grin.

Glancing at Willa, I'm jealous, wishing I could channel her tough cool. Then, praying he won't assume my unsteadiness has to do with him, I baby-step forward.

"Happy Fourth, Teddi. Willa."

He's clearly spent our away time basking, because even in night shadow, I see he's about two shades more beautiful than when last we met. I just stand there, mouth slightly open, feeling my cheeks darken as well.

Stepping between us, Willa says, "Oh, hey. Didn't expect to see you here. Figured you'd suffocated or something."

"Willa . . ." I wish, not for the first time, her braces included some kind of jaw-locking mechanism.

He regards her with a quizzical chin dip. "Suffocated?"

"Yeah, from having your head buried so far up your ass."

They assess each other. Aidan looks unsure if Willa's joking. I'm sure. She's not. That girl takes our sisterhood dead serious. When she heard about Ryan Hecht's Class-A Dickery, she plotted a revenge scheme worthy of Poe. Luckily, I found out before she lured him into a catacomb. She'd have landed in juvie for sure.

My wonky legs undermine my desire to push past Aidan and bolt for my front door. As if I'm wearing thirty-pound shoes, the best I can manage is a halting wobble. Attempting to turn away, I swoon again. Aidan and Willa each grab an elbow, supporting me.

Going limp as our picnic quilt, I visualize them each taking a pair of limbs, team folding me into quarters, stuffing my deflated form into the mesh bag. We stand in awkward kick line position for a minute more, until I'm stable enough to walk on my own.

"Sorry about that, guys. I felt a little dizzy for a sec. This heat . . ."

I don't mention my weird, psycho-vision. I can imagine Aidan's reaction. He'd probably call me crazy again. Instead, I turn to Willa and say, "Come on, let's get out of here. Binks must be climbing the walls."

Disregarding Aidan's pout, I link arms with Willa. Legs back to normal, I plod slowly anyway, half hoping he'll catch up. Stop us. Sweep me into his arms as fireworks explode in the sky. Nauseating.

Mounting the hill above the pool, I'm careful not to glance waterward. Last thing I need is another freaky visitation. I'd suggest we crash at Willa's place instead, but her folks are hosting a bunch of relatives for the holiday, a major houseful. That's partly why she was so psyched to sleep over in the first place.

Approaching the driveway, I feel Aidan's presence behind us. It takes every drop of determination I possess, plus Willa's vise grip on my wrist, to face forward.

At the park edge—the tiger lily border I call Binks's sniffing station—I hear my name.

Turning, I find Aidan a few yards away. Nic is with him. They both hold sparklers.

As I stand, speechless, Willa storms across the driveway. Squeezing Nic's arm, she drags him behind an oak. I should warn them about poison ivy, but I'm transfixed in Aidan's gaze. He comes no closer, regarding me from asphalt's edge.

Genuflecting, head lowered, he's balanced on one knee in the grass. Lifting his chin, he extends a hand toward me, and, barely perceptible, begins to stir the air, his sparkler trailing these fleeting shapes, almost too bright to look at.

Scarcely aware of Binks's barking, or of the hushed argument from behind the ancient tree, I recognize this as some half-assed attempt at grand romance, an iconic '80s movie moment, Aidan's *Say Anything*. Of course, he'd probably call it *Say Everything*. Frick, why do I find that so charming?

I've resolved to shut him down, go inside, slam the door. But then it clicks. He's spark writing. Unable to look away, I edge across the blacktop.

Aidan's arm sweeps and loops. Slowly, words take shape, sizzled into blackness: *Teddi I need you*. He swirls a final flourish, and briefly, this perfect heart hangs between us.

As it wafts upward into smoke, a tear tracks Aidan's cheek. Rising to his feet, he smiles, arms open to me. My own eyes pooling, I move toward him.

Just then, Willa stomps from behind the tree, Nic following her.

"—not what I meant, baby!"

"Just save it, Nic! And don't try to *baby* yourself out of this one!"

"Come on, Willa, if you'd give me a chance to—"

She turns to me. "Can you believe these two, Teddi? Mister Perfect has Nicky brainwashed or some damn thing!"

Trance broken, I turn attention to Willa as Aidan's sparkler spits its last faint stars.

"Wait, Willa. I don't get it."

She steps between us. "Neither did I, but apparently—"

Flinging his sparkler to the dirt, Aidan grinds the final glimmers with his heel.

As he walks off, Willa yells after him. "That's right, jackass, run away! You've caused enough trouble for one n—"

"Can't you ever just shut up?" Aidan towers over Willa, leaching ferocity.

Nic's jaw drops open like a busted mailbox.

I freeze.

Willa stands her ground as Aidan scowls down at her, fists clenching and unclenching. Then, rounding on Nic, she says, "Anything you want to say to this shithead?"

He coughs twice, hard, but manages only, "Uh."

"Typical."

Cracking his knuckles, Nic scuffs the ground with one sandal.

"Just go, Nicholas. I'll deal with you tomorrow."

Apparently relieved to be granted a tomorrow, he slopes away.

Shoulder to shoulder with me, Willa says, "So, that means it's in your hands, Teddi."

"What is?"

"My honor. You're not going to let this maniac talk to me that way, are you?"

Aidan makes no move to apologize, just looks from me to Willa with this stony expression. His nose wrinkles.

I stammer, "Willa, I . . . I don't think Aidan meant to . . . And . . . and you guys did sort of interrupt a special moment."

"Don't even tell me you're going to give him another chance."

"Wills, don't do this."

"Do what? Make you choose between your best friend and Roid Rage? Pretty simple choice."

It actually takes me a moment. Two sets of steely eyes boring into me, I weigh a lifetime of friendship against a boatload of romantic potential. I'm about to speak, not quite sure how to phrase my answer, when Aidan shakes his head.

"Skip it, Teddi. It's not a competition, whatever Medusa says. We'll figure it out another time." Stepping forward, he brushes lips against my forehead. "I'll call you."

Willa's eyes bulge. The girl's as fierce as Binks.

Pushing his luck, Aidan addresses her. "Give Nic a break. He's a good guy."

She shoots him a glare so withering, I'm amazed he doesn't turn to stone. Then she grabs my arm and we head inside.

14

Willa sprawls on my bed, hair a giant inkblot on the pillow. Her talent for falling asleep regardless of circumstance generally makes her a lousy sleepover guest. Tonight, I'm relieved when she fizzles to a stop and commences snoring.

She has reason to be tired after two hours of ranting. Aidan's crime was persuading Nic to break up our sleepover. I was initially flattered he'd tried to get me alone. Couldn't admit that to Willa, though. She was fixed on Aidan trying to "get rid of" her.

The more she griped about his "plot," the more I saw her point. After complete silence for two whole weeks, he shows up expecting . . . what, exactly? And he goes behind my back, gets Nic to help? Pretty sleazy, come to think of it.

But, oh, that sparkler thing. Kind of brilliant.

Anyway, I couldn't let Willa see I was conflicted. Cripes, I practically had to make a blood oath I'd pick her over him. Girlfriend has serious attachment issues.

My game of emotional Ping-Pong, coupled with repeated white lying to Willa, has me worn out. Splayed on my beanbag, I practice purging all Aidan thoughts. Lids closed, I breathe rhythmically, attempt to join Willa in dreamland. No luck.

Frustrated, I gaze at the ceiling.

Journal on my lap, the giraffe pencil rests atop splayed pages. Letting my vision melt into mid-distance, I inhale through my nose. Exhaling through my mouth, I begin to relax. Focused on the collage frame—I brought it up from the downstairs shelf—studying my school pictures, I move from grade eight backward.

Beginning the task of traveling back to age seven, I write.

They're giggling. New Girl leads. I call her that because Corey and I only just met her—even if she acts like they're best friends. Plus, she claims her name is Fawn, but I've never met anyone with that name, and everybody knows a fawn's a baby deer, not a person. I'd have believed it if she'd told us her name was "Fox" or "Snake." She has that sort of slippery menace.

Ever since she came around—has it only been a week?—things are different. It's all double-dares and you-scareds? We never play our games anymore. She's trying to get my neck broken with her challenges—Bet you can't jump from the top of the garage!—but it won't work. I have sense. And strength. And Brenda says, "Enough will for three seven-year-olds."

Brenda's my mom, but she lets me call her by her real name; sometimes she calls me "Little Sister." She says I'm as stubborn as her, and that's "major league stubborn." And she tells me it's no accident we're named Alder, and that's a tree. She says, even as a baby, if I made my mind up not to move, it was as if I'd put down roots.

Speaking of roots, we're playing this dumb game. Have been for the past four days. New Girl says the ground is acid, the only safe place for walking's on the rocks and roots that slither across the path.

It was a challenge, making our way around the pond without setting foot on grass or mud, but now I'm bored. Corey would play this stupid game forever, though. If she said so. He must be in love with her. Even shared his favorite sour apple candy, when I practically have to beg for one. Dummy.

And she's not so great. Sure, she's older—almost eleven—and pretends to know stuff, but I'm always catching her in lies. Like she says she lives by herself in a tent in the woods, but that can't be true. She's just a kid, double digits or not.

I followed her yesterday after Corey went home. Said she was going to ride the bus downtown, sneak into the movies. Corey and I never get to ride the bus on our own, and we sure wouldn't risk sneaking in. You could end up in jail.

I could tell he was impressed when she told her plans, even though he did his best to act all cool, pushing his chest out. Said he'd been sneaking into the movies since he was real little. He claimed he stole popcorn, too. Great lie. How could you steal popcorn, when they keep it behind the counter in that glass case?

And she pretended to believe him, or else she's just that stupid.

Anyway, I tracked her, like one of our old missions, diving behind bushes, low to the ground. She cut through yards, and even though I felt funny, I trailed her, crouching in gardens, behind sheds and pool fences. She never did go near the bus stop.

But she did head downtown. It got way harder to follow, once we left the neighborhood. There were fewer hiding places, and I had to be careful she didn't see me. I slipped behind buildings and parked cars, even pretended to be part of a family crossing the street.

I lost her for a few minutes, and when I spotted her again, I almost blew it. Came around the corner of this building, and she was sitting right in front of me. I was sure she saw me. Ducking back, I spied on her, but she just sat there.

I figured she was resting. She certainly wasn't anywhere near the movies on the stoop at Saint Anthony's. I usually avoided that place. It's not nice to say, but the people who hung around waiting to be fed creeped me out. And I didn't like remembering when I was real little, and Brenda and I went there for supper.

She said it was better taking handouts from strangers than from her parents, but I didn't think so. I always gagged on shame as we lined up with our Styrofoam plates. Some of the people seemed nice, but I never talked to anybody.

'Til the day I met Corey.

He plunked down at the long table, right across from me,

and said, "I'm Corey. I'm going to drive a FedEx truck when I get big. Let's be best friends."

After that, we just were. Not sure whether our shared dad-lessness helped bond us—I doubt we discussed it—but we did everything together. And seeing Corey made Saint Anthony's someplace I almost looked forward to going.

But this was different. No Corey. No Brenda. I was here to catch New Girl in one of her lies.

From behind the bricks, I watched her as she sat. She didn't seem interested in talking to anyone. Some people waved, some called to her. She wouldn't offer more than a word or two, even though she seemed to know them.

I felt jealous of how she could talk to anyone without being afraid. But I felt bad for her, too, acting so at home at the soup kitchen.

After a while, this guy came and sat next to her, right up close. I got a bad feeling then. Something changed. It was the way she was sitting, shoulders folded in, knees up under her chin. When he slid closer, tried putting his arm around her, she scooted to stoop's edge.

He seemed not to care that he was bothering her. Worse, it looked like he enjoyed it. His lips spread to reveal a wedge of teeth, some splotched, lots missing, but his eyes—blue ice—never smiled. Rubbing the top of her head with one large palm, he fuzzed her hair into a nest of snarls.

Then, snatching at the corduroy knapsack she always car-ried, he snapped it free of her shoulder, pawed inside. When she tried grabbing it back, he held it high above her, jiggling it, like teasing a dog.

Leaping at his hand, she yelled, "Give it back!" but he just laughed, some of the others joining in.

After a couple minutes, bored with pesking her, he bent low and said something in New Girl's ear. I couldn't hear, but she wasn't happy, whatever he'd said. Her eyes flashed same as when I told her I was sick of playing everything her way.

I knew I shouldn't go closer or I might get caught, but I was frantic to hear. As he gripped her waist, talking right in her face, I took my chance. Inching nearer, I squatted alongside the mailbox by the stairs. If she turned, she'd see me for sure. But so what? She didn't own the sidewalk. And if she got ashamed I'd seen her here, it would serve her right for telling her lies.

Even with my eyes closed, I couldn't have missed what happened next. The guy muttered something I couldn't make out, and she yelled, "You can't make me! You're my brother, not my father!"

So at least I'd learned one thing. New Girl was a liar, saying she lived by herself in the woods. She had a brother. Even though he looked nasty—grimy, wild haired, with that big, dirty smile—and bossed her around, I envied her for that.

It was lonely sometimes having nobody but Brenda. And of course, Corey. But if New Girl stuck around, I was afraid I'd lose him. Seemed Corey liked her better.

Grabbing her arm, New Girl's brother hauled her from the stoop so fast her feet came right off the ground. I could almost feel the tug in my own armpit. If he yanked any harder, her arm might snap, rip free like a chicken wing.

New Girl started yelling then, every kind of dirty word. Some of them I'd never even heard Brenda use, and she'd swear all crazy when she was mad. The worst part was no one in the lot seemed to care. A couple old guys actually started hooting. One yelled, "Show her who's boss, Eli!"

Giving New Girl a little shake, Eli winked and answered. "Oh, she knows I'm boss. You better believe, that's the one thing my little Fawn knows."

Fawn. So, she'd been telling the truth about that.

Knowing she'd told us her true name sort of made Fawn my real friend. Now I was anxious for her, wanted to do something to help. I figured if I stepped out from behind the mailbox and walked right up to her, her brother might let her alone.

But I didn't get the chance to find out. I took a few breaths for strength, and then it happened.

Still laughing, Eli dragged Fawn over to this car alongside the building. Ugly, rotten-vegetable green, it was so dirty you could hardly see in the windows. Fawn quit fighting then; when he opened the back door—reaching in through the window— she hopped right in.

Shaken by the car door slam in my head, I drop my pencil. The carved-wood shaft disappears beneath my bed in a wobbling roll. I hesitate before retrieving it.

I'm on spongy turf here, the land of dreams and echoes. Eleanor claims emotional truth is what's important, but does that mean I should believe whatever bubbles up from memory's bog?

I'm losing grip on the line between memory and fabrication, can't quite get traction. My mind skidding, I picture my thoughts leaving streaks like . . .

"Muddy flip-flops on the kitchen floor."

It barely registers that I've said that aloud. Sliding from the bean chair, I belly-crawl halfway beneath the bed. Spitting dust, I shove aside a Lego-stuffed shopping bag and reach toward my pencil.

Edging onto the bed, careful not to wake Willa, I prop pillows behind my back and open the book again, pressing lead point to page.

I begin writing, the words seeming to form within my hand, rather than my brain. I hardly look at the pencil as it scratches.

"Mama."

She nearly drops the heavy glass, amber liquid drenching the kitchen table. Standing, she lunges at me across the speckled tiles, forehead scrunched. She always starts angry, furious right off, when I get hurt. Skinned elbows earn a spanking, so as she comes closer, I back away.

"Teddi, stop!" Her shrill voice makes me wince.

Head down, I see my sandals have mucked the tiles—a crazy

hopscotch path painted in mud. Crawling the floor, I swipe with my palms, but as I smear the mud, the color darkens from brown to maroon. Lifting my hands palms-up, I frown at the biting scent of blood.

Mama lifts me, whispers, "All right. All right."

I don't resist as she strips my clothes, checks me all over. Carrying me through the living room, she lowers me into the empty tub. When she blasts the shower, I shrink into the far corner, where the spray can't catch me. Mama plugs the drain with the rubber cork thing. Concentrating on the shower curtain, I memorize rows of ocean fish.

Steam clouds surround us, bubble-gum smell rising as she scrubs my hair. Mama's hands come up redder each time she plunges them beneath the suds. Water so hot I want to scream.

Water so hot, scared I might melt.

Water so hot . . .

Why can't I stop shivering?

Mama lifts me from the tub, wraps me in her soft, white robe, carries me to the couch. Kissing my forehead, she says, "All right, baby. No one can hurt you now."

She pours liquid from the tall bottle into my giraffe mug, stirs in Splenda, makes me sip. Bitter . . .

I sleep.

Why isn't she here? Freaking Vermont of all places! She warned me there'd be no cell reception, said she'd check in tomorrow from a pay phone at the general store. What is she in, some time-warp colonial village?

I need her *now*. Need to ask her what happened. Who she was talking about. *Did* someone hurt me? Can't remember. When I approach the pond, I hit a cinder block wall. Memory slips from my grasp, a balloon string in the wind. A snake's tail through dark water.

I see Fawn and Corey, smell that chemical stink in the air. Not the usual swampy smell. There's a scream and I'm—

Running.

Branches whip me. The journey is gone.

The next solid thing, those sandal smears on the kitchen floor, shivering in the tub. The bath-scrubber against my skin. Choky brown liquid, bitter even with sweetener.

Then . . . nothing.

One other person might hold a clue to what happened, but we haven't spoken in almost nine years. I have to find Corey, because I'm certain of one thing.

Something terrible happened at the pond. Fawn never came back. And my memory of after is foggy as the bathroom when Mama soaked me in the tub.

Retrieving my laptop from the bedside table, I power on. My screen winks, the new screensaver—a stand of alder trees—sheds a pale glow across my bedspread.

Opening a browser, I log into my friend site, and tap search. When I type the name Corey Boatwright, thumbnails cascade down the left column. I study them one by one, hoping to catch an echo, the now version of Corey's childhood grin.

A few faces are possibles, though none strike a gut chord. I spot one potential Corey, from Alpharetta, Georgia. Something about the tilt of his head, the sparking eyes, calls to me. I click the thumbnail, his info displays. No match. He's ten years older than my Corey; plus, he's a winter baby. Corey's a Leo, same as me.

Moving on, some are girl Coreys, some are white. I rule them out, doubt he's changed that radically.

I spend twenty minutes scrutinizing faces, but none of the details match. There must be a faster, surer way.

Clicking to that Peopleseek site, I rifle my mental storage box, retrieve a pair of names, Corey's mom, his older brother.

Her name was Adele, same as the singer. There's a listing in Framingham, Massachusetts, for an Adele (Boatwright) Kingston. She'd be the right age. It's possible Corey's mom got married.

Below her name, another entry: Micah, age 19–24, same address. Has to be them, but there's no mention of Corey. I doubt she'd remember me, but Micah would. He used to tease Corey and me constantly.

When I click *more info*, a number displays. I'm tempted to call, but it's way past midnight. Switching back to the friend site, I type *Micah Boatwright Framingham MA* in the search box.

Jackpot: a photo. Older, obviously—goatee and glasses—but I'd recognize Micah anywhere, his grin the big-bro version of Corey's. Even with his page set to private, I see he's remained a Red Sox fan. His wall's plastered with their logo; in his thumbnail, he wears a Sox jacket.

I can't view his info, but there's nothing to stop me from messaging him.

Stomach souring, I stiffen, fingers stalled above the keyboard. Willa stirs beside me, and for a second I debate waking her. I mean, we share everything. She's the closest thing I've got to family. No offense to Brenda, who's barely more emotionally present when she's here than she is now, a couple states away.

My instinct to share is immediately eclipsed by the certainty I shouldn't. Willa's always resented Corey, my one friend who predates her. Though they never met, she has this peculiar competitive reflex; if I even mention him, she'll start listing things she and I did together as kids.

For some reason, shame rises, as if I'm betraying Willa by trying to track Corey down. I know that's irrational, but can't justify searching for him while sharing mattress space with her. Sliding off the bed, I settle atop my bean chair.

Committing to contact, the issue is: What to say? Reaching for pencil and journal, I jot. Reading through a few times, I make tweaks. Opting for short and sweet, I type my greeting into the message window:

Hi, Micah. Remember me? I was friends with your brother. Hoping you can put us in touch. Thanks! Teddi Alder

Suddenly queasy, I attach a photo of Corey and me. A blurry close-up of our spray-quenched faces, side by side at the park sprinkler.

With a deep breath, I send my greeting irretrievably on its way.

Glancing at the slumberlump, I jitter with anticipation; can hardly resist shaking Willa awake to share my news. But common sense tells me to dial down hope.

Who knows whether Micah will even see my message? And if he does, that's no guarantee he'll reply.

I'm about to log off, play it casual, force myself to sleep, when a red indicator pops up on my screen: MESSAGE RECEIVED!

Wow. Corey's brother. So strange. Will he remember me, the irritating tomboy with the *Blue's Clues* lunchbox? I carried it everywhere at six, stocked with crayons, Band-Aids, a spare juice box. Had to be self-reliant even then, with Brenda sometimes strung out for days.

The dialogue box pops up again, flashes at the bottom right of my screen: READ!

It's a start.

Drumming fingers on my chin, I gnaw my thumbnail, twist the pendant chain. Minutes tick. I'm about to give up, join Willa on the bed, when the alert box flashes: TYPING...

A blip signals, accompanied by a five-word question: *Is this a fucking joke?*

Not the response I expected from Micah. Sure, he always

seemed bugged by our general existence, but I imagined he'd be excited to hear from me after so long. Eager to tell his little brother about this online blast from his past.

Is he remembering how annoying we were, following his every move, two noisy shadows? The jokes we played.

I'm unsure how to reply. With a cheerful memory jog?— that time I surprised him with a pack of baseball cards for his birthday.

Mid-message, I stop typing. Maybe it's best to let it simmer, write back tomorrow. Catch him in a better mood.

I consider texting Aidan instead, the impulse of a reckless mind. As I reach for my phone, Willa sleep-grunts. Rolling toward me, she yawns.

"Whatcha doin', T Bear?"

"Nothing, Wills. Go back to sleep."

Powering off my laptop, I opt to take my own advice, forcing a yawn to match Willa's. My eyes water, but I doubt I'll dream tonight. I lie here, thoughts racing, as dawn lights my paisley panels.

15

Never did sleep. The combo of fireworks—the literal, the Aidan/Willa variety—and my dead end with Micah put me in overdrive. As I neared oblivion at daybreak, Binks howled me alert. Then Willa sprang up, prepped to resume her Aidan rant. Luckily, my hostile houseguest was beckoned home for family time.

I'd planned on an all-day veg, but, weary body at the mercy of boomerang brain, I kept returning to the laptop. Afraid to make matters worse with Micah, I held off replying.

Exhaustion, impervious to iced coffee, stood its ground, so I nearly skipped writers group tonight. When I arrived last minute, Marisol met me on the library steps, ready to bail if I decided not to show up.

From her miserable expression right now, I'd say she regrets my arrival. Fidgeting, Mari slips a strand of hair into her mouth, traces figure eights on her thigh. I envy her nervous energy; vitality's beyond me.

Eleanor repeats, "How about it, Marisol? We haven't heard much from you lately."

Letting the damp tendril drop from her lips, Marisol says, "But . . . it's really not good. I'm writing about my tia Adaluz, and for some reason, I started with this very bad poem. I'm not sure it works, and anyway, it's hardly a story yet. I just sort of—"

Eleanor interrupts, raising this cobalt-painted branch she calls the Serenity Stick. It's coiled with silver ribbon, and when she shakes it, tiny bells jingle. Marisol goes silent.

Eleanor asks, "What's Rule #1 of sharing our work? Kenneth?"

Standing, Ken answers as if reciting a pledge. "We must not self-judge. All work has merit, and we are least effective at finding the worth within our own words."

"Very good."

Todd springs up, waits for acknowledgment. When Eleanor nods in his direction, he adds, "She also broke Rule #2: Never explain the work. Just read exactly what's on the page."

With a tortured expression, Marisol says, "Okay, jeez, I'm really sorry."

Granting absolution with a quick shoulder pat, Eleanor asks Marisol to resume.

"From the top?"

"That sounds reasonable."

I offer a thumbs-up, and, searching through loose sheets of lined paper, Marisol begins.

> *"'My Tia's Special Gift'*
> *Aunt Adaluz has a gift*
> *But it's not adorned with bows*
> *She didn't get it in the mail*
> *It's not a ring or rose*
> *Her gift lies deep within her . . ."*

Struck with giggles, Marisol flushes deeply. "So then the poem just sort of ends, and I start the rest."

Eleanor answers, "Please continue."

Voice cracking, Marisol reads.

"Some aunts are magicians of spice, ruling over kitchens tinged with cinnamon, pungent with the bite of chilies and garlic. Others can sew a dress for quinceañera and a slipcover for the sofa in a single afternoon.

"There are soccer-star aunts, and I'm certain some nieces have architect tias, women whose dreams become wonders of steel and glass. Some have orthodontic aunts, psychiatric aunts, aunts who add endless columns of numbers, aunts who pilot taxicabs. Each of these women has her special gift."

As Marisol glances up to gauge our reaction, I steal a quick look around the circle. She has everyone's attention.

Eleanor whispers, "Go on."

"Tia Adaluz shares some of these gifts. My mother's older sister is forever stirring, rich-scented steam rising from her cast iron pot; always mid-project, she's sewn her way through miles of satin. And she is mad for Sudoku.

"But her true gift is one called *habla con espiritu*, spirit speak. This is a gift held cherished within our family, one shared by special women of each generation."

Picturing the SPIRIT-FUELED bumper sticker, I recall home-room whispers, "That girl, her aunt."

A throb of electricity circuits the group. A subtle intake of breath. Petra and Jeanine lean forward. Riding the shift in energy, Marisol assumes a storyteller tone, voice extra expressive.

"When Baby Luz was born, back on our island, there were signs, omens that pointed to her possessing the gift. As she entered the world—two minutes past midnight, on the Feast of All Souls—my abuelo's prize rooster, Pico, crowed exactly twice. And fell dead."

Savoring the gasp that escapes Ken, a small grin dances at the corner of Marisol's lips. She pauses to dramatically shuffle pages.

"During her early years, the family watched closely how the baby stopped mid-play, to babble to an invisible play-mate in an empty corner. They would gasp in awe to discover special objects—Abuela's silver hairbrush, a treasured clay Madonna—impossibly plucked from a locked drawer, the highest shelf, curled in the sleeping baby's fist.

"When she was seven, Luz nearly drowned. She claimed a boy with her exact eyes, the same twin moles on his cheek, had pulled her from the surf, carried her to shore. He told her his name was Felix, and said he had a message for her mama. 'Do not weep for me. I am happy with the others.' When Abuela showed Adaluz a picture of her dead brother, the girl said, 'That's him, the boy who saved me! He wants them to name the new baby *Felicia*, to honor him.'"

Folding back the page, Marisol adds, "One year later, my mother, Felicia, was born." The group "oohs" appreciatively, and she goes back to reading.

"Luz tried to cast off her gift. Some messages unnerved or confused her, not all the visitors were as welcome as her tio Felix. No, some visions terrified Adaluz. The most frightening she refused to discuss. For a time, she denied the second sight, claiming she wanted only to be 'normal.' Yet, she couldn't help sharing what she heard and saw, especially if it could help, might shield her family from harm.

"As Tia grew older, she embraced the gift as a part of her. People came for advice, to find misplaced articles: eyeglasses, earrings. A lover who had strayed. Somehow, she could usually help them.

"Eventually, my aunt accepted the dead; she made peace with the visitors. She says they speak within her chest, rather than into her ears. She feels their tickle, just behind her heart. Sometimes, they carry great weight. Sorrow. Often, she will whisper a name. When this happens, she knows to wait. To stop what she is doing. Put aside her puzzle. Turn down the stove burner. Stitch her last seam and wait. Because someone needs her.

"The messages are for those left behind; those Tia calls '*los que se quedan*, the ones who remain.' Many times, they seek Tia out. Other times, she goes in search of them.

"At first, she resisted this role; 'her great burden,' she called it. There was too much sadness, the regrets of those gone on, of those still here. But Tia found that, by acting as messenger, she could ease the ache for the souls on both sides of loss.

"Like the women before her, she came to embrace her gift, to cherish it. She jokes now that she is honored to have joined the family business.

"Some doubt her; some say she is a fake, but I know her journey, and I am proud. My tia Adaluz has a special gift. *Segunda vista*, a second sight. Spirit speak."

Typically, when someone finishes reading, the response goes one of two ways. We slide into auto applause; this might range from feeble-polite to prolonged and enthusiastic, depending on the particular piece.

The other reaction tends to be silence, often of the bewildered variety. In those cases, Eleanor, reluctant to influence group reaction with anything beyond the briefest commentary, challenges us with her standard call for "Thoughts? Comments?"

The immediate response to Marisol's piece is something of a departure. Before anyone else can react, Eleanor turns to me and says, "Well, Miss Alder, are you thinking what I'm thinking?"

On the spot, I stammer, "Umm, that was really . . . uh, great, Mari. The details were so vivid. You really took me someplace new."

Marisol says, "Thanks, Teddi."

I turn to Eleanor with a *How was that?* expression, and she surprises me by saying, "Actually, what I meant, Teddi, is that you really ought to set up a meeting with Marisol's aunt."

16

W ould you behave?"

Aidan has a compound case: uncontrollable giggles coupled with serious hand trouble. He keeps tickling, poking me, running his index finger along my thigh.

The attention's equal parts charming and maddening. Grabbing his wrist, I shoot him an irritated look. "You're going to get us kicked out!"

Willa got permission for us to sit in on *Twelfth Night* rehearsal. Miss LaRose, our school's drama teacher and the show's director, told her she'd love a visit from her former star. Willa said she made a big deal, telling the cast to "give it your all," that a "talented troupe alum would be paying a visit." But if Aid doesn't knock it off, we're guaranteed to get the boot.

He leans over and whistles gently in my ear, erupting in a burst of laughter. Willa spins in her seat two rows up; glaring death rays at Aidan and me, she goes, "Sssshhhhhhhhhh!"

Aidan calms, striking an angelic Cub Scout pose. Even so,

I'm worried he'll not only get us ejected but also undo the progress we've made these last few days. After their Fourth of July blowout, Willa refused to speak to Aidan, barely acknowledging his existence. This would not have been an issue, except she insisted on hanging with us every chance she got.

With Nic and Aid getting to be buds, this got uncomfortable fast, thanks to Willa's constant allegations. Whenever Nic spoke to Aidan, she'd roll her eyes and accuse him of "scheming again." Ultimately, optic nerve strain and the unnatural demands of the silent treatment proved overwhelming.

As the four of us sat at Sprinkles yesterday, Willa scooched next to Aidan and said, "You've been sufficiently punished. I forgive you. Besides, there's enough Teddi for us both. Friends?"

Aidan winked at me before saying, "Wait, the silent treatment was a punishment?" Nic did his best not to laugh 'til Willa did. After that, all was well.

So, reluctant to ruin this hard-won truce because of his fidget attack, I say, "Aid, it'll be a while before Nic runs his scene. Let's get some air."

Grinning, he says, "Air?" and blows across his open palm, causing my bangs to flutter.

"Come on!"

Pinching his ear, I pull him—angry-nun style—into the darkened aisle.

Aid continues laughing as we descend the stairs to the parking lot.

Once outside, I have to admit, he's kind of goofy-cute. He tries to tickle me, but I dash toward the grassy area near the school's side lot, Aidan in stumbling pursuit.

When he lunges, I turn tables, tackling him. We flop onto summer-crisp grass, a tumble of limbs and laughter.

"What is with you tonight?" I give him a quick ab poke.

He stops laughing. Rolling onto his back, he says, "I'm just happy, Teddi."

"Well, you're acting mental." I kiss him. "If I hadn't spent the day with you, I'd swear you were drunk."

"Nope, not drunk. High."

"What?"

"High. On love."

Turning onto his side, he runs his fingers through my hair. Then, burying his face against my neck, he delivers a massive, wet raspberry.

Squealing, I wriggle away, trying to catch my breath.

Aidan grabs the back of my shirt; laughing, he drags me toward him. My top hikes up in front, the dry grass scratchy against my stomach.

"Stop it!" Half laughing, I slap his hand, try to pry his fingers from my stretched tee.

His grip tightens, one arm wrapping, flipping, pinning me on my back. Straddling me, digging fingers into my sides, he tickles me senseless. I can't help but laugh; then, bucking, I struggle to escape, trapped beneath his weight.

"Aidan, stop!" Wrenching an arm free, I swing upward, deliver a smack to his left cheek.

He's stunned. Then he shakes his head and scowls. Leaning closer, his face pressed to mine, he says, "Come on, Teddi. Take a joke." His eyes glint. Glassy, unreadable.

A shiver of fear cuts through me. Fighting the urge to scream, in the firmest voice I can manage, I say, "Aidan, this is not funny. Let. Me. Up."

Just then, the side door opens; Willa peeks out, calling us. "Guys, come inside. They're starting from top of show, and Nic's in one of the first scenes. I don't want you ruining it, busting in in the middle."

Jumping up, Aidan offers his hand. I don't move, until he smiles, extra sincere, and asks, "You all right?"

I let him help me to my feet. Adjusting my shirt, I pick at the dry grass stuck to my torso.

Walking toward the stairs where Willa waits, Aidan tries to put his arm around me. I duck away.

At the bottom of the steps, he bows to Willa and says, "Your majesty, I'm glad we have made amends."

Willa grins. Abandoning her effort to remain stern, she says, "All right, goober. Just promise you'll pipe down."

"And keep your hands to yourself," I add. It comes out harsher than I intended. Willa raises an eyebrow.

Aidan makes an X over his chest. Leaning forward, eyes closed, he says, "Cross my stolen heart."

Instead of the kiss he's expecting, I poke his ribs and say, "Let's go, lover boy."

As we enter the auditorium, refrigerated air licks my skin; I shudder as we take our seats.

House lights cut, the only illumination comes from the exit signs and a single spot trained center stage. Miss LaRose addresses the cast, seated in a large oval onstage. "Okeydoke. You've worked hard this week. Let's see what we've got. From top of show. I want real commitment. Pay attention to each other! Consider this a performance." She indicates us. "After all, we have an audience."

Aidan smiles broadly, and I resist the urge to dive beneath my seat. After waving back at her, I turn to him with a serious look.

Miss LaRose continues. "Harper will be tinkering, so expect to be surprised by light and sound. We're testing effects for the prologue. Don't let it throw you. In fact, you might find it inspires your performance. If so, go for it. Now's the time to experiment. Ready?"

The oval contracts into a tight knot, and the group begins a barely audible hum. As they slowly rise to their feet, volume increasing, the hum becomes a nonsense-syllable chant, some kind of warm-up. Expression serious, Aidan murmurs in time.

Hopping from the stage, Miss LaRose sits in the front row and shouts, "Places for prologue!"

The circle breaks, actors scattering to various spots offstage.

Miss LaRose flashes a thumbs-up toward the tech table at the back of the auditorium, and the last lights go out.

Plunged into darkness, my brows stretch upward, eyes attempting to adjust.

Simulated lightning blinds me, followed by a loud rumble. I picture Binks's frenzied thunder response. In fact, right now, I can identify. Funhouse laughter escapes me as Aidan takes my hand.

As purple washes the stage, a group of actors enters. Some pose, arms entwined, creating the form of a boat; others unfurl fabric, undulating blue evoking the sea. The rest mime the motions of ship's passengers.

Miss LaRose shouts direction. "We'll have music here, more storm sounds, a burst of chaos. Feel the squalls! Really struggle!" The actors spin wildly, fabricating turmoil.

Following a thunder crack, the vessel blows to pieces; bodies whirl, storm-tossed debris.

My skin prickles as one young woman, a senior playing Viola, is wound in sheets of blue, then flung upward. Screeching, she flies free of the billows, briefly airborne. Landing atop taut fabric, cocooned again, she flails, a panicked swimmer fighting to surface.

Leaning forward, scalp tingling, I hold my breath. As lightning crackles, her hands grope toward me, her mouth a blank hole. Wind and rain crescendo, then subside. Fabric falling away, she sways inside a flickery circle. Like a flashlight beam.

Eyes pasted to hers, I'm lost in the scream. It's deafening.

Just before blackness engulfs us, I notice everyone's gawking. At me. Small wonder. Perched on my seat, pointing toward the figure onstage, I'm the one screaming.

Aidan literally carries me out of the auditorium.

Walking home, I'm about to explain why I freaked. Then he gives me this meant-to-be-soothing smile—usually reserved for the crazy person on the bus—and says, "So. That was a surprise."

My apology reflex kicks in. "Sorry."

At my door, he says, "Shit, I'm wiped. Feel like I went through something."

Suppressing my immediate response—*YOU went through something, asshole?*—I opt instead for "Call me."

Though he responds with a reassuring kiss and "You bet," I have my doubts.

I pass the night force-cuddling Binks 'til, unable to tolerate it any longer, he retreats.

Daylight and Willa invade my room simultaneously. When I answer my cell, she chirps, ultra-perky, "Feeling better this morning?"

"I'm fine."

"So. I fixed everything with Miss LaRose. Blamed your episode on excess hormones."

"I wish it were that simple."

"Teddi," she hesitates, careful, "what really happened?"

As I'm about to answer, my skin stipples with gooseflesh. Last night's scream echoing in my skull, I manage a weak "Not sure."

"What, T Bear?"

"Nothing. I thought I saw—"

"Teddi?" She waits for the rest. When I don't finish, she says, "'Kay, um, we'll talk soon."

Too late, I say, "Her. I was convinced it was her, Pool Girl, caught in the storm."

17

Can't quite believe I'm here. I've passed this place a trillion times going to school, or to Drunk Monkey, the thrift shop where Willa and I troll for discounted, brand-name merch. Each time, we debate ascending those cement steps, peering into the future, but neither of us ever has the guts—or the requisite twenty bucks—to actually do it. Still, I've always been curious.

Even when I was little, it was fascinating, the idea of a stranger figuring out life's path for a fee. I'd beg Brenda to come here the way other kids might pester for a playground trip. We never went. She always said she had "a hard enough time dealing with the present," that the future would "show its ugly puss soon enough."

But they say desperate times call for desperate measures. And, after my spontaneous performance at rehearsal last night, it's official:

I am Desperate.

For answers. For uninterrupted sleep. For a wee slice of

normal. If Marisol's aunt has the ability to offer even one of those, I'm in. Besides, it's my chance to finally find out what goes on behind that lavender door.

The house itself is nothing special. Sandwiched between a Sunoco station and Hair & Now, a defunct salon, it's a gray box with crooked shutters, dirty snowbanks out front well into spring. Summer brings yellow: dandelions surf the tiny yard, spill onto the sidewalk. These days, the neon sign's just part of the scenery.

It never occurred to me that somebody actually lives here. Or that the interior would be anything but creepy. It's not. The place is actually kind of adorable, bright, with floral curtains and butter-pale walls. No sign of a crystal ball.

Marisol's auntie's not what I expected either. Of course, I'm not quite sure what that was. My frame of reference for psychics is mostly limited to pop culture stereotypes: scary movie characters and, more recently, the Long Island variety.

Tia Adaluz doesn't fit either mold. I'm a little ashamed to admit I had other stereotypes in mind. Given her Latina roots, and Marisol's warning that her aunt was "a little unusual," I'd concocted this whole exotic-Santeria-priestess setup, totally expecting a glittery head wrap, kohl-rimmed eyes, animal carcasses strewn casually about a shadow-draped interior.

It's not that way at all. First off, the front room's totally normal, what they used to call *homey*. I won't deny being nervous as we waited together on the stoop. Marisol even looked anxious. When she tapped the screen door, I braced. I'm not sure for what. Drumbeats? Clouds of dry ice?

Whatever my preconceived notions, Adaluz deflates them, proving my imaginings wrong at once. I'd expected some intimidating figure—tall, icy—but she's teeny and she oozes warmth.

Smooshing Marisol's face against her chest, she plants a kiss amidst her curls. I'm anticipating the same greeting, but instead, stepping back, she looks me over and says, "You must be Teddi!" She has no accent, neither Spanish, nor—a little disappointing—Transylvanian. And she emits not the slightest malevolent vibe.

Taking my hand, she gives it a politician-worthy pump and says, "So good to meet you." Again, the most notable thing is an absence. No electric volt, no sizzling psychic connection. Just her doughy palm, slightly clammy.

I search her eyes, I suppose, for clairvoyant sparks. Again, my expect-o-meter fails. Not the heavy-lidded, makeup-ringed, wise-verging-on-sinister orbs I'd envisioned, they're, well, completely average. Granted, magnified by thick lenses, they look enormous. She blinks, and the effect reminds me of a butterfly wing. It's a relief when she slides the glasses atop her head, and her eyes emerge, normal human size.

They're kind, somehow sad. Pale/piercing was just below dark/broody on my expectation list, and they are fairly pale, a buttery caramel. They do not, however, appear to hold any special juju. Neither *lit from within* nor *mesmerizing*, right now, their expression's befuddled, probably because I haven't replied to her greeting.

Giving myself an interior nudge, I manage a reciprocal "Good to meet you, too, Mrs. Colón. Marisol's told me a lot about you."

"Well then, she must have told you my name is Adaluz. You may call me Tia. Or Luz. Most of Mari's friends do."

"Tia, yes. Thank you."

"For what? I haven't done a thing yet." She winks. "Will you girls have coffee?"

Marisol says, "Sure, Tia."

"None for me, thanks. I'm over my caffeine limit for the day."

"Ginger ale?"

"I'm all set, really."

"You are not here for refreshments."

"Not really."

"All right then. We should get to work. Come into the other room."

I step aside to let Marisol go first, but she shakes her head. "No, Teddi. It's best you and Tia do this alone."

"Alone?"

"Mari is right. She has a very strong signal; if she is in the room with us, I might have a hard time tuning her out."

I force a smile.

Marisol says, "Be right down the hall. I'll make a fresh pot. In case you change your mind when it's all over."

"All over." I only seem capable of parroting Marisol.

She winks. "Go easy on her, Titi. She seems a little freaked."

Tracking Marisol as she heads toward the kitchen, I feel the tiny hairs on my arms rise. Tia takes my hand, and I surrender to the warmth of her sad eyes, as she says, "Not to worry, Teddi. I am here to help."

Chasing each breath as we near a set of louvered doors down the hall, I bite my lip. I'm desperate to control this bubbling fear. The words *inner sanctum* repeat in my head. This is it.

Tia Luz strokes my hand, whispers, "Relax."

Again, I brace, gnawing my thumbnail, as she slides open the doors. Expecting beaded curtains, candles casting an otherworldly glow, I'm shocked to find Tia's sanctum as bright and ordinary as the rest of downstairs. A laundry/sewing room, it's a mix of wicker shelving and plastic bins. An ironing board leans against a row of cabinets. Two folding tables hold fabric and craft supplies.

"You'll pardon the mess. I wasn't expecting company."

I resist questioning her psychic prowess, though her failure to predict our arrival is less than promising.

Against the paneled wall is a small card table. Certainly large enough to support a crystal ball, it's currently cluttered with sewing magazines, scissors, a mess of paper patterns.

Leading me to the table, Tia Luz offers a chair by the window. Sitting, I notice this small ceramic bowl. Glazed in shades of turquoise and gold, it's rimmed with alternating cowrie shells and crudely etched cross shapes. At last, evidence of voodoo ritual: The container brims with slender bones. Meeting my gaze, Tia grins mysteriously.

As she lifts the bowl, my eyes widen. Transfixed, I wait for her to cast skeletal leavings across the tabletop, to read destiny in the scatter.

When she catches me staring, Tia winks. "Wings. I'm afraid you caught me at lunch."

So much for prophecy.

Hustling to the counter, she opens a cabinet and whisks the chicken bones into the wastebasket, placing one on a china saucer on the countertop.

"Dixie!" Tia clucks with her tongue, and a cat flashes across the room, leaping to dip her nose against the saucer. "Good girl," Tia coos, stroking gray fur. I'm sure Binks and I have battled this cat in the park. But, no, that one—a big tom—is considerably larger.

Bounding from counter to floor, Dixie upsets the saucer. With a lopsided twirl, it spins in slow-mo, before going airborne. I could easily catch the china plate, prevent its crash to tile. If I could move.

Something—the cat's swift grayness, the echo of whirling plate—has me stunned. My heart, my lungs, slide downward, my stomach lifting to accept their weight.

Vision clouding silver, whispers intrude. A muddle, voices

indistinguishable: Corey. Brenda. A deeper voice, somehow animal—familiar yet forgotten.

I grip table edge, afraid I'll repeat the saucer's impact with tile floor.

Stooping to retrieve the broken saucer, Tia says, "Are you sure you will not have a refreshment?" Her hand on my shoulder brings me back.

"No, thank you."

As Dixie skulks from the room, poultry rune clamped in her teeth, Tia's full attention turns to me.

"So, Teddi, Marisol tells me you have been seeing someone."

That phrase again, just how I described it to Eleanor. But the way Tia says it, as if we're gossiping about boys, I can't help but laugh. "I guess you could say that."

"You guess?"

"Well, someone. Or some *thing*."

"Can you describe this visitor?"

"Uh-huh."

"Tell me."

"I've been seeing this . . . girl. She shows up out of nowhere, leaves the same way. Like a puff of cold air."

"Did you know her?"

"How do you mean?"

"Is she a relative, a friend who has passed on?"

I fidget in the chair, fold arms across my chest. This isn't right.

"Aren't you supposed to tell me?"

Tia purses her lips; her brows lift—two exclamation points. "It is not a game, Teddi. Whatever Marisol told you, I have no need to prove my gift with some magic trick. If that is your expectation . . . well, I am no carnival attraction. If you seek to gain clarity from my *otra visión*, my special sight, you'll need to throw me a bone here."

She catches my sidelong glance at the chicken leg bowl.

"I mean cooperate."

"How exactly?"

"Talk to me. Open your mind. Stop trying to keep me out. Let me help."

Pressure builds behind my eyes, a windup to tears. I battle them back. Why is it so hard to accept that someone wants to help?

We face off for what seems an hour, is more likely a long two minutes.

Finally, with a *this-is-your-last-chance* expression, Tia says, "Let me see it, Teddi."

My right hand lifts toward my throat—total reflex—but I stop it, bringing it back to the tabletop with my left. Recrossing my arms, I say, "It?"

Tia answers, "The necklace, Teddi. The one you found. Is it a butterfly?" She narrows her eyes. "No. A flower."

Even as I say, "Marisol told you!" I inwardly admit that's nonsense, because I never told Mari about the pendant.

"Oh, Teddi, you disappoint me. You have so little belief? So little faith in your friend?"

"Faith?"

"Do you think my Marisol would bring you here as a trick, to deceive you?"

My head throbs, tears pulsing with each thud of my heart. Should I be able to hear my heartbeat so clearly?

"Yes, let it out. This visitor frightens, confuses, you. You are unready to hear her."

Rising from my seat, I stammer, "I'd . . . I'd better go—"

Tia slowly shakes her head, and though her lips never move, I hear her.

No, Teddi. Do not run. We can face this. Together. You and I.

Focusing on her kind eyes, I concentrate, passing a thought to her. *I'm afraid.*

I know. I am here.

What should I do, Tia?

Give me your hand.

She reaches across the table. This time when our fingers touch, I do feel something. Not electric exactly, fluid. Liquid energy flows from her stubby fingertips into mine.

I stop crying.

"Good." I'm startled when she speaks aloud again. "Now, do you trust me?"

I don't even have to mull it. The answer arrives practically before she finishes asking. "Completely."

Smiling, she says, "Show me."

This time, as my right hand rises, I don't stop it. Instead, my left lifts as well, stretching the collar of my top.

When I hold the daisy out to her, Tia gasps.

I shiver, spooked by the look on her face.

She pats my hand, then slides her chair to my side of the table, so we're elbow to elbow.

Gently, without speaking, Tia lifts the pendant from my palm. Raising it to her face, she studies the flower, tapping each petal with her fingernail, repeating the word "*triste.*"

Her eyes cross slightly as she raises the charm toward her face. I can't help leaning against her as the chain tightens between us.

We breathe in sync as I wait for her to speak.

Instead, she slumps against me, pressing her head to my chest, as if listening to my heart. Face upturned, eyes closed, she parts her lips. I strain to read her thoughts, but I'm unable.

Inhaling, eyes tight, Tia pops the daisy into her mouth like a cough drop.

Frozen by the strangeness of the moment, I hold my breath.

There's a rushing in my ears. A shriek—not my own—but whose?

I'm spinning, stomach in free fall.

Daisy balanced on her tongue, Tia begins speaking to me, but her voice is different, deeper, raspy. "*Lo veo.* I see him."

Plucking the pendant gently from her mouth, I ask, "Who, Tia?"

Without opening her eyes, she says, "There is no girl."

"What?"

"I hear a boy. Only a boy. He is calling, frightened. Adrift. He wishes to go home."

"What boy?"

Her eyes open. "Rah . . . Rahn?" Concentrating, she strokes the flower charm. "Could it be Ron?"

I shake my head and say, "What about Fawn? That sounds a little like Ron."

Tsking, Tia says, "Perhaps Rod?"

Anger rising, I snap. "I have no clue what you're talking about. I never knew a boy named Ron."

Tia answers calmly. "Names are tricky, Teddi. Approximate. And often the visitors come to me in Spanish."

Closing her eyes again, she exhales loudly. Slouched in her chair, holding the necklace, she says, "He is buried. Deep in your mind. He reaches for you. Begs you to find him."

I pull the daisy from her, stuff it back inside my shirt.

"This is crazy. I told you. It's a girl. I've been seeing a girl from the pool. This daisy belongs to her. She wants it back. I think she needs my help!"

Adaluz gives me a severe look. "No, Teddi. You are wrong." Staring past me, head tipped as if listening to music, she adds,

"I see no girl. It is the boy, this Ron—or could it be Rob?—who needs your help."

I shout, "Don't tell me what I saw!" Evading her gaze, I continue. "Forget it. I shouldn't have . . . coming here was a mistake."

Touching my face with her fingertips, Tia looks into me. "Do not worry, Teddi. In time, you will understand. He will come to you if you let him."

Stopping short of plugging my ears, I rise from my chair.

Tia grabs my arm. Eyes serious, she says, "The boy, this Ron. He needs you."

"No . . ."

"To free him."

"Free him?"

She nods. "By freeing him, you will free yourself. Once and for all. He wants you to see it, Teddi, wants you to tell."

I nearly knock my chair over as I push back from the table. Unable to look at Tia, I mumble a quick thank-you and flee the sewing room.

Marisol stands in the hallway, holding a green ceramic mug. Shaped like a smiling frog. When I see it, my feet stutter. Catching my balance mid-stumble, I practically mow her down racing past.

"Teddi, are you okay?"

Without turning back, I say, "No worries. I just need to get home."

Bursting through the front door, I swoon in afternoon sun. After a moment, I steady, but can't shake the feeling I'm being watched. Glancing back, I spot Marisol and her aunt, faces framed in the storm door. Mari's expression is blank, but Adaluz smiles. Slowly raising her right hand, she makes the sign of the cross.

18

Cross-legged on a moss-freckled stone, I study the water, pretend it's peaceful, knowing life wrestles death beneath the surface. As if to illustrate my point, two dragonflies get busy near my foot; then, with a soundless unfurling of wings, a huge gray bird appears. Darting at water's edge, it spears an unlucky frog before lifting to sky.

Hugging myself, I fail to subdue a shudder.

After my useless psychic reading, I headed straight here. The pond.

Regardless of Adaluz, I know what I know. Fawn or not, Pool Girl has a message, a memory for me. I need to put it on paper. To make it stop rattling in my head.

Eleanor claims, "There's solace in story—no matter how terrible."

I'm not sure she's right, but I have to try.

I will write it down.

Now.

Opening my journal, I face the blank sheet, mind spiraling.

But as I point pencil toward paper, some cerebral door slams shut. I disconnect, as if it's someone else's hand trembling above crisp white.

Eyes closed, I settle my mind, concentrate on sound, breathe in rhythm to the low insect buzz, the steady call of birds. Opening my eyes, I'm not at all surprised to find printing in the journal, the letters dark, rounded. Childlike.

It must be Tuesday. Garbage bins line Parkview, tipped and empty. Corey and I play that they're enemies—monsters or aliens.

Exhaling steadily, I press pencil to page, continue.

We meet Fawn by the pool fence like always, but she says, "I have a surprise. Today we spy."

Of course, Corey agrees, so I go along. No point arguing.

We cut through the park, sweat slithering my back as we cross the ball field.

"Ugh, not the pond again." Figure I'll try just once to change our course. "I'm sick of exploring there."

Fawn's eyes practically glow with excitement as she answers. "Today's special. I'm going to show you secrets."

That's it. There's no arguing Corey out of it.

We duck beneath coils of vine and branch onto the trail. I hear the glung of frogs, the chit-chit of marsh birds.

Corey and I start left along the trail, but Fawn stops us, stretching one spindly arm across our path. "Follow me. We need to go the back way." Lifting a branch, she slides under. Corey follows.

I see distant shimmer; can make out a line of lily stalks thrusting up yellow-bud periscopes. But there's something new. A smell. This chemical bite to the air. And, just loud enough to hear, music. Laughter.

"This way." Gripping Corey's hand, Fawn pulls him. They plunge deeper into the woods, giggling.

I have to run to keep up, jumping dry patch to stone to fallen tree, dodging marshy ground. We're circling the opposite way. As we go farther, the music gets louder. So does the whooping laughter. And that weird smell gets stronger. My eyes water.

Something feels wrong. Dangerous. I shiver in the heat. I'm about to suggest we turn back when Fawn whispers, "Almost there. Got to be extra quiet. No telling what he'll do if he catches us."

Low-hanging smoke caps the pond. Corey wheezes, can't help coughing. It's his asthma. The heat's bad enough, but this smog doesn't help.

Ssssshhhing him, Fawn claps a hand over Corey's mouth, her eyes round. I've never seen her for-real scared, even when Eli forced her into that car. But her tough mask slips, and I see it. Fear.

Then, she readjusts her expression; that gleam returns to her eyes. She mouths into Corey's ear, and he cracks up behind her grimy hand, his laughter ending in another coughing fit.

"We should go."

This time Fawn shushes me. She doesn't dare put her hand over my mouth, though. She must know I'd bite her finger clean off. Taking Corey's wrist, she leads him deeper in. I want to yell, make him come home with me, get him inside, so he can breathe some AC.

But he won't listen. And I couldn't deal with him picking her over me, so rather than force him to choose, I go along. The smoke's thicker up ahead; music's louder, too.

As I trail them through the woods, Fawn suddenly elbows Corey sideways. Crashing through a stand of fern, they crouch and belly-crawl.

Stooping behind them, I bite my tongue. Let them get poison ivy. Serves them right. Pushing aside a low-slung branch, I follow. Sweat peppers my forehead.

As we glide through the brush, smoke surrounds us. It's coming from Stone Loop, where Corey and I play on the broken-down picnic table.

Music thuds, and I notice the lack of other—usual—pond sound. No birds warble. The frogs are hushed. Even the bugs seem to have vanished. Must be the smoke, this potent mix of burning black licorice and Barbie hair. It makes me feel almost sleepy, as if my brain's wrapped in a wet, wool scarf.

My eyes sting as I creep closer.

Catching up to Corey and Fawn, I'm annoyed with their wild laughter, but can't help joining them. Then Fawn gets this serious look. Nostrils pulsing, she says, "This is it." Corey blinks solemnly, and they take turns peering through leaves.

Finally, eager to be included, I ask, "Guys, what is it?"

Corey turns slowly back to me. The look on his face is one I've never seen. His eyes shine, somehow frightened and hungry all at once.

Fawn shoves me onto my knees, pressing me through tickling ferns toward commotion. Eyes darting, I consume the scene rapid-fire.

A hibachi balances on one of the boulders. On it, a dented paint can fumes, the source of the greenish haze.

Two guys—bare chested, shoeless—sway in front of it, eating smoke.

A third, Fawn's brother, Eli, stands, his back to us. He's naked. I gape at the snarling wolf inked across his broad back, a demon, horned with blood-red eyes.

A girl I've seen at the pool—she's maybe sixteen—kneels before him, mouth open. Her bikini top hangs at her waist.

We shouldn't be seeing this, but I can't manage to move, to look away.

A surge of ancient guilt floods me. I feel dizzy. Journal closed, I place it beside me on the rock. Leaning forward, I dip my hands in the water, bring damp fingertips to temples. As I do, I recognize that sulfur smell, the one that almost made me puke at the library. This time, unable to muffle it, I gag, spit on the ground.

Sipping from my water bottle, I study the air. Late afternoon sun slats through branches, patterning the pond's pollen skin. Curls of algae punctuate a crimson koi that hovers, angel-like, just below.

Then, a havoc of wings and water, a squad of Canada geese land, paddlefeet churning the slime. Skimming in bowling-pin formation, they patrol; their calls are mechanical, more bark than birdsong.

Pivoting, they glide toward me, and I call to them, mimicking their rusted-hinge squonk. Floating closer, they bow in tandem. Their onyx caps, ivory chinstraps, synchronized head-bobs remind me of soldiers in some black-and-white documentary.

Crossing the surface, they startle the koi. It flits deep, disappears. As they advance, I'm wary, too, wondering if I'm on some hidden camera show, *When Geese Attack!*

As I contemplate grabbing my things and retreating, the lead goose snaps its neck, emits a sharp whistle. The others follow suit, hissing, woofing in flustered honks. I've spooked them.

Or something has.

Flattening, necks to water, they stare toward the woods, heads wagging violently. Then, a collective shriek, the group flaps wild. Lifting off, they scatter, fleeing the pond.

I call after them, "Was it something I said?" As I bend to collect my journal, I sense a presence. Spinning, I spot a figure in the shadows. Not Pool Girl, a guy.

He's tall, rangy. Menacing even at a distance, he just stands, feet planted wide. One hand's below his waist.

Fear-choked, I blurt the name before the thought's fully formed. "Eli?"

When he doesn't respond, I pocket-fumble, grasp my cell, promptly drop it.

With a mixture of relief and revulsion, I realize he's peeing in the bushes, hasn't noticed me. But for a sec, my fight/flight instincts were firing. Could it be him?

Dropping to the grass, I retrieve my phone and slide it in my pocket. Then, willing him to zip, I study him. The resemblance to Fawn's brother—general shape, hair color— is minor. Even accounting for the lapse in years, he looks too old to be Eli. Besides, on some gut-deep level, I'd know if it was him.

The guy finishes his business, and—resisting the urge to fish in my bag, toss him some hand sanitizer—I step forward. That's when I notice his hand. Toddler-small, fingers curled into a vague croissant shape. His eyes are deep brown; nothing like Eli's wicked ice-blue.

Noticing me, he does an automatic fly-check, smiles shyly. Then, baby-stepping toward me, he speaks. His voice is soft.

Extending his regular hand, he says, "My name is Carl. What's your name?"

Sidestepping the hygiene issue, I flash him a peace sign. "I'm Teddi."

As if reciting a script, he says, "Very pleased to meet you,

Teddi." Then, forehead rippling, he stops to consider. "Wait," covering his mouth with his baby hand, he giggles and says, "Teddi? Like the bear? That's funny."

"If you say so. Anyway, Carl, what brings you to the pond?"

Bending, he retrieves a plastic bag from the grass and shakes it, clanking the bottles and cans inside. "On my rounds. Collecting. Not much luck today."

"That's too bad."

"Yeah, used to be lots more cans and bottles back when the store was open. Course, you're too young to remember any of that."

I think better of telling him I live there. Though he seems harmless, you never can tell.

Clinking his bottle bag against his leg, he asks, "So, Teddi. What brings you to the pond today?"

Something in his voice makes me want to tell him everything. Instead, I say, "I've been trying to remember. Some stuff that happened when I was really small."

Dark eyes grave, he asks, "Bad stuff?"

When I don't answer, he whistles, a slight intake of air, and says, "I'm real sorry."

"Thanks, Carl."

"I'll pray for your friend, Teddi." And then he turns and just sort of fades into the tree line, leaving me shaking.

I call, "Carl, wait! How'd you know about my friend?" But

he's gone. Examining the ground, I note the shamble-tracks of his work boots, the dark circle where he'd peed.

So, that's a relief, he was real.

Or else, I just encountered Carl the Urinating Ghost.

Angel.

The word forms in my brain like an itch.

Scrubbing at my eyes to swipe it away, I mutter, "There are no angels in these woods, only ghosts. And devils."

After a few cleansing breaths, I return to the rock, open the journal, and reread the last sentence aloud. "We shouldn't be seeing this, but I can't manage to move, to look away."

Channeling Eleanor's brand of polished encouragement, I steeple fingers beneath my chin and whisper, "You can do this, Teddi. Keep going. Write it out."

Bracing for whatever's next, I continue.

Corey's "Eeww!" pierces my trance.

Her face right in close to his, Fawn says, "One day you'll learn, and you won't think it's so nasty." Clamping his mouth to hers, she grinds their lips together. As Corey tries to pull away, she flits her tongue into the space where his front teeth should be.

Pushing Fawn off, he looks sick. I actually think he's going to cry.

I touch his wrist and say, "Should we call the pool cop?"

Fawn yanks my hair. Tugging with her dirty fingers,

she says, "Do it and you'll end up in trouble, too. You babies shouldn't even be out here."

"We're not babies! Besides—"

"Besides what?" She leers. "It's just an adventure."

Giving my hair another tug, she laughs, and now I'm the one fighting tears.

Corey says, "Come on, Fawn, quit it. She didn't mean nothing."

Releasing my hair, Fawn turns on him. Balling her fists against his chest, she shoves, knocking Corey backward into a clump of skunk cabbage.

One of the hibachi guys shouts, "Hey! Who's over there?"

This time Fawn does slap her palm across my mouth. I don't bite, make no attempt to remove her hand. We're caught in silence as the music halts. The missing pond noise is even more noticeable now, but the stillness barely registers before Stone Loop erupts.

Eli's friends hustle to snuff the smoldering bucket. The girl squeals. I glimpse her between branches as she struggles with her bathing suit top.

The confusion lasts less than a minute before Eli ends it. Not bothering to cover himself, he stands mid-circle and bellows, "FAWN! I know you're out there, you shifty little bitch!"

The guys stop in their tracks, and Eli's girlfriend—if that's what she is—busts into loud sobs. Throwing a towel at her, he says, "Shut up or get lost, you dumb shit."

With one last explosion of tears, she yells, "Screw you!" and stamps down the path, the guys trailing behind.

Watching them go, Eli just laughs. Then he turns in our direction, and in this liquid singsong, he calls, "Little sister? Come out, come out, wherever you are."

A chill shakes me as all color drains from Fawn's face. I'm about to run when she pulls us into a desperate huddle and whispers, "Don't move." Then, before Corey or I can even think to stop her, she stands up and says, "Put your pants on, asshole."

"Why? It's nothing you ain't seen before."

As Eli stoops to gather his jeans, Corey and I shrink into fern, stare at the ground.

Pulling his pants on, Eli calls, "Get over here."

Careful not to disturb our leaf shield, Fawn picks through weeds and pricker branches to enter the clearing across from our hiding spot.

When she steps onto the flattened grass of Stone Loop, Eli turns to face her. "What you doin' way out here, baby girl?"

Like her namesake forest creature, Fawn looks ready to flee any second, but, voice strong, she answers, "I came to warn you. Saw a cop headed this way."

"That's a good little sis." Down on one knee, he opens his arms to her.

Apparently sensing no danger, she sits on her brother's knee, smoothes his wild hair. When Eli nuzzles Fawn's neck, Corey starts to rise, ready to defend her.

Grabbing him, I pull him close. As we watch—eyes bulged like Gordy the Frog on Corey's shirt—Fawn peers in our direction over Eli's shoulder. Waving us away, she mouths two words: GO. NOW.

I don't delay, but it takes a frantic moment tugging Corey's sleeve to get him to leave his friend. Practically begging with my eyes, I convince him to come with me.

Slowly at first, we press through brush, careful to make as little noise as possible. Then, when we're far enough so we're sure we can't be seen, we get to our feet and flee through the woods, gripping hands.

Finally stopping to catch our breath, something—shock at what we've just seen, relief at our escape—causes us to laugh.

Corey says, "Oh, man! Did you see his thing? So gross!"

"And the way the other two were sucking in that smoke?"

We can barely stand, we're laughing so hard, but our moment's cut short by a stifled scream from Stone Loop.

"Fawn!"

Again, I restrain Corey as he tries to fly back to Stone Loop to save her.

"She can take care of herself, Corey. Please let's go!"

"No, Teddi! We've got to—"

I nearly leap from the rock straight into pond water at the sudden pressure of a hand on my shoulder.

"Hey." Aidan stands behind me, grinning.

"My God, Aid! Are you trying to give me a heart attack?"

I'm startled a second time by a laugh from behind him.

Whirling on my butt, I see Nic's with him, waiting beside an arched willow.

"What are you guys doing here?"

They exchange a brief look; then Aidan says, "I was going to ask you the same question. This is not the safest place to be hanging out alone. Even in daylight."

"Well, thanks for caring, but I've been coming here since I was a kid. I'll survive."

"Fair enough."

"So, Nic, since Aidan didn't answer my question, I'll ask you. What brings you guys out here?"

When Nic falters, Aidan says, "Nicky wanted to run lines. Someplace private. I said I'd help. Right, Nic?"

Too energetically, Nic says, "Yep, that's it, lines."

They trade another odd glance, and I get the feeling I've missed some inside joke. I'm not sure why, but it makes me uneasy.

As I'm about to ask why they don't have a script, Aidan drops beside me. "So tell me. What are you doing here, Terry?"

The deliberate wrong name catches me off guard, makes me grin. Closing my journal, I say, "Just working on some writing."

Depositing a kiss on my forehead, Aidan stands. "Well, don't let us interrupt."

They turn toward the path that loops around the pond, and I call, "Hold up! Can we talk?"

Aidan stops. Nic takes a couple steps toward me, hands pocketed.

I feel a little guilty as I say, "Um, I meant just Aidan, actually."

Offering a shy smile, Nic raises his hands in a *no-prob* gesture.

Once he disappears down the trail, I stand, placing my hands on Aidan's shoulders. He's motionless; then his arms circle me.

"So, I've been missing you, boyfriend."

He looks away before producing a smile. Tilting his face to mine, he kisses me. Soft, nice. Then, hands straying down my back, more forcefully.

My own hands kneading the muscle of his shoulders, I kiss him back. Cheeks hot, I'm awash in the sensation of his hands on me, the warmth of his mouth.

Coming up for air, I press my fingertips against his jaw, rest my head on his chest. His heart pounds. Mine keeps pace.

I look into his eyes. He breaks contact, glances skyward. I get the feeling he wants to say something. Can't decide how.

"What is it, Aidan?"

"What's what?" He smiles, tries to kiss me again.

This time, I step away. Returning to the rock, I study the pond surface, waiting for him to speak. After a moment, I face him and say, "Something's wrong."

Aidan joins me on the flat rock; sitting, he takes my hand, pulls me down beside him.

Biting his lip, he sighs. "You said you miss me. But you don't even really know me."

Taking his hand, I kiss each knuckle. "Not as well as I want to."

Unexpected tears fill his eyes as he says, "I don't get it, Teddi. I feel . . . you're this amazing person and—I . . . just . . . if you could see inside me."

As he stands, panic constricts my ribs. I'm certain if I let him go, I won't see him again. Relying on my typical make-or-break tactic, I shoot for comic relief.

"Don't tell me! Those anger issues you mentioned are more serious than you're letting on. There are warrants for your arrest in seven states!"

It seems he might laugh, but then his expression shifts. Face going mask-blank, he backs off the rock edge, onto the path. "Why would you say that?"

I catch his wrist. Kissing his hand again, I say, "I'm sorry, Aid. I was totally kidding. I didn't mean anything."

He just squints at me, his face a cement wall. Then his features soften. "I get it. You were joking."

Sweeping a fringe of hair from his forehead, I say, "Please tell me."

"You don't know what's inside, Teddi, but—" his voice is hushed, tentative, "it's not good." He closes his eyes. "I'm afraid."

"Of what?"

"Hurting you. Messing things up. Mostly of being . . . forget it."

"Your father's son?" He nods. "You're not him, Aidan."

"I wish that were true, but, people are always saying I'm just like him, and . . ."

"You really believe we're all just a mashup of our parents' worst qualities?"

His miserable expression answers for him.

"Well, if that's true, you're the one who should worry. My mother's a disaster."

His smile's weak, but it's a start. Leading him back to the rock, I pull him into a sitting position, my lips brushing his forehead, cheeks, chin. Then, just as our mouths are about to meet, I ask, "Can you keep a secret?"

"Uh-huh."

Leaning close, I say, "I, um, think I sort of like you, Aidan Graham."

He's quiet, taking it in; then, brow furrowing, he says, "Well, this is awkward."

"Awkward?"

"Well, yeah. Because I'm pretty sure I'm in full-on love with you, Teddi Alder."

Barely stifling a gulp, I'm speechless, unsure how to react. The last guy to profess his love for me did so in the back of a

Mazda, his hand down my pants. Surprisingly, that relationship didn't pan out. While Aidan waits, I attempt to banish intrusive Hecht thoughts.

Finally, twining my fingers with his, I manage, "Uh, wow?"

Aidan says, "That's it?" Then, jaw tight, he stands. Wrenching a cattail from the bank, he grinds the brown spike in his fist. Pitching it into the water, he says, "Shit, Teddi!"

Jumping to my feet, I touch his back. He goes rigid, but when I wrap my arms around his waist, he loosens and says, "I'm sorry, Ted. I'm not mad. Not at you." Removing my hands, he steps away from me. "It's just. It's me. I'm so stupid."

"Stupid? No, you're sweet."

He rubs his cheekbones with the balls of his fists. "Great, I can hear exactly where this is headed. You're sweet, *but.*"

Taking his hands from his face, I hold them in my own and say, "But I'm not ready to say it back, Aid. I'm sorry, really. And I pray I won't regret *not* saying it, because I . . . I really may feel it. It's just—"

"Just what?"

The last thing I want is to bring up Pool Girl and all these crazy memories that have been surfacing, but he needs an answer. "It's not even about you, Aidan. Honest."

"Oh, come on, Teddi! Please don't say, 'It's not you, it's me.' Even I've stopped using that shit line." Turning, he stomps off. Then pacing back, he says, "If you don't want to be with me, say so."

"Aidan, I'd be crazy not to want to be with you. You're like a for-real Prince Charming."

Volume rising, he says, "Well, you're acting more like I'm the frog."

Battling back tears, I answer, "Don't say that."

Face red, Aidan shouts, "Look, you get to decide what you will and won't say, but you don't get to tell me what I can say."

"I didn't mean—"

Lunging, he pokes his finger in my face. "If I'm such a prince, why are you treating me like some frog? SOME FUCKING FROG!"

Terror floods me; I bat his hand away. Arms wheeling, I strike him in the chest and neck. I'm not sure how long I flail, but I'm out of breath when Aidan slaps me.

Huffing out shock, I sit down hard.

Eyes trained on the pond, I experience this momentary disconnect. I'm on the ground; he's standing over me. How did I get here?

Aidan's voice is choked, quavering. "My God, Teddi. I hit you. Oh God, I didn't mean to hit you! Oh shit, oh shit!"

Barely above a whisper, I answer, "Don't, Aidan. I'm okay."

When he bends to help me up, I wince back, and for just an instant, he looks like he might hit me again. Without warning, he starts to sob, dropping next to me.

Cradling Aidan's head in my lap, I comfort him. He finally calms, and I tilt his face to mine, kiss him gently on the cheek.

Then I say, "You'd better go find Nic. You have lines to run, don't you?"

Aidan just gapes at me. After a moment, uncertainty creasing his brow, he asks, "Are we all right?"

Shaking my head no, I answer. "I'd say we need some time apart, Aidan."

Features gathered into this pleading look, he says, "I never meant to hurt you, Teddi."

Staring past him at the water, I say, "Nobody ever *means* to hurt anyone, Aidan. Not usually. Even when I was little, I don't think anyone ever *meant* to hurt me. But that didn't stop it from hurting."

"I don't understand."

I shock him by laughing. How do I explain I don't understand anything anymore?

Aidan's face takes on that dark cast I've come to recognize as stifled rage. Scarily soft, he says, "Don't laugh at me." It sounds like a threat.

Anger breeds anger and, pulse beating in my throat, I say, "God, Aidan! I'm not laughing at you. I just. I have some things to figure out."

"About me?"

"Not . . . exclusively. There are . . . there are some things I haven't told you."

"What things?"

I brace for his reaction. "Marisol's aunt. This friend from when I was little. I'm not sure what happened to him."

His expression slides from confusion to concern.

"And it all has something to do with the girl from the pool. She's the link. I know she's trying to help me, to tell me what happened to Corey."

As if I've kidney-punched him, Aidan changes. Compassion draining from his face, kindness eclipsed, he's wordless.

Rising, I touch his shoulder. "Aidan, what is it?"

Voice cold, he says, "This again? For real?"

"For real."

Exhaling frustration, he says, "Good-bye, Teddi." Then, turning his back, he calls for Nic as he trudges pondward.

19

After the pond, I'm close to calling Willa, but as I imagine rehashing the Aidan fiasco, I admit I haven't got the energy for it. Or for Willa's reaction, which will almost certainly be as dramatic as the event itself. Instead, I commence drowning sorrow in Forever Fudge. Flatulence be damned.

The sugar crash finally hits. Hard. I conk, and I'm out 'til early afternoon when Willa calls, to discuss a "semi-big matter." She feigns chipper, but I can tell something major's up. Ironically, she suggests we meet for ice cream. Pocketing some lactose pills, I slip through Bren's den without alerting mother bear, and head to Sprinkles.

Slouched in her plastic chair, it's obvious Praline Pirouette's not sufficient to lift Willa's spirits.

When I ask, "What's your parasite?" friend-code for "What's eating you?" Willa just grunts, shoveling a spoonful.

Scooping whipped cream with a peanut butter cup, I ask, "Is it Nicky, Wills?"

She slams her spoon on the plexi tabletop with force enough to snap it in two. "Wow, who died and made you clairvoyant?"

"It doesn't take a mind reader. Your face is a billboard. What's up? Is he still obsessed with the show?"

Shoulders shaking, Willa struggles to swallow a glob of butterscotch without choking. Then she answers. "He's obsessed, but not with the play."

"What do you mean? Don't tell me he's fallen for a costar. That'd be entirely too predictable."

"I wish it were that simple."

Magenta splotches each of Willa's cheeks. Fighting the urge to call her Raggedy Ann, I reach across the table. She resists, fingers curling into a stiff fist, but, refusing to let go, I hold her hand.

Breaking down, she blurts, "I've lost him, Teddi. And I don't know if I want him back."

"How, Willa? And why?"

She shakes her head, black ringlets sproinging, and says, "Dick."

"I beg your pardon."

"He's a dick, Teddi. Nic the Dick." She gets up, pitching her half-eaten ice cream into the trash. Returning, she spreads a napkin on the tabletop and sags, resting her face against it.

I wait for her to speak. When she doesn't, I spread a napkin next to hers and lay my head alongside. Touching my nose to Willa's, I say, "Talk to me."

She groans. "Oh, T Bear, what's the point? It'll just upset you."

Straightening in my seat, I pull her upright. "Willa, why are you worrying about my feelings? If I can help, that's what counts! Besides, you've spent more than your share of time lately listening to me gripe about Aidan."

At the mention of his name, my heart hiccups, and oddly, Willa's cheek patches darken. As she bites her bottom lip, a fresh tear plinks from her chin, seeping into her napkin.

Swiping the next tear with my thumb, I say, "What is it, Wills?"

"Aidan—"

Over the shushing sound in my ears, I ask, "What about him?"

Breath shivering out in a thin stream, Willa studies the tabletop and says, "Nic is, like, fixated on Aidan or something."

"Fixated?"

"Yeah, if I didn't know better, I'd swear he's obsessed with your boyfriend."

I resist joking that's one more thing they have in common, because she's genuinely bugged. I also don't say anything about running into them at the pond, or my episode with Aidan, figuring it'd only make things worse. And, honestly, I'm still struggling to process that. Instead, I just wait as Willa traces shapes on the sticky glass tabletop.

Shoulders drooping, she says, "He's been spending way

too much time with Aidan. He's got this insipid boy crush or something."

"You're shitting me."

"I am most definitely not shitting you, Teddi."

"So your boyfriend is crushing on my boyfr—" thinking back to the pond, I finish with "*ex*-boyfriend?"

She doesn't react to *ex*, proving she's neck-deep in her own woe. I repeat, "*Crushing? On Aidan?*"

"Utterly. But platonic, some bro-fatuation." Voice trailing, she rests her chin on her hand.

Unsure whether I want an answer, I persist. "What makes you think so?"

Wadding her napkin into a ball, she says, "Well, aside from the damn play, all Nic talks about lately is Aidan." She sticks a finger in her mouth, adjusting an elastic. "He blew me off last night. We were supposed to catch Penalty Box live." Flattening her napkin on the table, she smoothes it with her hand.

"Supposed to?"

"He never picked me up."

"You're kidding. Did he give you a reason?"

"No, and I texted him about fifty times. He says he was wiped, that he crashed right after rehearsal. Claims his phone was set to silent."

"Sounds legit."

"Sure, but it doesn't excuse him not getting back to me."

"Well, did he have an explanation?"

Dabbing another tear, she says, "Yeah. Aidan showed up around midnight, and they went to his place to play video games. When I asked Nic why he never called, he said he forgot about Penalty Box. Thought it was tonight."

"But you don't believe him?"

"I don't know what to believe. He'd been hyped about that concert for weeks. But Aidan shows up and—BAM!—forget Willa. He doesn't even seem sorry. The old Nic would've been all puppy-sweet apology. But since he's been hanging with Aidan, he's . . . different."

Despite my own Aidan issues, I say, "Or it could be the play."

"Teddi, please don't defend Aidan. Just, please. It's bad enough he tried . . ."

Something tells me to ditch my sundae and hightail it home. Instead, I ask, "Tried what?"

She looks down then, bracing herself. I know I should brace, too. Or leave before she has a chance to continue. Instead, I repeat, "Tried what, Willa?"

Chocolate eyes wide, she answers, "Aidan tried to kiss me."

At first, I'm sure she's joking, but that doesn't account for the tears. Still, my initial response is a laugh.

Expression clouding, Willa says, "You think it's funny?"

Unsure how to respond, I just stare at her. Then, carefully weighing my words, I deliver probably the worst imaginable response. "You're lying."

For just a second, I hope Willa might laugh, too, until we

both register what I said. And that apparently I meant it. There's no going back.

Barely audible, Willa asks, "What did you just say?"

Swinging into full-scale bitch mode, I glower, arms bolted across my chest.

She repeats, this time at full volume, "What did you say to me, Teddi?"

"You heard me."

Crimson patches reappear, along with a wounded expression that gives me instant guilt. I know core-deep Willa's not lying, but admitting this truth would open a massive can of bad for Aidan and me. And if our pond squabble was any indication, the last thing we need's more bad.

Thinking back to the Fourth of July, I realize Willa was right. It *is* a choice between her and Aidan. And ass that I am, I seem determined to choose poorly.

I have one last chance to fix the situation. So of course, when Willa says, "Teddi, be reasonable. Why would I lie?" I reply, "Because you're jealous."

This is so outrageous she does laugh. I join her, until she says, "Don't you even want to hear the details?"

I answer, "I'd prefer to save the fiction for SUMMERTEENS. But if you're set on sharing a story, go for it. Tell me about the time Aidan Graham tried to kiss you."

Instead of flinging a fistful of rude back at me, Willa takes the high road. That's another reason I know she's telling the truth. It's obvious it's hurting her to share info that will hurt me.

Frowning, she says, "He was drunk. Or something. He'd gotten Nic all messed up, too. It was yesterday, after supper. They said they saw you writing by the pond."

"Oh."

Along with proving her story, this detail propels me into new territory, some Land of Magnified Emotion. Pressure building, I close my eyes. As I knead my temple, my right thumb slips automatically between my teeth.

Willa keeps talking. ". . . upset or something."

Opening my eyes, I dab my bloody cuticle with a napkin.

"Anyway, they showed up at my house—wasted. Nic was being a total ass. He never could handle booze. And Aidan took me aside . . . and—" She stares at her hands.

"And?"

"Teddi, he says he's worried about you, because you've been acting . . ." voice barely audible, she says, ". . . unstable."

"Unstable?"

"His word, not mine."

It occurs to me just maybe she agrees.

"And then he suddenly kissed you?"

"Not exactly."

"What, then?"

She loses herself, shredding her napkin. Then she continues. "We walked Nic home. Luckily, his folks weren't around, so we were able to get him inside. He was all sloppy. Giggling, falling down. I helped him to bed. He kept saying how much he loves me. And how great Aidan is."

"Yeah, Aidan's a real gem. So, when do you get to the part where Mister Wonderful was so overcome with desire he couldn't help trying to kiss you?"

For the first time, Willa looks seriously pissed. "Is it that hard to imagine Aidan Graham could find me attractive?"

Because we've never fought over a guy, or because I'm a natural at Petty Bitch, I don't pause to consider ground rules, or what constitutes cruel. I blurt, "Honestly? You are so not his usual type."

No longer committed to the high road, Willa hooks a left onto Low Lane. Leaning back, she says, "Oh, right. I hear he's developed a taste for neurotics who fart when they eat ice cream. And who betray their friends."

Rising, she topples her plastic chair, and stalks off. I almost call after her, but the whole experience has me stunned. Afraid what might come out of my mouth next.

Ditching dairy debris in the big striped barrel, I waver in the Sprinkles lot. The last thing I want is a Brenda run-in, so home's out. Some small, insane part of me envisions going to Aidan's to confront him. Then I acknowledge how asinine that is.

Instead, I wander toward the library. We have the night off from SUMMERTEENS, but I cross Literate Green anyway.

Halfway up the walk, I see the sign: CLOSED FOR A/C REPAIR. REOPENING TOMORROW.

Drifting down the street, I settle on Hale's.

At the counter, waiting for my Caffrappe, their specialty concoction, I hear, "Hey, stranger."

Swiveling, I spot him beyond the bookshelves. He's sprawled, one leg draped over the arm of the old couch. Instantly relieved, I have this impulse to run to him.

Thankfully, my sandals show some restraint, sticking momentarily to the weathered wood floor. Grabbing my drink, I offer a shy chin tip, and Ed says, "Come on back, grab a seat."

As I approach, he clears a spot, hefting a pile of books onto the kilim-draped trunk that serves as coffee table.

We sit hip to hip in easy silence, until he asks, "Soooo, what made you think to look for me here?"

"As if." I laugh.

When Ed winks, I challenge him with "Where's Glade?"

He counters, "Where's Aidan?"

"Asked you first."

Ruffling fingers through his hair, he says, "She's got a date."

"With . . ."

"Someone else."

"Interesting."

We sit, unspeaking. As Ed reaches for a magazine, his leg brushes mine, the hairs on his calf tickling my kneecap. I will my leg to stay put.

Breaking the silence, he says, "Constant struggle. Classic on-again-off-again."

"I can identify. It's what we get for dating above our rank."

"I'm not following."

"Face it, Ed. We've hooked some major fish. Aidan's perfection with an eight-pack and a tan. And Glade, well . . ."

"So you're saying I'm not worthy. That I'm Quasimodo or something? Thanks."

"No! Look, you and I are attractive by any standard. You're like, a solid eight-and-a-quarter, but you've got to admit, those two are off the scale."

Thankfully, he laughs, so I continue. "Their kind . . . not that they don't have challenges, but . . . they live by a separate set of rules, different expectations."

"It's true. Take my sister. In seventeen years, I've never heard Eleanor belch. She doesn't sweat. Magic just happens for her. Glade's the same; enchantment trails wherever she goes."

"She's a Disney princess."

"Yeah . . . and," he pauses, looks away, "I suppose Aidan's a real-life prince, huh?"

My bitter laugh surprises him.

"What's funny?"

I sigh. "Prince Charming's a hollow concept, Ed. The whole idea of a perfect guy to sweep your troubles away? It's horse-shit. Besides, I'm hardly a damsel. I've taken care of myself as long as I can remember."

"That's admirable, I guess. But even strong people some-times need support." He places his hand on mine. "Or protec-tion."

When I slide my hand away, his palm cups my knee. Noting the image—a soulful eye, the number twelve—inked on Ed's wrist, I meet his gaze. Flushing, he moves his hand.

I catch us both off guard, leaning in, brushing my lips against Ed's. He stays perfectly steady, eyes open. I feel the heat of his face. As I shift my weight, the leather couch makes a flatulent squawk, killing the moment.

Cracking his knuckles, Ed says, "Wow. That . . . I'm glad we finally got it over with . . . was nice."

Immediately regretting the kiss, I go mute.

Straightening the book pile, Ed says, "So. What were we talking about?"

"I'm sorry."

"Don't apologize, Teddi. Two slightly better-than-average-looking teens grappling with turbulent relationships? A rebound kiss was inevitable. But it's a bad idea."

"I know."

"I mean, you have real feelings for Aidan, right?"

I nod.

"And Glade and me—"

"You're right, Ed. I don't know what came over me. Must be your cologne."

"Or my size eight-and-a-quarter magnetism."

"Right. Um, I should go." Slurping my Caffrappe, I stand.

"Teddi, wait." Face a map of concern, Ed says, "The other night at SUMMERTEENS you said Aidan wasn't the problem."

"That's right."

"But you two *are* having problems?"

"It's just . . . it turns out perfection really is only epidermal." I perch on the couch arm. "I should know better than to have expectations, you know?"

His eyes narrow. "Teddi, what did he do?"

I look away.

Punching a cushion, he says, "Dammit! I knew I should've warned you. If that prick hurt you—"

"Calm down, Ed. I'm fine. Anyway, how could you have warned me? You just met Aidan."

"Like I said the other night, I know his type. And I've," looking away, he says, "heard some things. He . . . seems . . ." Clearing his throat, he takes my hand again. "Just be careful."

"Why are you saying this?"

"Because I can't stand by and watch it happen, and because—" He stops himself.

"What?"

"If things were different, you and I . . ."

I cut him off. "Whoa there, Edlenson. No point pondering what-ifs." Then, ignoring the stone in my stomach, I smile. "Catch you later, Joy."

Ed manages a strained half smirk and says, "You bet."

I head home for a much needed quilt burrow, just me and my thoughts. Hours later, I'm tangled in bedding and confusion.

Postpond, I'm not sure Aidan and I are worth another attempt. Closing my eyes, I picture him. Eyes raging, screaming at me.

If Aid and I are done, I pray Willa's salvageable. Because what I said—"You're lying"—may have changed us. Permanently. Even as I accused her, I knew Willa would never lie about Aidan kissing her. I'd deserve it if she never spoke to me again.

Thoughts of Ed are a jumble. What made me kiss him? Am I so off the rails I've blown our shot at friendship?

I've managed to torpedo three relationships in rapid succession. Impressive feat? Or further proof I'm losing my grip?

20

This afternoon, the sky fell. Fine, it's water, but it's been coming down for hours. A true deluge. Binks flipped out as rain hammered the aluminum siding; his relentless pacing had me ready to snap. So, sealed in my room, I blasted the TV, successfully drowning him out. Now I feel guilty.

When I get downstairs, he's reached critical volume. Practically sloshing, he circles, nips my heels. He's ready to bust, so I skip the search for Brenda's rain poncho. Clipping leash to collar, I open the door, and we step into sheeting storm.

Binks has this wacky-when-wet gene; he morphs into a complete spaz when he comes into contact with water. Bracing for the inevitable yank, I sprint after him across mushy grass.

Feet luging sideways, sinking ankle-deep in mud, I scream, "Binks!" and jerk his leash so hard he pinwheels in the air. It barely fazes him. He's immediately flying top speed again, and it's impossible to keep my Crocs on. Kicking out of them, leaving them half sunk in sog, I skid after the little maniac.

Rounding the corner of the pool fence, my feet slide, almost skiing, and the leash flies from my hand. I nearly face-plant, but somehow, miraculously, I recover. For once, Binks doesn't take advantage of the situation to fly to freedom.

He stops, panting, a devious spark in his eyes. Then, snuffling the mud furiously, he flings himself on his back in a manic wriggle-roll. By the time I get to him, he's a living chocolate bunny.

Scooping his leash from the grass, I decide to head past the basketball court to the kiddie pool. Even in this rain, the fountain will be on full spray. It runs 24/7, rain or shine, from June 30 through Labor Day, a colossal waste of water—and total E. coli breeding ground—tots love.

I figure I'll let Binks paddle and de-muck before bringing him home. As we cross the field beyond the baseball diamond, thunder blasts the sky, and Binks curls into a quaking cower. If he weren't filthy, I'd pick him up for comfort. Instead, saying, "Okay, Ironman. Let's move," I drag him through the grass.

Nearing the sprinkler, I'm shocked to spot someone else braving this weather. Kneeling at pool's edge, she's beyond soaked, and not just due to rain. She's not dressed for swimming; her clothes puddle—a failed parachute—but as I watch, she wades slowly toward the center of the pool, where the water's about three feet deep.

She submerges; then, surfacing, floats on her back. I hear

her voice but can't decipher what she's saying as she drifts. A sudden flurry of limbs, she thrashes, and I almost call out. Before I can, she stops, stands, repeats the process.

Finally, she glides back toward pool edge, lips moving. They're the only feature I can make out. The rest of her face is hidden by her large hood. It and the cape she wears make her look time-travelish, as if she's been beamed into Sylvan Park from a previous century.

Not wanting to frighten her, I announce our approach before Binks has a chance to bark her out of her trance. Raising my hand, I call, "Unusual weather. Isn't it?"

Startled anyway, she almost slips stepping from pool onto equally wet grass. Facing me, she folds back her hood, and I recognize her. It's Tamika, the senior playing Viola in *Twelfth Night*. We had trig together my freshman year. I doubt she'll remember me.

Dipping her chin, she says, "Gosh! You caught me practicing. I must've looked like a real whacko!"

"No, not at all."

She peels off her robe, twists water out of it. Wringing her dripping braid, she says, "I'm trying to get the hang of what Viola would feel, after the shipwreck. All disoriented, dumped in the water fully clothed. The method-actor thing, y'know?"

"Sure."

Gazing skyward, she says, "Storm's finally over." As Binks snarls, she says, "Cute dog."

"Thanks." I give his leash a tug, and he looks up as if to say, *Just doing my job.*

"It's Teddi, right?"

"Um, yeah. Good memory. Trig class?"

She looks embarrassed. "Oh . . . sure. But I was really remembering you from the other night." When I don't respond, she continues. "At rehearsal. You're the one who screamed."

"Oh, God. I am so sorry about that. I probably ruined your whole practice."

She laughs. "No, no! It was actually the highlight. I admit it threw me, but Miss LaRose rolled with it. We had a whole discussion about audience unpredictability. She said we need to expect the occasional oddball reaction."

"Ouch."

"Um . . . that came out wrong."

"No, I get it. I'm glad my psychotic break proved useful."

She eyes the sidewalk that leads to civilization. Probably debating whether to run for it.

"Kidding."

After a pause, she says, "Sure." I'm not certain she's convinced, 'til she laughs and says, "So. You were there with Aidan Graham."

She waits as if some response is required, though that was more statement than question. I grant a noncommittal "Yup."

She leans closer. "It was really romantic the way he carried you out."

"That's one way to spin it."

"Teddi . . . if you don't mind my asking, are you two a couple?"

I search for the perfect response. None comes.

Tamika says, "Oh, that was rude, huh? Guess it's none of my damn business."

"No worries. I'm just . . . our relationship status is . . . questionable, right now. Let's say we're experiencing technical difficulties. That's all."

"Oh. Well, good luck. You make a cute couple. Of course, you do have an unfair advantage with Mr. Hotness on your team."

Eager to change subjects, I say, "So, the play looks cool. Can't wait to see it. I'm friends with Willa and Nic." A crinkle forms between her brows, so I follow up with "Your cast mates."

"Uh-huh." She sucks in her bottom lip. After a long silence, accompanied by further braid wringing, she says, "I'm guessing you don't know."

"Know what?"

"Nic got kicked out of the play."

"What? Why?"

"I wasn't there; had to work. But I heard he showed up late, out of control. Swearing, arguing with Miss LaRose. He actually tried to pick a fight with my friend Vinnie."

"That's impossible. Nic's never been in a fight. He's basically the mellowest guy ever!"

"Maybe, but two crew guys had to literally pull him off

Vinnie. Miss LaRose tried calming Nic down, and he called her"—she lowers her voice—"the c-word. She was furious, and she's usually so calm. Vin says Nic had to be shitfaced. Stoned or whatnot."

I just stand, like someone's kicked me in the gut, until Tamika says, "Teddi, I'm sorry to blurt it all out this way. I'm surprised you didn't know."

"That's insane! Nicolas Andrewski does not do drugs."

Riled by my unexpected temper, Binks flattens in the grass, growling again.

"Sorry." Tamika takes a backward step. "Just telling you what I heard."

"No, I'm sorry." Stooping to pat Binks, I say, "I didn't mean to yell. It's just . . . a lot. When did this happen?"

"Gosh, a few nights ago. Just after the rehearsal you visited."

I shake my head. "That can't be right. I was with Willa yesterday, and she complained about Nic being obsessed with the play. She said he's at rehearsal every night. She never mentioned any of this."

"Strange. I mean, she must know, right? Could be she's covering for him. Or else she's too embarrassed to tell you?"

"Willa's my best friend. She tells me everything."

"I don't know what to say. Maybe he hasn't told her. She has a real small part, so she hasn't been at rehearsal either. I bet he's trying to figure out a way to break it to her."

I just stand there, stunned, until Tamika says, "Listen, I'd better get home. I'm really sorry, Teddi. I dropped a real bomb on you, didn't I?"

"You sort of did. But I'll be fine. I just need to talk to my friends. Find out what the hell's going on."

Tamika's hug catches me off guard. Binks must sense I need it. He just sits there, no toothy menace.

I watch her shrink into the distance as she follows the path toward Parkview. Then, lifting Binks, I carry him to water's edge. Plopping him in, I say, "Time for a swim, buddy. I almost forgot the whole reason we came here."

He rolls his eyes as if to answer, *Small wonder. That was a major mindscrew, don't you think?*

21

Finished reading, Jeanine returns to her seat. With a dainty thumbs-up, Petra says, "Nice job, JC." The rest of the group claps sluggishly.

The newly fixed AC limps along, burping sporadic puffs. The storm had zero impact on temps; with the air in here pudding-thick, we're a troupe of pit-stank zombies—all except Eleanor.

Enthusiastic in the face of swelter, she exclaims, "Solid work, Miss Costa! The shift in time comes across more vividly. Questions? Comments?"

When no one responds, Eleanor says, "Alrighty, then. Let's call it a night. Unless anyone objects to adjourning twenty minutes early due to heat."

There are no objections. The gang splits quickly, Ken and Todd debating how the library basement could possibly be so hot, given "the inherent buoyancy of heat."

Ed slouches in the doorway, shaking his head as they pass.

He gestures me out to the hall. As I cross the stained carpet, Marisol approaches, tentative, serious.

Our interaction tonight was all business, nothing but writing, and strained. We haven't really spoken since the reading with her aunt. I worry how much Adaluz shared with her. I don't suppose there's such a thing as psychic/client privilege; that's probably just with doctors. And I doubt mediums take a priestly vow.

We "hey" in synch, and then Mari says, "Don't take this wrong, but . . ."

"What is it?"

"Just so you know, my aunt didn't tell me anything about . . . you know. The other day."

"Really?"

"I thought you must be wondering."

It dawns on me Mari may have inherited the family talent.

"Thanks for telling me. I did feel funny about it. I'm afraid I acted kind of wenchy."

"I doubt that."

"I told her it was stupid coming to her for help. That she was wrong about what she saw."

"Oh." She stops to examine the mole on her wrist.

"I'm sorry, Mari."

"It's no big deal."

I look at my shoes. "For real, she didn't say anything?"

"Nope."

"I think I owe her an apology."

Marisol smiles. "Not necessary. Lots of people refuse to accept what Tia tells them. But she's usually right. Anyway, she's not one to get angry over that stuff."

"That's a relief."

Sliding a small purple envelope from her binder, Marisol hands it to me. "She did ask me to give you this."

"It's not a bill, is it? I felt bad cheating her out of the twenty bucks."

"No, Teddi, she'd never charge one of my friends. Actually, Tia doesn't like taking money. She says it 'cheapens her gift,' and has the capacity to 'taint the message.' But it's how she put her daughter through radiology school."

"Seriously?"

I wait for her to continue, but it suddenly feels like we've maxed out all the words, neither quite sure what to say. Thankfully, Ed comes to the rescue.

"So, not that I was eavesdropping, but now that we've confirmed radiology's a growing field; Marisol's aunt isn't holding some psychic grudge; and cash can interfere with communication from the spirit world—a concept I find fascinating, by the way—would you two hug it out already, so I can talk to Teddi?"

Laughing, we step toward one another with open arms. As we embrace, Ed says, "My work here is done."

Marisol excuses herself, and I turn to Ed and ask, "So, what's up?"

He's about to answer, but then he really looks at me. "Hey, are you all right? You seem a little . . . off lately."

I can't help going on the defensive. "Nice of you to notice."

"Wow, sorry, I just—"

"No worries. I just haven't been sleeping. I have a lot on my mind."

He hesitates a moment too long, focused anywhere but on me.

"Ed, is something wrong?"

"No, I just wanted to . . . um . . . see how you're doing. And, uh, ask if you want to grab something to eat." He looks ultra-serious. "I mean, unless you and Aidan have other plans."

When I say, "I haven't spoken to Aidan lately," his features shift, disappointment and hope caught in a standoff, stranding his face on the border of doofy.

I say, "Try not to look so happy about it. And I didn't say yes to grabbing something."

"Oh." Hands in pockets, he smirks.

"I hope I didn't give you the wrong idea, Ed."

Smirk eclipsed by confusion, he says, "How do you mean?"

Lowering my voice, I answer, "At Hale's. The kiss?" Unable to read his expression, I continue. "It's just, things aren't perfect with Aidan, but I'm hoping to iron them out. So there's no point complicating the situation. Agreed?"

Not bothering to hide his smile, he says, "Sure, sure. I'll text Glade and let her know it's a no. Too bad, she was looking forward to seeing you again."

"Glade?"

"Yeah." Smirk returning, he says, "Wait! You didn't think I was asking you out just now. Like, on a date?"

Feeling my face go eight shades of pink, I manage a strangled laugh and sputter, "What? Ha! Too funny. Of course not! God, a date!"

Now it's Marisol's turn to come to the rescue. Spotting my discomfort from across the room, she's at my elbow. She asks, "Ready, Teddi?"

Ed says, "This isn't a poetry workshop, Marisol. Easy with the rhyming."

Following a polite laugh, we say good night to Ed and Eleanor, and head upstairs. Mari offers a ride, but I tell her I'm going to stay a few minutes longer to read over my writing. No need to admit I'm reluctant to leave early, in case Aidan comes looking for me.

As Marisol passes through the double doors, I decide to hit the private study room. Spreading my stuff on the table, I page through my journal, read over what I've written tonight.

It's crap.

Eleanor challenged us to upend our writing routine, to veer from our typical creative path. Tonight's prompt involved taking on a persona, writing in a whole new form and voice.

We were supposed to create dialogue in that new voice, and Eleanor suggested argument as a way to provide an innate sense of drama.

Thumbing through the pages I scratched together in—of course—Brenda's voice, I have to admit Eleanor was right about one thing, the inherent drama of a fight.

I've written a heated mother/daughter exchange. For creativity sake, I refrained from calling the mom Brenda, went with Linda. At one point, the girl, Frankie—short for Francesca, because *her* mother put some thought into naming her—calls her mom selfish, and Linda replies, "Are you shitting me, Frankie? You've got nerve saying that to the person who's devoted her life to wiping your nose, not to mention your ass."

Ken objected to the language. Explaining it wasn't so much the words, he clarified. "It just doesn't sound believable. What mother would talk to her daughter that way?"

Must be nice to have such a rosy outlook on parent/child dynamics.

Sighing, I check my cell. No messages, and class time was officially over fifteen minutes ago. If Aid were going to show up, he'd have been here by now.

I'm stalling, avoiding the envelope from Adaluz. Taking it from my journal, I flip it over. Holding it to the overhead, anticipating the contents, I imagine Willa saying, "Just open it, Teddi!"

The back flap is sealed with an Our Lady of Guadalupe

decal. Counting the stars patterning her mantle, I peel off the image and stick it to the inside of my journal. Then, lifting the flap, I slide out the piece of stationery. In keeping with the envelope and label, it's purple, featuring a larger Mary.

Opening the card, I'm struck by Tia Luz's tiny lettering. It fills the sheet in perfectly straight lines.

Dear Teddi,

I upset you the other day. Forgive me. I should not have pushed. The spirits can be imprecise, and as I told you, I sometimes hear them in Spanish, la lengua de mi alma. *I've puzzled it, and while you are sure you see a girl, a boy speaks to me. It does seem I was wrong about the name.*

"No kidding."

It only sounded like Ron. But it was not a name at all. He's saying "rana." Silly to miss it. Foolish, second-guessing my Spanish. So think, Teddi. Rana. Frog. *Does this mean something to you? The boy says it will. He drew a picture. I'm afraid he had to rely on my meager artistic talents (see back). Be well, Teddi. Be in touch.*

God Bless, Tia

When I overturn the card, I'm assaulted. An intense stink—of smoke and swamp—causes me to spin, looking for the source. I expect a smoldering bookshelf, but nothing's amiss. Next, the cicada buzz building and building in my ears, I hear the voice. Wild, gravelly, it gnaws inside my skull as it screams, "Fuckin' bullfrog!"

On the edge of blackout, I fold in my chair. Sliding from my hand, the Guadalupe letter lands, Mary side down. I tremble. Smiling up from the back, with his bulbous, goofy eyes, is Tia's drawing. It's Gordy, the cereal frog from Corey's T-shirt.

22

Last night was a smudge of upset. In fact, ever since Tia's drawing, I've been jangled, afraid to contemplate the Gordy picture's meaning. I was tempted to contact Corey's brother the minute I got home, so he could put me in touch with my friend.

And I knew I should call Willa to see whether she'd heard about Nic and the play. Instead, seriously close to overload, I went into defensive sleep mode. Winding my worry in bedsheets, I crashed 'til noon. For once, it sort of worked. I know I had a bunch of crazy-as-shit dreams, but I'm fortunate not to remember a single one.

I sort of expected to hear from Aidan today. Thought he'd at least text, to find out if Willa spilled the details about his attempted smooch. Unless he doesn't care about my reaction. I've imagined a hundred scenarios for that kiss, each worse than the one before.

Knowing would be better, but every time I start dialing Willa, I feel a gush of guilt-induced nausea, along the lines of "how dare I focus on anything other than Corey" after Luz's message.

I try again to erase her Gordy sketch from memory. If I could wipe away these last weeks entirely, I'd do it. Whoever established the link between ignorance and bliss was genius.

But there's no going back. I need to know.

It's been days since Micah's virtual "Piss off!" so, just before sunrise, I log in to the friend site for the millionth time, hoping for a follow-up. Zilch. Tossing caution, I type:

Hey, Micah. To clarify: NO, it wasn't a "fucking joke." Apparently, you're not thrilled to hear from me. I get it. We were pretty obnoxious. Sorry for all those annoying tricks we played. General tagging along, lame questions. But we were kids. And we sort of looked up to you.

Anyway, I really need to get in touch with your brother. Can you help?

After typing my cell number, and signing *Corey's friend, Teddi,* I brace myself and hit enter.

Barely a minute passes before my phone shimmies on the nightstand. I practically fall off the bed lunging for it, bracing as I check the screen.

It's Willa.

I'm just not ready to engage her, doubt I can without spilling what I've learned about Nic. I consider swiping decline.

But that might be why she's calling, maybe she found out about the play and needs to vent. This might make me a bad friend, but the last thing I want is to hear about her problems.

Then again, this could be our chance to fix things.

Snatching my phone, I'm about to tap accept when voice mail beeps. This is better. I'll let Willa stew. After all, she was mighty quick with that farting betrayal comment.

I watch the clock, anticipating the final blip signaling her message is complete.

"That was quick."

I give it a minute, assuming she'll call again, to leave a signature multipart meander.

The phone sits silent.

Picking it up, I log into messages, zoom through robo-lady's "You have one new voice mail," and press 1.

Willa's voice is super bright. "Teddi, pick up." A chip bag crinkles. "T Bear . . . I'm sorry. But we cannot let Douche-Meister G. come between us. Not happening." Huffing, she pauses. "Look, we need to discuss the kiss . . . to . . . rate his technique. Kidding." She laughs. "Call me!" Then, just before the tone, she says, "It's Willa."

That last part was meant to be funny, but humor's premature. Especially because she evidently hasn't found out about Nic yet. That'll be a trauma-fest.

Rolling my eyes, I say, "What to do with you, Wills?" Even though I know the answer is *make up*, I'm not ready yet.

Backing out of voice mail, I place my cell in its charger.

I spend the next several hours couchbound, tandem-plowing through daytime TV shows, boxed snack crackers, and a two-liter root beer. Binks and I will need our sodium levels checked if this ennui keeps up. But something about the mindlessness of soaps and game shows, the persistent crunch and sugary goodness, helps to block out Aidan's face, Willa's voice.

During the six o'clock news, I succumb to the laptop's siren call. Checking the friend site again, I confirm expectation. Micah silence continues. Deciding to go for broke—what do I have to lose?—I message again. This time, abandoning self-deprecating humor and any attempt to be cordial, I type:

> *Micah, don't be a dick. Message me. Or text. Otherwise,*
> *so help me God, I'm calling your mother. Teddi*

I type my cell number again and hit enter.

When I return from the bathroom (all that root beer), the friend site indicator flashes red. I click it to find a one-word plea from Micah.

Don't!

My reply is almost as brief.

Call me!!

I expect him to blow me off, make an excuse, persist playing Dodge Teddi. What I do not expect is an invitation. But as I study the laptop, waiting for some curt reply, a screen chat speech bubble pulses in the left corner. When I hover my cursor over it, Micah's picture appears, along with the word *Chit?*

Stomach leaping, my immediate impulse is to power off. Instead, after checking my shirtfront for snack remains, I release my hair from its messy bun. Then, strapping on my emotional Kevlar vest, I type *Chat!*

I always feel like someone's shoved me through velvet curtains into a spotlight when I screen chat with someone new. It's like this plunge into ultimate exposure, my image filling their screen. And catching my face in thumbnail totally throws me.

Tonight, discomfort's compounded by context. Last time Micah laid eyes on me, I was a prepubescent weirdo. Now I'm, well, a postpubescent weirdo. One who's stalked and threatened him into communicating.

We both gasp as our faces flicker into focus on each other's screens. I feel my cheeks redden when Micah says, "Wow, you really grew up."

"You're looking pretty adult yourself."

As if to prove it, he raises a beer bottle to his lips. "Yup."

We go quiet, and I question whether it was wise, forcing him to contact me.

Micah must feel the same about inviting me to screen chat. After a speechless minute, he says, "Look, I better go. I've got work in half an hour."

I launch into stall talk. "Oh, you've got a job?"

"Yeah, we're off assistance. Surprised?"

"That's not what I meant. It's just . . . all these years. What do you do?"

"I deliver pizzas. Don't pretend you give a shit." His smile's brief, joyless. "Look, it was . . . all right. Talking to you, but—"

Desperate to keep his attention, I leap. "I'm in a writers' group, and—"

"Congratulations."

"—I've been working on a story about Corey and me."

He makes a point of looking disinterested, but his hand shakes as he swigs his beer.

"There's stuff I can't quite remember, but . . . if I could just talk to him . . ."

Micah's expression robs me of words. Chin trembling, he says, "You really don't know."

"Know what?"

"Corey's gone."

"What do you mean 'gone'? Where?"

"Just . . . *gone.*"

"Wait. When?"

"I don't fucking believe this." His image blurs as he pushes back from the table. "It was in the papers, on the news when it happened."

"When what happened?"

From off-screen he says, "When my brother disappeared."

As if I've taken a jackboot to the stomach, I struggle to

breathe. The room spins. Steadying myself, I ask, "When did this happen?"

"When we were kids." Sitting, he comes back into focus. "When we still lived there."

"But . . . that makes no sense. There was no search? No investigation? I mean, a kid doesn't go missing and that's the end of it. The cops had to have looked for him."

"They did, for a while." Peeling the label off his bottle, he continues, "But we weren't exactly"—his voice takes on a rasp that echoes Corey's—"the sort of family people cared about."

"What do you mean?"

Glaring from my screen, he says, "Are you serious? Single welfare mom, two raggedy-ass kids?" His laugh is brief, brittle. "Plus, Corey was a couple shades too dark to matter much."

Picturing my friend holding a bunch of wildflowers, I can't believe anyone could feel that way. "We're best friends. He matters to me."

Raising a fist, he says, "Black lives, right?"

"My mother and I were in the same situation back then, Micah. If it had been me missing, you really think my complexion would have made a difference?"

"Only to the people who counted." He makes this sucking sound through his teeth, the way his mother would when she caught Corey acting foolish, *telling tales*. Tipping back, face out of frame, he guzzles his beer. Then he adds, "It's too late now. Maybe if your mother let you help that summer."

My temples pound. "My mother?"

"She wouldn't let you come out the house." Eyes glinting, his volume ticks up a notch. "My mom wanted to talk to you. She kept saying, 'If anybody knows where Corey is, Little Teddi does,' but your mother said you needed rest."

"Micah, I—"

"Look. It's not your fault. She was probably trying to keep you out of it. It was a crazy time." He takes a final gulp of beer. "One we don't talk about anymore."

"So you're saying your little brother vanished. And nobody did a thing to find him?"

"The cops mostly focused on my mother. And the guy she had living with us at the time."

"How could they think your mother—"

"Come on, Teddi, don't you watch TV? Family members are always suspects. Mom's boyfriend? Classic."

"Wow."

"They tried to pin it on Corey's dad next. Had this idea Corey'd gone off with him. I remember when they questioned the bastard. He was even on the news. The way he cried over his 'little Naphtali'—"

"Naphtali?"

"Corey's real first name. After his father. Asshole played concerned parent for the cameras like it was an episode of

Crime Scene. As if he was ever really interested in Corey."

"I can't believe you're referencing some TV show! What's the matter with you?"

"Fuck you, Teddi! Just—" He's about to throw his beer bottle, reconsiders.

"I'm sorry. It's just. I don't know how to process this, Micah."

"Yeah well, try processing it from my end." He rests his forehead against his folded hands, voice taking on that Corey rasp. "It got harder and harder to live with the possibility—"

I whisper, "That he was really gone?"

Micah chews his lip. "No. That he was . . . alive. It was so exhausting pretending he might . . . c-come h-home." He swipes a sleeve across his face. "But I did it. For her. For years. Said I was sure he'd be back in time for his birthday. Or hers.

"She even kept a bowl of those shitty sour apple candies 'for when he came home.' And we hung his stocking every Christmas. I have years of candy canes stashed in my sock drawer. Fucked up, huh?"

"I think it means you still have hope."

"I wanted it as much as my mother, for a while. But I never believed in it the way she did. She never once said he might be dead. Not to me. She kept coming back to his father. That's partly why we moved to Framingham. Bastard had family here," he makes that sound with his teeth, "so my mother figured . . ."

"What, Micah?"

"She was holding out hope his father's family really did have Corey. It would have meant he was alive."

"Is that so impossible?"

He isn't listening anymore. Doesn't acknowledge my question. Rocking side to side, he says, "I started praying they'd find his body. Used to go looking for it. Even after we moved. I'd ride my bike for miles; wander the woods, sneak into basements. I was determined I'd rescue my brother's bones. *That* became my hope. I strapped Corey's old backpack to my handlebars. Told her it was to keep him with me, but really, I planned to use it to carry him home. That probably sounds crazy . . ."

It sort of does.

". . . but I realized the only way to get my mother to live her life—our life—again was to get her to admit he was dead. So I had to bring his bones home to her."

"My God, Micah. I can't imagine what that was like."

"No. You can't. But even without his body, my mother and I finally managed to move on."

"How?"

He must read accusation on my face, because his twists with anger. "It wasn't easy. Especially for her. She insisted for a long time Corey was coming back. For me, it was tougher living with that possibility. I chose to face facts. I decided early on he . . . wasn't."

"Coming back?"

He answers extra slow, wants me to absorb every word. "That he wasn't alive."

"But how could you be positive if no one ever found him?"

"Same way I know there's no Santa Claus, no tooth fairy. I grew up, Teddi. I recognized the stupidity of hope. Stopped wasting my time on the impossible."

"But, Micah, it *is* possible. Corey could be—"

"Are you crazy? It's almost nine years." He looms so close to the screen I can see red squiggles in the whites of his eyes.

Gripping the corners of the laptop, I lift Micah's face even closer and say, "It's possible! Those women in Cleveland were missing more than ten years! But they came home!"

Leaning back, he folds his arms across his chest. "Different story, different ending."

"How can you be sure?"

"I told you, I got past it. And I don't need some shit pep talk or whatever this is. My brother's dead. I've made peace. If me and my mother can put him to rest, you ought to be able to do the same."

"I can't give up on Corey. Not yet. Why are you so sure he's . . . gone?"

"Dead, Teddi. Not gone. Dead. Corey is dead. You believe what you need to, but leave us out of it. My brother is dead. I just know."

THE PRECIOUS DREADFUL

My screen goes black. He's slammed the laptop, the way he slammed the door on possibility. It's not hard to see why. I busted into his life through memory's mist, reopening a wound that—no matter how he might argue—is incapable of healing.

23

I drag my broken spirit upstairs. On the bed, I rock and hum, anything to tune him out, but Micah's voice drills through my brain. I refuse to accept what he said. I'd know if Corey were truly gone, I'd sense it. But when I think of him, it's as if he's right here, sure, out of reach, but vivid. Alive.

Treading a sea of emotion, I submerge consciousness in loud music and memory foam. Earbuds snug, I sandwich my head between pillows. It's a valiant attempt, except most of what I'm trying to seal out is already inside my skull.

One benefit of faux hibernation: Brenda steers clear when she finally rolls in around two. I sense her for a moment, lingering outside my bedroom. But from her perspective, the swaddled hump must appear to be sleeping, so she drifts away, wordless. I hear her creak back downstairs; the TV comes on. Small favors.

We haven't spoken much since her return from the land of maple syrup. According to her brief description, Vermont was marked by neither catastrophe nor epiphany. She's resigned to third-wheel status with Mandy and Dev.

No doubt, she drank her fill; she slept most of that first day back, couch-snoring loud enough to keep Binks in perpetual agitation. This whole week, she's been powered down. Not sure whether she's depressed or exhausted. Selfishly, I have no desire to find out. She's easier to take at half mast, and I've got enough going on without Brenda's emotions seasoning the mix.

Although I'd been worked up over it while she was gone, asking about the journal passage seems pointless now. Even if she remembers muddy flip-flops, scalding bathwater, liquor in the giraffe mug, I doubt she'll give a straight answer. The truth matters, but it looks like I'll need to uncover it alone. Which is handy, because, honestly, who else have I got?

"Joy the Troll." It's Mirror Teddi. I roll over to tune her out.

Her intentions are pure, but she's been interfering all night, and I'm not amused.

She does have a point, though. Joy—okay, Ed—would take me seriously. I know I could trust him to help shoulder this load. He seems to genuinely care about me, shows not a hint of Aidanesque kick-start temper.

"Yish, Aidan. This might be a good time to call him. To resolve the whole kiss business."

"I wonder, Miss Buttinski, if you might allow me to wallow in private—maybe get a little sleep."

Silence.

Great, now she's mad. Emerging from pillow cave, I waggle fingers at my reflection and whisper an apology.

Plucking out my earbuds, I slide them onto the nightstand. Then, lids sinking, I drift.

Sleep's an elusive beast. I finally spot her stooped in the clouded corner. I can't make out her features; they're in constant motion, a shifting mask composed of many elements: Corey, Aidan, Fawn.

The creature, strangely entrancing, draws me close. I feel no fear as she takes my hand.

Hers is an odd composite of paw and paddle. As she grasps my wrist, I shiver at her fingers, wet-tacky. Bringing her hand to my face, I study the glistening digits, just four, webbed, with slightly bulbous ends. She touches my cheek. I feel a slight pluck, the tips adhering briefly to my skin.

Shimmering, she darts away, and I track her antlered form. I know where we're headed. But the journey is new. Where I'd ordinarily open my closet and stoop through the tiny door, access now requires passage down a corridor of gloom and leaf.

When she speaks, it's as if her voice—a trilling croak—originates within my head. Sounds twirl like smoke, forming word-shapes. Really, a single word, repeated: "Follow."

I do and, pelt rustling, she guides me through fringes of frond and vine. The path is straight, paved with scuffed checkerboard tiles. I note streaks of mud—and darker stuff. The smeared flip-flop tracks make me tremor. She draws me close, whispers, "Steady."

As we travel the path, branches part, beckoning. I marvel at the vines and trunks as they curl against themselves, creating sinuous letterforms.

I say, "The woods are writing," and my companion nods.

But when I pause to puzzle meaning from the barky script, she urges me forward. Training hazel eyes on mine, she says, "Your story lives here, but only you can write it."

"Eleanor?"

Shushing me, the creature draws back, face cloaked in sheets of alder.

And I'm alone.

Then, from farther along the path, her voice summons. "Your answers lie this way."

I spot three figures. Before they swim into focus, I know. It's Corey, Fawn, Younger Me. They twirl, wrists linked, squealing. It's some game, and their laughter calms me—until they chant, "All fall down!"

Springing forward, to warn them of acid ground, I scream, "Stay on the rocks, the roots!" Beside me again, sticky fingers smoothing my brow, my guide says, "They can't hear."

As I walk past, the children fall silent, palms raised in greeting. When I reach for them, they recoil, shrink, reappearing ahead.

We arrive in the storage area, but it's morphed, a fusion of real—stacked boxes, exposed two-by-fours—and imagined. Impossibly, the entire park's enclosed in this abandoned room.

The children's tracks stop short at chain link.

Pool fence rises.

Grasping metal, fingers curled through wire diamonds, I mean to climb. But, looking upward, I see the fence has no end. Against the black above, a form spins, suspended. Face barely visible through a mask of spider silk, Aidan's mouth hangs slack. But I hear his silent plea, at nerve level repeating, "Save me, Teddi."

Willa and Nic hang beside him, each in a separate casing, asleep. Calling their names, I begin scaling, but the fence extends, lifts my friends from sight. Falling, sobbing, I sink through soaked earth.

More sensed than seen, my guide materializes again. Caressing my shoulder in comfort, she says, "Don't let them distract you. These threads are unimportant."

It should be impossible for me to leave them, dangling in danger, but her touch soothes. Directing attention within the fence, I anticipate pool water, rippling in the floodlight beam, but reality tricks expectation. The deck fragments, cement heaving into bands of mud and vegetation. The scent's all wrong, too, not chlorine, but a gassy-wet aura, the steamed-cabbage stink of pond.

Palms to fence, I reel forward as the links dissolve. Shocked, I'm standing mid-pond. Water bugs dash arrows, leading me toward the rectangular bulk at the stagnant center.

Waves lap my ankles as Eli's car surfaces. At first, it looks hazy, but that's because it's the exact scuz shade of pond slime. Rolling upright, the car floats closer, back fender brushing my hip. The driver-side doors seem to pulse as rivers of shadow spill down them, sending rings across pond skin.

Catching my reflection in the side window—warped, dull— I'm not surprised to discover I'm wearing my Scooby tank. I step closer, then stop, thrown by a metallic click as the trunk lifts. As tentacles of unease tighten, I seek assurance from my escort. She's gone.

Fear somehow dragging me, I lean into the trunk, curious at movement. Before I know what I'm doing, I'm elbow-deep in goo. Drawing back, I puzzle at the brown mess that slicks my forearms, horrified to see tadpoles, hundreds, stuck to my skin in wriggling sleeves. Retching, I pluck them off, ignoring the squish as I pull them free.

About to plunge under to clean the remaining slime, I find I'm no longer standing in water, but seated in the backseat of Eli's car. He's up front; his ice eyes track me in the rearview. The seatback's transparent. Through it, I see the horror inked into his back, the slobbering wolf's head, its ram horns, and red, red eyes.

Turning toward me, Eli leers. "Where to?"

"Home?" I'm simultaneously reassured to hear Corey's rasp and reluctant to face him. Scared what I'll find, I cover my eyes.

When I finally look, it's not Corey at all, but his old

backpack. The zipper tempts me; dread prevents me looking inside. I shove the bag to the floor. When I pull my hand back, it's thick with blood. Rubbing it against the cracked seat, I jump at a sudden rap on the window.

Through smeary glass, I see her, my guide. Arms extended, she gestures me outside.

Swinging the heavy door, I step warily, bare feet pricked by coarse cement. Pool deck. I spin in a quick circle to find her, but again, I'm alone. Then I notice the petite figure in the shallow end. Pool Girl.

I call out, but she doesn't react, simply continues her slow ascent of the stairs. I move backward across the deck. Hand extended behind me, I fumble for the fence.

She steps onto concrete, a train of dark slickness trailing her small form.

Fear-numbed, I twine fingers through the wire diamonds of chain link. As the child glides closer, glistening in the security beam, details swim into focus. Weed-draped, hunched, she leaks a new malevolence. My nostrils fill with pond odor— mud and broccoli—as she nears. I can't look away, though I'm terrified to see her face.

Head down, features obscured by snarled hair, the thing gropes toward me. I see the yellowed workings of bare knuckles, flesh hung in strips below her wrists, forearms bloated, blackened. I'm unable to release my grip, despite fence wire beginning to slice my palms.

Bone fingers fanning toward me, the girl clutches at my neck. Terror blocks my esophagus, until I realize she's come to claim the daisy. This low drone, an insect lullaby, vibrates in my head. As she lifts my hair, a flat calm, a sense of connection, overcomes me. Freeing the charm from beneath my shirt, she clasps it to her chest.

The hum in my ears crescendos into a cicada buzz as her head lifts. Fearing her face, I train eyes on the sandaled feet— so familiar. When she whispers, "Mama," I'm powerless. Looking up, I see.

The slim body.

The Scooby shirt.

Her bloodied palms.

As her blond hair falls back, I find myself in her face—I'm seven, eyes wild, horror-glazed.

I shriek awake.

Confused, I realize I'm at the foot of Brenda's empty bed. My feet are wet, urine puddled between them. Binks shivers next to me; the low whine seeping from him is identical to my own.

Before I can buckle to the floor, I grip Brenda's iron footboard, steadying. My other hand seeks the flower shape where it hangs between my breasts. For a crazy moment, I'm sure it's gone, that Pool Girl did reclaim it. Calming, I realize the daisy's merely flipped around, dangling down my back.

Approaching the bureau, I see *her* for a breath's length, peering out from *my* sockets. Touching the mirror cheek, I whisper, "My God, Pool Girl is Little Teddi. She's me." With cold fingers I stroke my own face, speak into my curled fist. "I'm her."

24

Staring at the screen, awash in infomercial static, I chase oblivion. What I really crave is sleep. But it's no use. When Brenda came upstairs to find me by her bed, it was like a stranger had pushed open my stall door mid-pee.

Luckily, in her typical, postwork state of marination, Brenda's question—"Wha' the hell's goin' on here?"—was easily addressed. I'm not proud to say I pinned the puddle on Binks.

After a quick mop-up, I fled to my room. Brain on code red, I alternated between pacing and lying open-eyed for the next few hours. After witnessing sunrise, I slid into oblivion 'til late afternoon. By the time I woke, Binks *had* wet the floor. Out of bladder-panic or simple payback, I don't know. Either way, I couldn't fault him.

Brenda and I finally crossed paths this evening as she left for work. She made me promise to "keep a closer eye on that friggin' dog," adding, "Little pisser can't be trusted." I nodded, said I planned on staying in tonight.

And so, here I sit, hours later, plastered to screen, trying to numb my head. No luck. When Micah's words cease replaying, I obsess over Pool Girl, trying to comprehend what it might mean, how she could be me.

And then there's Gordy. If I blink, or my focus strays from the television, I'm instantly fixed on that damned frog drawing, wondering how Tia could know. If it is Corey trying to contact me, does that mean what his brother said is true? That he's really . . . gone?

The minute I succeed at banishing Gordy, Fawn's face intrudes. She's waving Corey and me away. And then, as we run, her scream slices through the woods.

Corey and I never saw Fawn—or Eli—after that. And we promised we'd never tell what we did see. Not ever. To anyone. But I needed to tell. Climb into Mama's lap and speak it out, so she could help. Could report it. Tell the cops a girl named Fawn was in danger.

But when I got home that day, Brenda was in a rough way. I crept in to find her at the kitchen table, a metal box spilling relics, photos spread out like solitaire.

When I asked, "What's that, Mama, what are you looking at?" she knelt on the floor beside me. She'd been crying, and she just kept repeating, "Baby, it's you and me. All we'll ever need. Just you and me."

I tried to look at the pictures, but she swept them back into the box.

Knees to chest, I lean against the couch pillow, shut my

eyes. When I do, it's there, as if it's sprouted from nothing, on the coffee table. The metal box.

Open eyes bringing absence, I say, "I have to find it."

I'm not sure why, but I know with a certainty I haven't felt in days. The lockbox. It holds answers.

Jumping from the couch, I'm newly energized. It's twelve thirty. Brenda won't be home for a couple hours. Binks groans. Tossing him Cinnamon Girl, I say, "Get busy, pal." Then I head up to Brenda's room.

It's a mess, as usual, but that could work to my advantage. I doubt she'll have any idea if I disrupt things, and I can always claim I was tidying, to make up for Binks's accident. Can't fault a girl for housework.

Brenda used to keep the box on the bottom shelf of her bedside table. I can picture it so vividly. Sometimes in the wee hours, cutting through her room to pee, I'd catch her on the bed, sifting contents. She'd shoot me an aggravated look, then lob some remark about my erratic sleep habits. And she'd always snap the lid shut 'til I left.

But it hasn't been on the shelf for a while. That space is now her go-to for stashing empties. I check the obvious places: closet shelf, beneath the bed, bureau drawers. The box is nowhere. Surveying the room a final time, I realize how sad, how small the boundaries of my mother's universe have become.

Crossing to the door, I take one last look back, landing on the framed photo atop Brenda's dresser. It's a picture from her high school graduation. She's legit happy in her wrinkled maroon robe. Giving a thumbs-up with her left hand, she balances ten-month-old Teddi on her hip.

Red-faced, the baby squints, mouth in a stop-action yowl. I imagine the looks Brenda must have gotten. From teachers. From other kids' parents. And, of course, from her own. It had to be a complicated commencement day. Then, right after, Papa bailed.

I wonder if Donor Dad was the one who took this pic. As many times as I've seen the photo, I've never imagined him snapping it. That could explain her genuine smile. Sad.

All right, I don't have time for second-hand sentiment. Replacing the frame, I knead my forehead, hoping to activate intuition. I've got to zero in, picture where those other photographs might be.

As soon as the image infiltrates my head, I wish to dismiss it, because if I'm right, retrieving the strongbox will require another expedition through my closet portal. And I'm not sure I can venture into the realm of the spiders again.

I mentally scramble to block the afterimage, but it ignites the back of my eyelids bright as neon: marker-inscribed labels—SCRAPBOOKS/PHOTOS/JUNK—scrawled in Brenda's angry hand on a pair of cardboard boxes in the unfinished storeroom. I see them stacked against the wall, wedged between my old dollhouse and Pharaoh the bouncy horse.

Terror pins me, hunkering, to the wall. Listing all the reasons

I shouldn't set foot in the storeroom, I fail to talk myself out of needing the metal box. If I'm right about my connection to Pool Girl, I doubt I'll see her again. But I can't help imagining her— or worse, Eli—waiting, eager, swathed in dark.

Finally, a wet nose punctures my fright shell. It's Binks between my feet, gazing up. As I tousle his head, he yips, nudges my shin as if to say, *Stop stalling, Teddi. Man up, now.* It's pretty bad when your cockapoo calls you out as a coward.

"You're right, big guy. I can do this."

Trudging to my room, I snatch a bucket hat off the hook by my mirror, mound my hair atop my head, and cram the hat over it, hoping to keep eight-legged interlopers at bay. Then I scoop house keys from my dresser.

I may have committed to going back in that funhouse, but I can at least enter from the other end. Rather than ducking through Wonderland doorway, battling cobwebbed blackness, I head downstairs, step outside, and trek to the building's rear.

Sliding my key into the bolt is a second challenge, because hardly anyone's unlocked this door from outside since Brenda's father opened it for deliveries. I jam the key in, jiggle 'til the mechanism grinds, gives way. Pushing the door wide, I shine my flashlight, piercing the murk. I reach into the fuse box and trip all the switches.

The overheads hum briefly, ancient fluorescent tubes crackling, before winking to life. I wait for them to steady; then, pulling the door closed, bolting it, I edge forward.

Simultaneously trying to look nowhere and everywhere, I anticipate a monster in each corner, behind every piece of furniture or equipment. "Get in and get out. Get in and get out." It's my mantra as I survey the clutter.

Mantra or not, I'm freaked. Along with the fact that one of my first spectral sightings occurred here, it's hard not to get distracted by the wealth of shit we've accumulated. Shallow breathing to minimize filth inhalation, I pick my way toward the spot where most of our stuff is heaped. It's clear this area's stint as storage dump predates us.

A tower of furniture climbs one wall. Rocking chairs and twin bamboo side tables balance like acrobats atop an antique vanity. Everything's ratty, scratched, sealed beneath a lifetime of cobwebs and ceiling dust.

Sucking breath, I squeeze between a chest of drawers and an old metal walker. My butt catches the edge of a vinyl tarp, dragging it—and a milk glass pitcher—to the floor with a thud. "Shit!"

I spin, surveying damage. Thankfully, the pitcher's in one piece. Sliding it back against the wall, I spot my old friend Pharaoh. Next to him, cardboard boxes I hope contain my quarry.

Stopping to pat my horse's muzzle, I swab grime from his soft, brown eyes. In them, I see Corey's, ablaze with fear and hunger like that last time in the woods with Fawn. Then they fade to a milky haze, their warmth draining.

"Where are you, Corey?"

A sob batters my rib cage, but I contain it by pinching my upper lip hard as I can take. It's a charley horse cure, but I've found it works to harness untamed emotion. Pulling a calming breath, I press my forehead to Pharaoh's, my hat brim folding against his dull white star.

Then I turn my attention to the boxes. They sit as I remember, one atop the other. Instinct—Tia Luz might call it something else—tells me the metal box waits within the bottom one. I listen. As I lift the top box to place it on the floor, one of those skeevy, gazillion-legged creatures Willa calls eyelash bugs skitters over my hand. Shrieking, I drop the box back in place.

F-bombs and vigorous hand-flaps soothing me, I make a second attempt, successfully lowering box number one to the floor. Dragging the bottom carton from the wall, I pick at the packing tape, loosening it enough to yank a strip free. I unfold the cardboard flaps. Ignoring the musty smell, and the possibility of an eyelash colony within, I peer inside.

Old magazines, dog-eared school portraits, and my ancient drawings—sort of touching she saved those—share space with the promised scrapbooks. I hit the jackpot underneath. Buried there is the stainless steel container of memory. Hopeful it holds those long-ago snapshots, I wrestle the lid.

It's locked.

Another f-bomb session ensues. Lucky as I was to find it,

there's no way in hell "instinct's" going to lead me to the key. If I were the heroine of some film noir, I'd use a bobby pin from my perfect hairdo to deftly pop the latch. Sadly, no such useful instrument resides beneath my ultra-chic, denim hat.

I give the box a violent shake; then, channeling calm, I actually look at it. Made of the flimsiest metal, barely thicker than a tuna can, it shouldn't be too hard to break open.

Declaring, "My kingdom for a can opener," I balance the box on Pharaoh's back and commence pacing. As much as these crammed and crusty quarters will allow.

On one pass, I catch my reflection in a blistered mirror and, barely aware I'd started, I deliberately stop mid-chew. Assessing my thumb, I find the nail split and ragged; the cuticle bleeds. The thumb itself is two-tone. Apparently, I've consumed a hearty portion of store crud while stress-gnawing.

"That's it. I've got to develop a more hygienic tension habit."

Cleaning my tongue on the hem of my tee, I lean closer to the vanity mirror. Looking in her eyes, I say, "Think, Teddi."

Ever helpful, my reflection suggests, "What about the drawer?"

Glancing down, I grasp brass handles and rattle the drawer open. It's littered with loose hardware: picture hangers, screws, these slender L-shaped tools. Allen wrenches? I scoop a handful of debris and, snatching the box from Pharaoh's back, I go to work.

Gently first, I prod and scrape. Starting with the smallest

wrench, I jab the long end of the L in the keyhole. It slides in easily, then lodges. Unable to pull it back out, I curse under my breath and yank with all the strength I possess in my thumb and forefinger. It's stuck. Giving a final twist, I exhale relief as it gives. Up close, I see the wrench has snapped; a small sliver of metal protrudes from the lock.

Generating Zen thoughts, I channel my energy in a positive direction. Frustration's no help. Feigning relaxation, I plant my left foot, and, yogi-style, slowly raise the right, my legs a giant number four. Exhaling, I locate my center. Then, lifting the box above my head, I hold the pose for a ten-count before lowering my foot smoothly to the floor.

I inhale through my nose, eyes closed.

Then, with all the force I can muster, I slam the lockbox downward, bashing it repeatedly against the steel body of the Mister Sno ice-grinding machine. So much for serenity.

Stopping to regain breath, I inspect for destruction. The box is badly dented, and two tiny tacks have loosened, the handle drooping at an angle. Otherwise, it's survived the beatdown remarkably intact.

Facing Pharaoh, I say, "Sorry you had to witness that, friend."

He reserves judgment.

For a moment, I contemplate resorting to the big guns—Grandpa Alder's table saw stands against the opposite wall—but, leery of leaving this craphole minus a digit or three, I rethink.

The tuna can image resurfaces and, though this freaking container is certainly more impenetrable than your basic tin of Bumble Bee, it gives me an idea.

"I'll bet there's something in the kitchen I can use."

Pharaoh seems to whinny agreement. Or he wants me gone so he can hibernate in relative peace. I consider returning the storage area to its original state; then, rather than waste a single, precious, Brenda-free moment, I decide as-is condition will suffice.

After shoving aside the cardboard bins, I squeeze back through the debris field. Switches tripping, I plunge Pharaoh into blackness and bolt the door.

Outside, I behave as if I've pulled a heist. Hyperaware, I race around the building, fully expecting to be intercepted by . . . someone—beat cop, cat burglar, roving skunk—but I make it to the front door without incident, treasure clutched to thumping heart.

Binks scrabbles at the other side of the glass for me to open the door. When I step inside, he power-leaps into my arms, nearly knocking the box from my grasp. Placing the metal cube gently on the floor, ironic after the way I whaled on it moments ago, I ruffle his fur, hoping to calm him.

Once he finally plunks on his bed, I sprint to the kitchen, rip open the junk drawer, and collect an impressive array of dangerous utensils. Moving to the table, I set to work with the studied precision of a neurosurgeon.

If I'm being honest, I try every implement—from metal shish kebob spear to meat mallet—to stab, hack, and bludgeon my way into the box. Ultimately, after piercing the lid with a corkscrew, I open a ragged gash, using an old school, hand-crank can opener.

Cautiously folding serrated metal into accordion creases, I uncover a potpourri of Alder artifacts. First up, a zipper bag containing trace elements of Baby Teddi: my newborn hospital bracelet; a quartet of sepia baby teeth; and—blurg—what could only be an umbilical snip, all cocooned within a fuzzed clump of baby hair. Eerie, like a fossil, or some fetish trophy. Serial killer party sack? I pretend it's a normal display of parental nostalgia. Pushing it aside, I'm thankful not to have encountered a full-on mummified placenta.

A little leery, queasy even, about continuing, I commit to digging deeper. Pushing aside baby relics, I uncover a plastic bag from Always 18, a long-gone mall store. Mindful of the gashed lid's jagged edges, I lift the bag. Inside is a Tigger greeting card; it's stuffed with loose-leaf pages, sticky notes, fast food napkins, candy wrappers.

It seems like an arbitrary batch, 'til I notice the writing. Everything, including the wrapper scraps, is inscribed with this messy, left-leaning scribble. There are dates, song titles, '90s catch phrases, and the initials B.A. + G.V. My "parents."

Ugh. I've unearthed some sort of romantic keepsake, a memento from Papa Sperm. Though on one level I find it more repulsive, if slightly less disturbing, than that umbilical sachet, on a deeper stratum it's just damn sad. I'm a little angry she's kept it. And surprised to realize Brenda's still able to disappoint. I thought I'd moved past expectation, at least where she's concerned.

Shouldn't these tokens have succumbed to a ritualistic burning a decade ago? I make a mental note that, if things with Aidan continue to fizzle, I will systematically destroy all remnants of him, rather than risk looking absurd to some future daughter at some future date.

Cramming Brenda's adolescent shame back into the Always 18 sack, I shift the remaining lockbox contents, revealing a flat, manila rectangle. The envelope lines the metal bottom; lifting it out, I note Brenda's inscription: RECEIPTS.

"Yeah, right."

I know better than to believe she'd ever save receipts. Bending the tiny clasp, I feel this hiccup of certainty. All anticipation has led me to this. Opening the envelope, I tip out the small bundle of photos, held fast with a blue elastic.

As I unwrap it, my mind stretches with the rubber. I see Brenda sweeping these very pictures into the box, tossing the elastic in on top.

Jaw tight, I confront the top photo.

The back's labeled: MOM AND DAD'S 25TH. Brenda's parents pose next to a cake table, all bride-and-groomish. They look to be about fifty, way younger than I ever remember, and atypically happy, as well. They always seemed to be baked inside this crust of disdain, and I was afraid to know what was underneath.

Of course, I only knew them post-BBS, Brenda's Big Scandal. Well, obviously, because technically I *am* Brenda's Big Scandal. Speaking of Mom, she's in the picture, too, looking a lot like me, the couple-years-ago version. Must be around fourteen. From her expression, this bash is the last place she wants to be. I do some quick math, figuring, at this point, she's only a year from meeting her destiny, my future dad.

I skip to the next photo, wherein Baby Teddi makes her unremarkable debut. This one's familiar, a wallet version of one Mom keeps on the living room entertainment unit. It's my first Christmas pic; I look like a velvet-trimmed turnip. I stick it facedown.

Shuffling through the rest of the photos is like some mind-bending card game. They're in no specific order, so Picture Teddi rebounds from infancy to a sullen nearly ten, and back to toddlerhood. No formal portraits are included, besides that unfortunate yule pic. These are the candid shots that tell the warty tale of my early years.

I spread them on the table, mindless of chronology. I'm not so much interested in my image anyway, or even Brenda's. It's the supporting characters who pull focus, demanding to be seen.

One photo shows me with Corey and his mom. Brenda's scissored the picture down. Skillfully cropping the brick façade and most of the sign above our heads, she's almost managed to purge context. Except the Saint Anthony's symbol is semi-visible by Corey's ear. Besides, I'd recognize this place anywhere: the soup kitchen steps.

Examining the image, I guesstimate particulars. Summer, late afternoon. I can't pretend to recall this moment exactly, but it had to be around the time Corey and I met. We both look so small. His mother laughs, head thrown back, as Corey clowns for the camera. Little Teddi gazes at him like a groupie, as if she's in the presence of some magic creature.

It's a cute scene, and looking at it, I feel like someone's gift-wrapped my heart in barbed wire. Breath hitching, I blot tears and stash this photo underneath the others.

Mercifully, there's no sign of Corey in the next one. But that's the only mercy.

Brenda, in a fairly shocking tube top and micro-shorts, straddles a motorcycle. My pimply father sits in front of her, bastard grin blazing. I'm tiny, wearing only a diaper—no shirt, no shoes. No helmet. Bio-Daddy's perched me between the handlebars. It's a disconcerting mashup: domestic bliss coupled with shockingly poor judgment. This could serve as the totem image for our family unit.

But another figure hovers just behind. I shudder in my seat.

Tall, thin, handsome in a predatory way, he's left of Brenda, his large hand cupping her bare shoulder. Distracted, he eyes a tattered Elmo doll in his other.

He's a little younger, several shades cleaner, but it's him: Eli. And there, materializing beside his thigh, an eye, an angular cheek, a mass of hair converge. It's Fawn. She must be about five. Even that young, she's unmistakable, her face somehow hard.

But it doesn't make sense. I have no memory of Fawn until later, Corey and I meeting her when we were six or seven. And she was eleven. What does it mean that she and Eli were participants in my babyhood?

Flipping the picture, I hope for a clue on back, courtesy of Brenda's pen. For once, she comes through. Her scribble reads ME AND BABY T, GEOFF'S BIKE. FUN DAY WITH G'S BUDDY ELI. FUN-NER NIGHT.

Suddenly, I'm sick. Shoving my chair back, I lunge for the counter, hang my head over the sink. I ache to block my memory of Eli naked by the pond, but it's all I can see, and for a horrible moment, it's Brenda kneeling eagerly in front of him.

My gut burning, I force the mirage away. I have to focus all my will on not puking. Retreating for a few minutes into the sound of gushing water, I'm able to calm my stomach. Though the nausea passes, I can't shake this dread.

Back at the table, I sift through more photos. There are others with Brenda and Teen Dad, but fortunately, no further appearances by Eli or Fawn. Nothing rivals the motorcycle shot for sheer shock value. For this, I am thankful.

But that doesn't stop me wondering what it means. My mind

keeps trying to connect dots in ways that make terrible sense. The trouble is they revolve around my mother as some drug whore servicing Eli, and God knows who else, to score a high. I'm not willing to accept that. Much as I've struggled with the fact that she screwed up and had me at sixteen, I've always chalked that up to bad judgment, to romance, to sexual immaturity.

Her futile belief in one true love.

But it gets a little trickier to buy that angle if she was involved with Eli. The words *FUNNER NIGHT* keep echoing, and I realize my only option if I want the whole truth is to talk to her. Pleasant prospect.

She'll be home soon. I should meet her at the door with the photo, ask her point-blank, "So, what was it like, screwing for drugs?"

That'd be awesome. A real moment of mother/daughter closeness. Brenda's voice playing in my head, "worthless slut like your mother," I bury my face in my hands.

Binks snuffles my hair. Looking into his sad eyes, I almost smile for his benefit, but can't quite manage it. Lifting him onto my lap, I sob for Corey, for Brenda, for my own sorry life.

Finally, moisture depleted, I reach for a napkin. Rubbing my eyes, I say, "Thanks, Binksy. I'm better now." Of course, I'm not, but, looking to salvage my dignity, Binks plays along.

I glance clockward. Feels like I've been here for hours, blubbering, but it's just quarter past one. Not bad. I managed this whole freaky, life-altering treasure hunt in under an hour.

Rubber banding the pictures back into a neat pile, I slide them inside the envelope. When they catch on something, I put the photos aside. Peering in, I notice a smaller packet.

Upending the manila, I tap it gently, and a white envelope dislodges, dropping out onto the table. As panic inflates my chest, I squelch it. After all, what could be worse than the discoveries I've already made?

Turning the envelope over, I find the back flap tucked rather than glue-sealed. Inserting my finger, I free the creased triangle and remove the contents.

A paper clip joins a cluster of news clippings. Removing it from the smudged paper, I warily unfold the pages.

"My God."

Binks looks up at me with concern as I scan the first headline. SEARCH CONTINUES FOR MISSING LOCAL BOY. Below the bold print is the photo of a face I've known forever. Beneath the picture, a name I've learned only recently: *Naphtali C. Boatwright.*

There are few details, aside from a brief reference to "the mother's boyfriend" and the fact that "Naphtali was last seen by his brother, Micah, in the company of a young neighborhood friend." They don't name names, but it's obvious they mean me.

Folding the page, I glimpse the next headline: COULD PLAYMATE HOLD KEY TO DISAPPEARANCE? I do read this entire article. Again, they don't mention me specifically, but it says, "Police interviewed the girl's mother, who insists her daughter was home sick the day of Boatwright's disappearance. She also claims, 'My daughter hasn't spent much time with Corey lately. She's been sick a lot this summer.' Refusing to allow her daughter to be questioned, she told police, 'I won't put my girl through that. She's not feeling right. And she's lost her best friend. My heart goes out to Adele and her older boy. They're good people.'"

So Micah was right. Brenda kept me out of it, told them I was sick, that I couldn't talk. God, please let me remember. I don't recall ever being sick for more than a couple days. And she lied about me and Corey not spending time together. We were inseparable that last summer. Just the two of us. Until Fawn.

And then she was gone after the pond, and—

"So was Corey. Could he have gone with her and Eli?"

Binks glances up, shaken by my voice.

I pat his head, scan through the rest of the clippings. They get smaller as the story heads from summer toward fall with no resolution. The final one, hardly bigger than a sticky note, dated September 21, is only a paragraph long, titled SEARCH FOR LOCAL BOY SUSPENDED.

Micah's comment—"a couple shades too dark to matter"—echoing, I wipe my eyes. This sad, little packet is evidence of the pitiful search for my best friend. Folding the pages in half, I secure them with the paper clip. Wishing I could forget having seen them, I slide the whole batch, pictures and all, back into the manila holder.

My brain free-falls, colliding with memory. That last day at the pond, Corey and me laughing after we escaped Eli. Then, Fawn's scream. But what came next? My mind skips to kitchen, to Brenda and the metal box.

Then nothing.

Until the muddy floor. But I have no reference point for that, no concept of when it happened. Or what happened, how my hands ended up bleeding. It's like some online video that freezes up, cutting past all the important stuff.

I sit, helpless, for the first time wishing for Pool Girl. If she *is* me, there could be some way she can help me remember.

"The daisy."

Slipping the chain over my head, I dangle the pendant between my fingers, where it swings like a magician's charm.

Focused on the painted flower, I slow my breath and whisper, "Concentrate, Teddi."

Vision dimming, flicks of green and fly-buzz fill my head. I'm close, can feel the heat of that day, see Corey crouched ahead. But again, recall slips from my reach. I keep coming back to the bath, but I can't access whatever it was that got me there.

Mind tickled by a feather of memory, I see Brenda's hands. After she lifted me from the water, I must've slept. But how long?

Days?

Weeks?

How could it have been weeks?

There's nothing.

Was I in some sort of mental hibernation? Shock?

The next clear memory I latch onto is out of sequence, a months-long gap later.

It was like waking up right there in Mrs. Goulet's class. Jack-o-lanterns on the windows. Corey's empty desk. The shocked joy on Mrs. G.'s face when I asked Chelsea to pass the orange safety scissors. What was it Mrs. Goulet said?

"Teddi, it's good to finally have you back."

Again, I do this mental stretch, trying to reach backward from the classroom, to see what came before. But it's no use. I keep getting stuck at Mrs. Goulet.

The way her voice cracked. How she embraced me in front of the whole class. And Chelsea, holding my hand in the lunch line, solemn-eyed, saying, "It was like you were under an evil spell."

A new image blooms. I'm in my uniform, Brenda holding me. Crying, she says, "Baby, you're talking. Thank God, you're talking."

When I tell her Corey's not in school, she starts to weep again; then she says, "Corey and his family had to go, Teddi. They had to go away."

Gushing tears, I ask her why.

Real low, she answers, "To be near his grandma."

I ask, "When will they be back?" and Brenda says, "We'll

see them again one day." Then she says, "Enough questions. Now, let's get you a snack."

I don't say a word, but I wonder. *How could his family have split us up, left without giving us a chance for good-bye?*

Pulling my journal toward me on the table, I consider writing, but I can't even open the cover.

Wiping my eyes, I say, "Why did she lie? Sure, to protect me. But all these years later, why is she still pretending?"

Then Binks barks and I snap back to this moment, my memories kitchen-table caged.

"Dammit, Binks!"

It's not 'til he howls at me, then practically draws a map to the front door, that I notice the unmistakable rumble-sputter of Dev's Saturn in the distance.

"Oh, shit!"

Scooping everything from the table, I say, "Thanks for the warning, buddy. Sorry to yell!" Then, unable to trust my behavior in Brenda's presence, I retreat upstairs.

25

There's no escape.

From my room, I hear Brenda teasing Binks, calling him "Cockapisser," cackling as if it's the best joke ever. Her volume alone tells me she's way over her limit. Then the shower blasts, a sure sign she's looking to sober up before turning in.

Even with the journal cracked open on the bed, I can't focus enough to start writing. The close call with the strongbox has me jittery. It's safely back in the storage area—sort of. When I got up here, I yanked open the little door, stashed it on the steps. Good enough for now.

But Brenda's off-key singing—that Seal song "Kiss from a Rose"—does nothing to promote reflection. She shuts the water, and I hear her tromp through the kitchen, can tell she's tripped over Binks by the way she hollers. She's perfected the art of stream-of-consciousness cussing. Poor Binks. I hear her flop into a kitchen chair, and then she's silent, thank God.

I'm about to open the journal for another attempt, when she bellows.

"Teddi! Down here now!"

I debate whether to obey, or just lay low, hoping her mood will pass. Before I can decide, she's mounting the stairs. Hiding my journal under the covers, I'm straightening the bed as Brenda appears in my doorway.

Seething, she clutches something in her hand.

My stomach hits the floor as she thrusts the object toward me. "What the fuck is this, and where the fuck did you get it?"

Before I can generate a real response, "Oh, God" slips from my mouth.

Brenda advances on me, waving plastic. My umbilical stump and hospital bracelet jostle inside the bag as she rams it toward my face, yelling, "I asked where you got this!"

When I don't answer, Brenda pushes past me, collapses on my bed. Letting the bag drop to the floor, she covers her face with her hands and says, "How much do you know?"

Stunned, I'm afraid to respond.

Sniffling loudly, she wipes her nose with her fist and points to the desk chair. "Sit."

I do, and Brenda surprises me by collapsing on the rug in front of me, burying her tear-slick face against my ankles. Floored by the strangeness of the moment, I'm suddenly sobbing.

Through tears, I ask, "Why?"

When she doesn't respond, I pull my feet away, angry. She springs back as if I've kicked her.

I want to.

She repeats, "How much do you know?"

Rather than answer, I cross the room, slide open my closet door. Unlatching the hook and eye, I bend, retrieving the strongbox from the stairs. Brenda has to know I've been rummaging in it, but she recoils anyway—shocked—when I present it to her, shocked again when I ask, "What have you been hiding?"

"I tried, Teddi. I tried."

"Tried what?"

"To be a good mother, the type you deserved. But, remember, I was just a kid myself."

"I know all that, your standard sob story. But what I want to know is—"

Hands clapped over her ears, she emits this shriek that brings Binks sprinting. I've never seen her like this. Don't know what to make of it.

Slowly, like she's a bird I might scare off, I sit beside her. Opening the box, I say quietly, "I've been remembering. When I was little."

Eyes flaring, she says, "Please, Teddi. Stop."

God, she's infuriating. The way she snivels, a strand of snot dangling to her chin.

I snatch the tissue box from the nightstand, slap it on the

bed next to her, and say, "Wipe your nose and meet me down-stairs. We need to talk."

As I wait for her—at least fifteen minutes—I go through the lockbox again, spreading its contents on the kitchen table, re-creating the scene from when I was little, these same photos laid out in rows.

Only this time, Brenda comes to me.

Standing beside the table, she wears a little girl expression as she says, "So. I'm sorry about before. I should know better than to mix beer and tequila shots on a work night."

When I don't respond, she says, "You caught me off guard. That's all. I'm better now."

"I'm not."

"Why are you being like this?"

"Like what, Mother? Like someone who wants to finally be told the truth? Not just hints and pieces?"

Sitting beside me, she wrings her hands. Trying to keep her voice even, to file off the angry edge, she says, "Exactly what truth is it you want from me?"

I barely know where to start. There are Fawn and Corey, of course, and the lies Brenda told to the paper. I want to know what happened after the bath, and most important, right before. I want it all, but I can't begin to figure out where to start, so it surprises me when I blurt, "Eli. How did you know him?"

She's not prepared for that. Her eyes dart away, and she's on the verge of tears again. But then, jaw muscle twitching, she says, "Eli was a mistake. A bad one." Looking at me, she starts to shake.

"What . . . kind of . . . mistake?"

Her eyes cloud as she says, "The worst kind. Luckily, I only made it once."

"Once?"

"Yes, and once was one time too many. There was a high price to pay."

The kitchen tilts at an odd angle. Sweat breaks on my forehead, and my mouth goes dry as it hits me with horrible certainty. Gripping the table edge, squinting through tears, I ask, "Was Eli . . . my father?"

Her slap of laughter jolts me.

"God! Teddi, no. Holy shit."

I nearly slide off my chair, limp with relief. "You're sure?"

She reddens. "Yes, I am quite certain of your paternity."

"But you said there was a price to pay, so I thought—"

"I know what you thought, but the price was more a personal one." No longer talking to me, she looks a world away. Hugging herself, she continues. "The cost was steep, and it took a long time to pay off."

When I touch her wrist, she snaps back to now, saying, "Look, I don't want you getting the wrong idea, Teddi. There weren't that many guys."

"But Eli was one of them?"

"Yes. He was Geoff's . . . your," she forces herself to say it, "your father's 'best bud,' his cousin, actually."

"So we *are* related."

"I suppose, by marriage. But you don't share blood."

Blood—a flash—my bleeding hands.

I'm not sure why I want to hurt her, but I must, because I say, "But you and Eli shared other bodily fluids."

Rapping the table, she says, "Teddi, you are not too old for me to smack."

I grant her a grudging "Sorry." Then, as she starts to relax, I say, "So tell me all about it."

"I will not. I will say it was after your father took off. You were about a year old. I was lonely, and Eli was someone to turn to. Familiar. And he," her face goes soft as she admits, "he always had plenty of . . . stuff . . . to help ease the ache."

"Drugs?"

"Yeah. Drugs."

The high price. But, relieved he's not my father, I have no real desire to hear more about Eli. Well, except for one thing. "Do you remember Fawn?"

Brenda blinks hard, like I've pitched sand in her eyes. Then she says, "Why are you asking about all this, Teddi? It was half your life ago."

"Do you remember her?"

"Yes! I remember her, dirty little thing, nasty little mouth. When she started running around with—" She stops herself,

257

backpedals. "Well, you were just a baby, too young for her to influence, thank God."

"Why are you lying?"

"Teddi, I will not be talked to like that. I am your mother."

"Sorry. Why are you lying, Mother?"

She pushes her chair back from the table, but I grab her wrist before she can stand.

"I've started remembering. I know Fawn came back when Corey and I were seven. I thought—until I found this photo," I hold it to her face; she refuses to look, "—that was the first time I'd met her."

"Oh." She picks at her nightshirt, unraveling the hem.

"Mom, please. Be honest with me. I'm afraid something terrible happened to her, and I'm just trying to find out what. Will you help me?"

"I can't." She starts crying again, even harder than when she was drunk upstairs. She keeps repeating, "Oh, Teddi. I was such a mess back then. Such a mess."

"Try. Please, Mama. Try."

When I say it, she gets this pitiful expression, not anger or sorrow, but a sort of wonder, as if she's seeing me for the first time. Then she says, "You haven't called me Mama in years."

I take her hands. "I need your help. To remember. I'll bet we can do it together."

A tear catches in her lower lashes.

Wiping it away, I say, "Wait here."

Racing upstairs, I return with my journal. Opening to the latest entry, I read to her. She doesn't want to hear it, says it's "too much." But I insist, and Brenda reluctantly agrees.

She gnaws her lip, trying hard to keep it together. When I mention the smoke at Stone Loop, she says, "Oh, God." Face streaked with guilt, she continues, "You never should have been wandering out there. It's a dangerous place."

I look into her eyes, not needing to say it: She should have known what I was up to, where I was, at seven.

She says, "I'm sorry."

"I know."

"Go on."

Eyes trained on the page, I read the next part, about the hibachi guys, the paint can belching smoke. When I describe Eli's snarling tattoo, Brenda shudders in her seat.

I say, "There's more."

"I figured." Her focus straying toward the fridge, she says, "Honey, I could really use a—"

Stopping her before she can say "beer"—or retrieve one of those fruity malt drinks she pretends are suitable for breakfast—I stare her down. Then I return to the journal.

I can't help glancing at Brenda as I describe the topless girl. Eyes squeezed shut, a tear slips down her cheek. When I get to the part where Eli bellows, her lids fly open.

"My God, Teddi! He didn't hurt you, did he?" She asks it through a curtain of fear.

"I don't know."

Brenda's shaking brings Binks to the table. Lifting onto hind legs, he rests his chin against her thigh. Her fingers twining through his curly coat, she exhales. "Is there more?"

"A little." I finish reading, both of us frustrated at the cliff-hanger ending. It goes beyond the fact that Aidan interrupted my entry. I honestly can't see much past this point.

I tell her the next thing I recall is coming home to find her at the table with the metal box.

She's embarrassed not to be able to summon the memory. Looking away, she says, "I was in a bad place back then."

"Yes. I was going to tell you what happened in the woods. About Fawn screaming. But you were crying when I came home."

"I was?"

"You usually were." I smile, and she looks grateful for one of my dark humor moments. When I follow with "Do you remember what it was about?" frustration invades her voice.

"Teddi, it was a long time ago. How should I know? It was probably just the latest romantic disaster. I don't see what it has to do with—"

"Look, my memories are this knotted ball of yarn I'm trying to unravel! We both know you're keeping things from me, Brenda. Are you going to help me or not?"

Standing, she crosses to the refrigerator, opens it, lifts out a bottle. Turning back to me, she says, "Want one?"

I look at her in silence, hoping the disgust on my face is clear.

Popping the cap, Brenda drains half the beer in one long slug. Then she says, "So you think Eli might have hurt Fawn?"

"I'm not sure what to think."

For some reason, I'm afraid to bring up the next memory, the sandal smear, the blood, the bath. I'm surprised when Brenda does.

"Teddi, do you remember a different day? Coming home? You were muddy. I gave you a bath." She's clearly fishing; after saying it, she looks at me expectantly, like she's uttered the magic words that might cause me to transform into a sack of rubies—or to spontaneously combust.

Shooting for nonchalant, I ask, "Just muddy?"

When I say it, she flinches; then she takes another long pull on her bottle. Tracing the writing on the label with her fingernail, she answers, "Yes, mud. Do you remember?"

I suppress the urge to call her a liar again, can tell it would just scare her off. Instead, I say, "Kinda sorta. Fill me in?"

Relief unmistakable, she replies, "I guess you'd been playing at the pond that day, too. You came home caked with mud, exhausted. I scrubbed you down. Not much more to tell."

This time I can't ignore it. But I keep my voice level, friendly even, as I say, "Please stop lying to me, Brenda. This is so fucking important. If you don't help me figure it out, I swear I will never speak to you again."

"What is it you expect from me, Teddi?"

"Only the truth."

"Hardest thing of all." She sighs. "Don't you get it? I've spent most of my life running from that very thing."

"Mom, seriously, I do care about your issues, the drinking, the self-loathing, the whole spectacularly-bad-choices-in-relationships thing. And we can have a full-on therapy session, for real. Just not tonight, okay?" I turn to Binks. "Did that sound bitchy?"

Happily, Brenda chooses to grin rather than belt me. Then she says, "I'll do what I can. But I can't promise you I'll remember anything that will help. Where do we start?"

"Mud Day is as good a place as any," I say it with my typical offhand attitude, but the crack in my voice gives me away.

She says, "You're sure?"

Eyes pooling, I tell her what I remember. "After Corey and I ran from the pond that day, I came home and found you crying."

Looking impatient, she says, "We've already covered that."

"I'm just setting the scene."

"What's next?"

"That's the problem. My next actual memory is of running, but it's patchy. I'm not clear where—or what I'm running from. Just this feeling, like my heart's about to rip through my chest. And the mud."

"Yes."

I leave the table. Moving toward the center of the kitchen, I drop to all fours, trying to extract memory from the physical. "I stooped to wipe the floor, and my hands were bleeding. They didn't hurt, but they were bleeding."

"No, Teddi. They weren't."

"Brenda, it's practically the one thing I'm sure of. My hands were bleeding."

"NO!" I think she surprises herself as much as she shocks Binks and me. "Your hands were bloody, not bleeding. Bloody."

"But whose—"

"It was terrifying. You busting in the door like you'd just run some horrible race, caked with mud, leaves in your hair. And then when I saw the blood on you. My God."

She's seeing it as vividly as I have been.

"You thought I was angry with you, Teddi, but really I was scared. Terrified. I thought my baby was hurt. You have no idea what that's like. I thought someone had . . ." Voice breaking, she takes a quick mouthful of beer and gargles at the back of her throat before continuing. "I thought you were going to die. And even though it was a challenge raising you on my own—and sometimes, God forgive me, I wished—"

I finish the thought for her. "You'd never had me?"

She looks ashamed, but she nods.

"Wow."

"Teddi, I—"

"No, it's all good. I asked for honesty."

"Let me finish. When I thought I might lose you, I knew my world would end. Cliché, I admit, but true."

"Thanks."

Taking another swallow from the bottle, she continues.

"There was so much blood, like you'd rolled in it, I was sure you were really hurt. But when I checked you over, you were okay. Just a few pricker scratches, some scuffs from where you must've fallen."

"So whose blood was it?" *It was Fawn.* Her face blooms in my head. *You heard her scream.*

"I didn't have time to bother about that. I raced you to the bathroom. Got you right in the tub."

"Did I say anything? About Fawn. Or Eli, maybe?"

She shakes her head. "Baby, you didn't say a thing besides 'Mama.' And that's all you said. For weeks."

"Weeks."

"Weeks and weeks. You were in some kind of shock. I couldn't imagine what you must have gone through."

"What did the doctors say?"

She doesn't answer. Getting up, she grabs another beer. Even from behind, I can see she's crying again by the way her shoulders shake as she grips the sink edge.

"Brenda? Please tell me you took me to the hospital."

Lurching forward, she vomits. Blasting water, she rinses and spits. Spinning on me, fumbling the beer, she sends it flying, shrieking, "You need to understand! I couldn't!"

She tries to dash for the bottle, but I block her. "What are you talking about?"

"I was afraid I'd lose you. I couldn't let that happen!"

"Lose me how?"

"God, Teddi. You're a smart girl. Think for a minute. Alcoholic single mother, known drug user. With my reputation, pregnant at sixteen, I wasn't exactly up for Mother of the Year. Would it really surprise you to learn we were in the system?"

"What system?"

"Child Protective Services. Want a laugh? It was your grandparents who first reported me. They were determined to see me fail, those two. Well, I nearly lost you once; I wasn't going to let it happen again. Not when I'd given up everything to keep you."

"What are you talking about 'nearly lost me once'? When did you nearly lose me?"

She leads me to the couch, sits by me. Afraid to miss out on what he interprets as affection, Binks jumps up, sandwiching between us. I try to push him down, but Brenda says, "No. Let him be."

Then, crushing him to her chest like a plush toy, she says. "Losing you had always been the plan, you know. When I got pregnant, my parents made arrangements for me to give you away. They got me to sign the paperwork and everything. But when you were born, when I saw your feet . . . Your ears were perfect little seashells. Well. I knew I couldn't go through with the adoption."

Realization slides onto the couch between us. Sensing its heavy presence, Binks hops down to make room.

I put my arms around Brenda and say, "What did you mean you gave up everything to keep me?"

"Never mind that."

"No, you owe me this. If you're trying to be noble, to protect me by burying the truth, I just want to say, that's a bullshit attitude."

"Fine, though I don't understand how it could possibly help you to hear this. When I decided to keep you, my parents cut me off, refused to pay for college. And my boyfriend, yeah, your dear father, he found out pretty quick . . ."

"What?"

"He couldn't handle the whole baby thing, I'm afraid. Specifically, the fact that I 'seemed to care more about the baby than about him.' Which was true incidentally." She laughs.

I feel like I'm meeting her for the first time, and I can't help saying, "You know something? I think you are."

"What, a loser? A drunk who fucked up two lives monumentally?"

"Noble. I think you're noble."

She manages the sorriest smile and says, "Well, I doubt Child Services would've shared that opinion, so I—" Sobs wrack her thin frame. "I did the best I could. After the bath. I held you, rocked you. I spoon-fed you again, like when you were a baby. And when the cops came around asking questions about Corey—"

"You lied."

"Teddi, don't hate me. There was nothing else for me to do."

"But we might have helped find him! Maybe we could have helped Fawn, too. And the blood, whose blood was I wearing?"

"None of that mattered to me. All I knew was if I told them you'd been out roaming the neighborhood, came home covered in blood, they'd have taken you away from me. And I couldn't let that happen. So I took care of you, and when it came time for school, I braided your hair, sent you off, and hoped for the best."

"I remember Mrs. Goulet's class. How surprised she was when I talked."

"Well, it had been a rough few weeks. No one knew quite what to do with you. But Mrs. Goulet was such a nice lady. She was my teacher, too, you know. She understood how hard it must have been for you, your best friend missing and all."

"Mom, I know he's alive. I really do. His brother doesn't believe it's possible, but I have to believe it. Please say you believe it, too."

Smoothing my hair, she smiles, but it falls short, not quite reaching her eyes. Then she says, "Anything's possible, Teddi. You just have to want it hard enough."

26

The moon is a dirty fingernail; it rips a hole in the black fabric sky. Binks and I hug the tree line. He snuffles the grass methodically. I yawn. Another sweaty, post-midnight stroll.

Brenda texted earlier tonight, to tell me she won't be home until tomorrow afternoon. She claimed she's pulling a double at the college, helping set up for some event. Not sure I buy it. I suspect it's her way of avoiding further recollection.

Truthfully, I'm relieved at the thought of some alone time. Now that I've had almost twenty-four hours to stew over our talk, I'm even more conflicted. Part of me wants to stick with noble, focus my energy on seeing her that way. She did make all these sacrifices.

But on the other hand, what kind of person sabotages the search for a missing child to protect herself and her kid? She could've made an anonymous tip. And she conveniently left out the part where she was drunk at the table, and gave me a mug full of who-knows-what.

And I'm not entirely sure I buy her claim that she and Eli were a one-shot deal, especially since she mentioned how he always had drugs for her.

Eli.

Just thinking of him causes this cinder block of unease to lodge in my stomach.

Roaming the park in a semi-trance, my mind ricochets Brenda to Corey to Eli to Fawn. It's maddening. Even with all I've found out, I don't feel much closer to answering the big questions. What happened to Corey? To Fawn? I'm holding on to that thin sliver of hope—that Corey's safe—that I'll somehow find him.

Like I mentioned to Brenda, I need to believe. And I need enough hope to balance out Micah's total lack.

Binks has dragged me farther than I intended, way down past the pool. Tugging his leash, I call, "Come on, Binkster. Time to head back!"

He pauses. But when he spots the cat, there's no stopping him. It's the big gray tiger I call Pirate for the black patch around his eye, the crooked grin.

Binks hollers; hurtling forward, he speeds to the end of his lead, nearly popping my shoulder out of joint. If not for the padded handle, my fingers might've been severed. As it is, I may be looking at a wrist sprain.

"Shit, Binks!"

I'm barely able to keep my balance, nearly tumble down the

grassy hill. As for Binks, he's a fluffy missile, twenty-seven pounds of cockapoo fury. His collar snaps free of the leash, and the idiot literally somersaults as the taut lead releases. Grasping that he's loose, he slows for just a second, looking back guiltily, before streaking toward the woods after his target.

Then, as I begin to pray there are no skunks lurking, the cat hairpins. I feel a punch of nausea as they take off down the slope toward Parkview.

This time of night, traffic on our street is thin, but there's never any regard for speed limit—or the children-at-play sign. Vehicles seem to materialize with no warning, ripping around the curve beyond the bus stop.

Like the minivan bearing down now.

"BINKS!"

He shows no sign of having heard me, laser-focused on the cat as it flees toward the road. The driver doesn't bother braking, rockets by.

The fear ball in my stomach melting rapidly into annoyance, I holler "Binks!" again.

This time he stops just long enough to glance in my direction. Then he bolts catward. I pray Pirate will do the sensible feline thing and head straight up one of the roadside oaks, but instead, he summons some deep reserve of macho kitty hormone and decides to stand his ground. Binks is caught off guard by Pirate's hiss. He stops short, allowing me to get close enough to make a grab for his collar.

In a comic standoff, the three of us regard one another like cautious gunslingers. Then, just as I go for Binks, Pirate—in one fluid motion—swipes him across the snout and snakes toward the road, Binks in crazed pursuit.

I barely have time to register the Forester, or to process the muffled *whump* as front tire impacts fur.

When I make it to the curb, I'm winded, shaking.

The SUV is eerily silent as it speeds into the distance. Taillights winking out, it rounds the bend toward Aurora.

I avoid looking at the small figure wrecked in the gutter, until the sudden movement and metallic clacking draw my gaze.

A low mewling wraps me in dread. I realize it's coming from me. Taking a single step toward the writhing creature, my knees lock, and I drop, crumpled on the curb edge.

Striving for a clinical, bio-lab attitude, I study the spear of bone pushing through matted fur, the slick pink of some exposed organ. I refuse to acknowledge the growing puddle of red.

When I lean forward to assess the damage, his hind end spasms, reeling like a gruesome mechanical toy. Kinking, wormlike, his tail flicks skyward. Again, I hesitate, caught between grief and revulsion. I'm inching closer to the broken form when his rear legs kick again, then fall still. Final firings of stray neurons, a death dance. The last spark fades from his eyes.

Through sobs, I feel a nudge against my hip. Binks whimpers, earnest cocker eyes shifting from me to the dying Pirate, as the cat shudders out one last rasp.

Wrapping Binks in my arms, I teeter backward, my butt striking sidewalk. Burying my face against his thudding ribs, I avoid the spreading blood pool.

"Corey."

I shiver as his name escapes my tongue. I've tried to think him safe since the phone call from his brother. But now it's all spinning in on me. I spit into the gutter, throat burning. I can't unsee them: Corey's brown eyes filmed with blood, their light dying out like Pirate's.

"No. Not Corey."

How can I be picturing my friend in this moment?

You know exactly how, Teddi. Know what it is to watch the life seep from a friend's skull like yolk. Remember it. You are ready.

I spin to see who's there, but the voice is in my head. Not my own, Tia Adaluz. Trying to block her, I whip my head side to side, stand, and stumble from the curb.

Binks nuzzles, kibble breath warm on my neck. I squeeze him beyond his tolerance level, but he doesn't nip or growl the way he normally does when he's fed up with affection.

As I plod through the park toward home, he watches over my shoulder, as if expecting Pirate to follow. Then, he whines quietly, his eyes seeming to brim with remorse.

"It's okay, Binks. It wasn't your fault. He was too far gone. You couldn't have saved him."

Again, I picture Corey's face, the skin gone ashy, his plump lips caked in blood.

27

Binks finally relaxes after a marathon soothing session and two caps full of homeopathic Pup-Eazzz. Snoring at the foot of my bed, he intermittently snivels in his sleep. I hope he's not dreaming of poor Pirate.

After dosing my traumatized pup and securing him in the house, I dragged back to the curb, armed with a shovel and pasta pot of scalding water. It was a gruesome, heave-inducing task, but I couldn't leave Pirate in the road to be pulverized by a succession of passing cars. I kept envisioning little kids showing up tomorrow to swim, only to be greeted by a heap of gore outside the pool entrance.

Managing to scrape the majority of cat pelt from the gutter, I carried him to the dumpster behind the community house, his stiff body shovel-balanced. Fighting a moan, I hoisted him in. Then I tried to scour the blood away with a few splashes of hot water. It was only marginally effective. Still, a smeary stain's preferable to an authentic, road-plastered corpse.

Tears cresting again, I do my best to tamp them down. I've

been trying with limited success to erase the dual images of Pirate and Corey from my head for the past hour.

Binks grunts. He looks serene, curled in a donut shape between my feet. I, however, have been powerless to conjure even a semblance of sleep. Immune to a double dose of night-time pain reliever, I lie here, fixated on the alarm clock.

Every time I close my eyes, I backslide toward the pond. My head is a choir of discord, this jumble of voices, pictures. Some terrify; others carry an enormous weight of sorrow. Corey's voice is toughest. It starts out rasp-joyous, half laughter, but dissolves to choke and gurgle.

Clearest is Tia Adaluz. Her words weave through the rest. They blot out pond sound, Eli's beast howl. She's poised, ada-mant. But somehow, I find her voice most frightening of all, because she keeps repeating the same command.

Remember it, Teddi. You must remember.

I want my mother, but it's useless. She might as well still be miles away. Trying once more to spawn sleep, I scrunch my eyes. Burying head beneath pillow, I cry, sing, pray. In the midst of sucking my thumb for comfort, I admit it's no use.

Throwing off covers, I pace the room, stalling at my win-dow, to study the moon. A thin scrim of cloud intersects its rusted sliver, transforming it into a menacing, gap-toothed smile.

Shuddering, I grab my phone and dial Aidan. Reconsider-ing, I hit end call before it can ring, and scroll my contacts list. Willa's number goes direct to voice mail. But I can't begin to formulate words, let alone a full message. The SUMMERTEENS folks are out, though I am tempted to ring Eleanor. Or Ed.

Just thinking of them brings the journal to mind. It's there, in the satchel, resting in the center of my bean chair.

Waiting for me.

But the book already holds its fill of awful. And I can't possibly write down what I've begun remembering. It's too shattered, indistinct, each vague chunk a horror.

Again, clear as if she were standing in the room with me, I hear Tia's voice. *Remember it, Teddi. For him, for your friend. And for yourself. Remember.*

"Shut up!"

On my knees, I mash my lip to my teeth, trying to use pain to summon peace, crazy as that sounds.

It's not working.

Instead, I pummel my thighs with livid fists. Watching bruises form, I analyze the shapes, grateful not to find a single frog. Finally, exhausted, I pull the spare blanket from my bottom drawer and curl into myself on the floor.

As I begin to drift, I hear the word *REMEMBER*, loud as if someone's screamed it in my ear.

This time the voice is Corey's. He's angry. Frightened.

Grinding knuckles into my eyelids does nothing to purge the image of his face. His cheeks are speckled with black-eyed

Susan pollen, same as my earlier vision. But then the flecks deepen, spread together into a sticky mask.

I choke back a scream.

Weeping, I crawl to the beanbag, rip open my satchel, pull out the leather book and pencil. My body draped across the vinyl mound, I wipe my nose with the back of my hand. Then I open the journal to a fresh page. Steeling for what's to come, I whisper, "Remember, Teddi. For Corey."

And then I write.

> *We're back at the pond. Can't believe Fawn and Corey want to risk it, spying on her brother again, after what happened last time. When I tried to argue them out of coming, Fawn chanted, "Chicken Baby, Chicken Baby!" I couldn't care what she thinks of me, but I started sniffling when Corey joined her.*
>
> *He put his arm around my neck then and said, "I'm sorry, Teddi. We don't have to do it if you don't want to." Then, low in my ear, he said, "You're my best friend, not her. For always."*
>
> *That was all that mattered. Shoving him, I said, "Let's go, then."*

Turning the tear-splotched page, I reach for a tissue. After dabbing my cheeks, I check my reflection, shocked by the face in the mirror. It's me, but I look seven years old again. Like Pool Girl, but not scary this time. Terrified.

Touching fingers to glass, I say, "You can do this, Teddi.

Remembering can't be half as bad as living it. And you did that. You did it and you were so little."

Climbing back on the bed, I scoop Binks onto my lap. When I squeeze his furry shape to calm my nerves, he squirms on the edge of sleep.

I kiss his forehead.

Open the journal.

Write.

We're crouched near the big stones, picking through splinters of broken glass and little baggies, when Fawn's brother bursts through thorny brush. Scratches ribbon his forearms and cheeks. Eyes lit, wild, he's smiling, the same jagged grin he wore that day at the soup kitchen. But there's no humor in it, not even the mean type I saw in the parking lot.

He looks . . .

I'm stuck for a moment, struggling for the right word. Suddenly, it's in my head. I write the word in my book, and Binks flinches as I speak it to the dim room.

"Rabid."

He looks rabid.

Then, he's on us.

Fawn tries to protect me, throwing her spindly body between us, but Eli tosses her aside. Her brief spark of courage flicks out as she crumbles alongside the old picnic table, head in her hands.

He comes at me again—fists clenching, unclenching—close enough that I smell his breath, this eggy mix of alcohol and decay.

Arms shielding my head, I brace for his blows.

But a scream from behind distracts Eli just long enough that I'm able to dash aside, diving for cover behind one of the trees that share my name.

Eli grunts as Corey grabs him around the waist. They oof in unison as Eli's big feet tangle, crashing them to the dirt.

For a moment it seems to be over, as if Eli's decided to let it go. Standing slowly, palms upward, he says, "No harm, hot shot. You took me down fair and square."

When he grins again, Corey laughs, his front-tooth gap seeming to wink.

I want to warn him, but I'm petrified, mashed to the trunk, finding brief comfort in the press of bark against my cheek.

Eli bends, extending a hand to Corey where he sits on the ground. "Come on, little man." He winks. "Friends?"

Smiling up at him, Corey reaches out his hand, and the world goes dark.

Rejecting memory, I drop the journal on my comforter, as if it's a scorpion primed to strike. The giraffe pencil seems to brand my palm. Snapping it in two, I fling the pieces beneath my bed.

Penciled or not, the memories hiss, demanding to be seen.

Pacing my room, I'm desperate to resist the open book, but it taunts me in the blurred light. I've dared myself too deep to stop.

Scrabbling through floor dust, I retrieve the pencil halves.

Sprawled on the bed with the sharpened end, I continue writing.

After helping Corey to his feet, Eli smiles at me. Then, slamming Corey backward, Eli pins him against a tree.

"What were you doing, you little shit? Spying?"

Corey can't answer, can barely speak with Eli's ropey forearm pressed to his Adam's apple.

Fawn makes this sound, a low moan, from beneath the picnic bench. Where are her guts now when we need them?

Peeling my cheek from the tree, I take a halting step forward. Eli turns on me again, and I stop at the sight of his eyes. Gone black, all pupil, they sear through me, and I feel warmth trickle down my thigh.

Eli growls, the sound freezing me in my tracks. Even when he turns back to Corey, I'm paralyzed. Then, I spot a rock, Frisbee-sized, half sunk in dirt.

On my knees, I dig at moss and muck with my fingernails, freeing the rock. All instinct, I throw it as hard as I can. Aiming for Eli's head, I don't factor in the height difference, or the fact that he's yards away.

Missing my target, the stone connects with the small of Eli's back, just below the tattoo. Howling outrage, he swings his fist behind him, feeling for damage.

Corey takes advantage of Eli's distraction; arms pinwheeling, he kicks to free himself.

It works.

Eli curses, calling Corey "Fucking little nutsack." Under different circumstances, we might laugh at that, but not now.

Our escape efforts have sent Eli over the edge. He's actually foaming, saliva swinging from his chin in a frothy web, as he turns on his sister.

Before Corey or I can react, Eli's flung himself to the ground. Raking his big hand beneath the table, he takes hold of Fawn's ankle.

I expect her to scream, punch, bite, but Fawn keeps eerily quiet—it's as if someone's removed her batteries—as her brother hauls her across the dirt toward pond's edge.

Hands on Corey's wrists, I lock eyes with him. I've never seen such fear. He just stares, like he doesn't recognize, or even see me. Squeezing his wrists harder, I shake him, fingernails leaving tracks. I pray the pain will pull him back to me.

As Corey flinches, I pour all my force into a one-syllable command: "RUN!"

But, shaking his head, he pulls free of my grip and screams, "We can't leave her!" Then he launches headfirst into Eli's back.

The monster stumbles, bringing one heavy boot down on his

sister's thigh. Fawn screeches agony, but then she just lies there. Facedown.

I'm wondering whether she's dead or unconscious, when I hear her moan, frail as some wounded creature. I barely have a chance to wonder whether actual fawns make that same noise when all thought is eclipsed by Corey's shriek.

Eli's lifted him off his feet. Beast bellowing, he swings violently, hurling Corey airborne. A wet thwack sends clouds of dragonflies out over the pond as my friend lands chest-first in the brack.

Spluttering, Corey pulls himself onto the slick bank, but Eli stops him. Straddling Corey's back, Eli pushes his head under. Corey thrashes, losing a sneaker. As his legs jerk, he churns the scummy surface with his arms.

Then my friend goes still.

Backing off, Eli hoots as Corey's limp form spirals slowly at pond's edge.

I hold my breath, praying for my friend to stand.

Finally, with a single, explosive cough, Corey lifts his head. Slogging up the muddy bank again, he collapses, inches from Eli's feet.

From my spot on the bed, I watch the rest unfold in front of me. My pencil nub can barely keep up as the dreadful scene plays out.

Lunging, Eli twists grimy fingers through Corey's hair. His face goes purple as he shouts, "What are you, a fuckin' bullfrog?"

Lifting Corey's head, he says, "Let's finish this."

Unable to move or scream, I finally stumble toward them as Eli spots the rock. It's big brother to the one I threw at him; that seems hours ago. He works it free, rocking it until—with a wet slurp—it loosens from the pond bank.

Next, fists raised high, Eli trains his icy glare on me for just a second, long enough to chill me with that horror-show grin. Then, with a force that pitches him forward into ooze, he slams the stone down, striking Corey's skull.

Binks yips. I'm squeezing him, fingers snarling his fur, as I rock on the floor next to the bed. I have no idea how much time has passed, how we got down here. I release him. Retreating to the bean chair, he shoots me an annoyed look, closes his eyes.

I confront the journal, splayed on the bed. Standing, I flip it faceup, read over the last paragraph, and implode. Grinding my giraffe's eraser end into the page, I scrub. As I obliterate the words, I command my memory to vanish with them.

It's no use. Micah was right.

My best friend is dead.

Murdered.

And I watched it happen.

Suddenly calm, I'm truth-stunned. Smoothing the page, I scribe the ruined letters with my broken pencil, etching Corey's fate back onto paper.

"There's more." It's Mirror Teddi.

"This is enough for one night." It's a plea more than a statement, but she shakes her head, dark eyes sad.

"Finish, Teddi."

I turn the page, not expecting to have anything to add. It's been more than eight years, and I've never once remembered anything beyond the pond—and then the arrival home.

Until now.

Standing over Corey, Eli says, "God dammit, Fawn! Look what you made me go and do."

As he grabs his sister's forearm to lift her, flinging her over his shoulder, I try again to be invisible against the alder trunk.

Opening my eyes, I find them gone. Crying as I crawl to Corey at pond's edge, I keep repeating, "God, let him not be dead."

Bending over my friend, I try to pretend his head isn't caved, tell myself one side's not crumpled in. Laying my hand on his forehead, it scares me how fast my palm turns red. His eyes stay closed. That means he is dead. I know from TV. But as I press my fingers to his chest, smoothing the wet fabric of his Gordy tee, Corey's eyes flutter open.

Just for an instant, his lips move; he's struggling to speak. But I can barely hear him. I lean down close to catch the words.

He says, "Teddi, sorry I called you Chicken Baby." Sucking shallow breaths, he winces. "You were real brave."

I answer, "No, Corey. You're the hero. You saved me and Fawn."

He must like that because, just before his eyes go milky dim, half his face smiles, and he says, "Hero? Like Croc Hunter."

As I whisper, "I love you, Corey," and cradle his head—my hands slick with blood and something thicker—he silently mouths my name. Then, as I beg God to leave him with me, my best friend dies.

So I have my answer. Corey is gone.

Forever-gone.

I want nothing more than to close the journal. Or even better, take it outside and burn it, pretend it and its contents never existed. But this isn't over. Images continue flooding my head. I need to drain them off, exorcise memory, if only onto paper. Pencil to page, I keep going.

"You can't go, Corey. I can still save you." The words spill out angry, but really, I'm so scared.

Picturing what I've seen on Brenda's hospital shows, I press my mouth to Corey's. I don't let the blood on his lips bother me as I blow. And I try not to imagine what Micah would say if he caught me and Corey on the ground, our faces mushed together like boyfriend and girlfriend.

After a while, I can tell it's no use. That Corey's eyes will never go back to brown, will never spark with laughter. Never spot another snakeskin, never twinkle at the sight of the ice cream truck. Never see me.

Ever again.

I try lifting him, can't leave his body—it's strange, Corey being a body not a person anymore—here on the ground. He's heavy, but I might be able to drag him out of the woods, run for help.

As I'm deciding what to do, I hear the voice again. Eli. And there are others, maybe those same ones from last time.

My joints lock; I'm pasted flat with fear. I remember how Corey fought me, refused to leave Fawn. Chose not to run away. To protect his friend.

Lifting his head, I press his face to my chest, not caring about the dark smear on my shirt. Holding him, I whisper, "I won't leave you."

Then Eli yells, "Over here!"

And I run.

Ripping through branches, not caring about spiders or mud or poison ivy, I'm aware only of the smack of my sandals, the tug of thorn and vine. Bloodied fists swinging, focusing on sky through the trees, I run. For my life.

So I ran off, left him dead by the pond. Now that I've seen it, I'm betting there's no forgetting that part. Ever again.

I don't need to write what came next. It's already recorded here, minus the run home. And I have so little memory of that. Just fragments: sandals slapping, leaf and blood.

Did no one see me? I must have looked like something from a horror movie.

The next clear image is the muddied kitchen.

Brenda at the table.

Heat of the bath; soft, white robe; the bitter mug.

Finally, sleep.

Sleep.

If ever I've needed to sleep, it's now, but I'm wracked by waves of recall. Corey's whisper, his caved-in skull. Their voices coming for me.

I fling the journal against the wall, startling Binks awake. Yipping once, he scuttles downstairs.

Reality in shreds, I fall on the bed. Sorrow-gagging, I pray for sleep's arms to enfold me.

28

Elbows on the table, I work to meet the gluey challenge in the black, plasti-tray. It's one of Brenda's microwave dinners. I use the term *dinner* in the loosest possible sense. Nine grams of protein, under 300 calories. Anti-delectable.

Binks presses his chin firmly to my knee, in hyperbeg mode. My boy's operating strictly on habit. I can't imagine he finds the smell enticing.

I'm honestly not hungry. I've barely consumed a thing today, beyond a few sips of ginger ale and some cracker nibbles when Brenda insisted. But she's mostly left me alone.

I am empty.

But, ironically, it feels as if there's no space inside me. Grief's crowded out my organs, its bulk crushing them paper-flat. I'm inside out. If I did eat anything, it would just seep, pooling on the floor, leaving my guts raw, exposed.

But rational sense says I must eat. And Creamy Tuna Medley it is. It's my first real attempt at anything in the last two days.

The contents brim, a mass of pale noodles, studded with neon peas, the sporadic blob of tuna rubble. A thin, brown crust collects in one corner. Piercing it with my spoon, I stir.

This aggressive, gassy smell rises from the tray. *Swamp.* Stomach rebelling, I belch disgust, bend and scoop, dumping the slop in Binks's dish.

He gives it a quick sniff, shoots me an *oh-hell-no*, and heads to the couch. Leaving the lump to congeal, I turn back to the counter. My journal's there beside the plastic film from the top of the tuna tray. I'm close to tossing both in the garbage, but don't.

Although I haven't been brave enough to look inside, I've kept the journal with me every second since that last entry. As though it's turned sacred. Become some depository of horrible truths. Outlining the Celtic-knotted cover, as if my finger's roaming a mini-labyrinth, I try to clear my head.

The last two days have been a blur. I told Brenda my stomach's gone rogue, warned her away when she tried to check on me, saying, "Stay back! If I'm contage, believe me, you do not want to catch this!"

As if it's possible to catch what I've got. Which is what, exactly? Horror? Revulsion? Despair? Insanity? Acceptance? My personalized five stages of grief. Honestly, acceptance is the most horrible possibility of all.

Brenda has hung back quite effectively. I'm sure she suspects it's my past, not my stomach, that's gurgling, but she's chosen to take me at my word. Can't blame her for seizing any

opportunity to disengage. Her distance has allowed me to burrow deeper into sheets, into numbness. For this, I am thankful.

But numbness takes effort to sustain. I'm hoarse from humming to block out the sounds. Of Eli's gang crashing through
trees. Of the bathtub blasting its scalding stream.

Worst of all, the sound of the rock coming down on Corey.

The thud.

The rupture.

Sure, I'm only imagining that sound—a ceramic jug
exploding—but it's real enough.

I barely manage to remain afloat by talking myself out
of belief. It's possible, isn't it, that my journal entries aren't
memories at all, but some kind of fabrication? Spontaneous
generation, cells dividing or something? My brain hopped up
on imagination.

Isn't that the point of SUMMERTEENS? Writing stories.
Creating *fictions*. Making shit up. What if my mind somehow
got too good at it, doesn't know how to stop?

"No, Teddi."

The voice is Corey's. I've been hearing him plenty these
past two days. His little boy rasp. I wonder how he'd sound
now, at nearly sixteen—if he'd had the chance to get here. If he
weren't bashed and dead gone. Maybe he'd sound like Micah.

"God, Micah. I've got to tell him." I say it out loud, and it's
funny, because I've barely spoken at all since writing that last
passage.

Lifting my laptop lid, my hands shake. I press it shut. "No. I can't do this. It's too horrible to be true. Too much to think, never mind tell."

"Too much to keep." Now it's Mirror Teddi. She's been talking, too. It's possible I truly am losing my mind. Who'd have believed that might be preferable to finding out the truth?

I speak to my reflection in the microwave door. "Corey is dead." I see the words form against smoked glass, feel them settle in my chest. They hold the weight of truth.

Who can I tell?

Not Brenda. Not yet. I have too many questions for her. About what she really knew. And when. If I open my mouth to say, "I've remembered what happened to Corey," what's likely to come out is "If you were a better mother, my friend might not be dead."

Of course, Micah would probably say something similar to me. "If you were a better friend . . ." But that's not fair.

A laugh, this bitter bleat, slips out at that ludicrous concept called *fair*.

I imagine Willa saying, "Get a grip, girl."

She, at least, would be a help. To hold on to, to cry with. But I'm not willing to fasten this anchor around her neck just yet. Not Willa's.

Or anyone else's.

It's why I've stayed home, in bed mostly, only getting up to use the bathroom and see to Binks. When sleep *has* come, it's flattened me. But mercifully, there have been no dreams.

I pick up my phone, debate turning it back on. But who would I call? I shut it off in the first place to avoid talking, to avoid Willa's messages. To avoid the certainty that Aidan would—or wouldn't ever—contact me.

And I recorded a new message, about having the flu, said I'd be in touch when I'm feeling better. I posted a gut bug status online, too—very thorough—just to buy some peace. As if peace will ever be possible again.

SUMMERTEENS starts in a little under four hours. I skipped last night, don't think I can face them tonight either, though a part of me wants to. I'd take center circle, stand on a chair, transfix the crew with my latest selection. I'd call it "Pond of Horrors." I'm sure it would get a major reaction.

Realizing I've been gawping at my phone as if it's morphed into some exotic and dangerous creature in my palm, I put it down.

Opening my journal just wide enough to slip out the workshop contact list folded inside the cover, I slide my finger down the page. I'm searching for Eleanor's number.

I opt for the kitchen phone, punching in her digits before I can lose my nerve. As it rings, I suspend breath, praying I get a machine.

Quite the opposite. On the fourth ring, someone answers. It's a guy. No surprise Eleanor has a boyfriend. Flummoxed, I only manage "Uh" before ending the call.

Barely a minute later, the phone chirps in its cradle. I let the machine handle it. Brenda's bored mumble advises the caller to leave a message. After a short pause, I hear his voice.

"Hello? Teddi, did you just call?" It's Ed. I resist grabbing the phone, and he continues. "If you're there, pick up. I just want to make sure everything's okay. I . . . everyone missed you last night. I hope . . . we'll . . . see you at workshop tonight. 'Kay, later."

I should call him back, tell him I won't be making it to the library. That I'm contemplating never leaving the house again. That I'm not sure I belong out in the world anymore, now that the world has changed so fundamentally.

But of course, I don't.

Some stupid part of me apparently continues to operate under the delusion that things—manners and relationships and people's feelings—matter. I mean, I get it. That's all bullshit. *Nothing* really matters. But that'd be sort of hard to explain to somebody, especially when he's just calling to check on you. Just calling to be nice.

As I stand at the kitchen counter, aching to decode the meaning of it all and coming up empty, my eyes return to my cell. Curiosity getting the best of me, I press the button and watch the screen illuminate. Against the alder leaf background, a little yellow envelope winks. When I tap it, a number swirls up and out, hovering center-screen. Eight messages.

Scrolling through the list, I see only two—one voice mail, one text—are from Willa. She's shown remarkable restraint.

I listen to the voice mail. She says she wants to make things right between us, that we should meet at Sprinkles to "exorcise the bad mojo" as soon as I'm better. The text is typical Wills, a laughing selfie with Nic, captioned **Freedom! We both quit 12th Night!**

Hmm, *We quit*, not *Nic got booted.* Wonder what he told her.

My heart stumbles when I see the other six messages are from Aidan. I'm wary of the voice mails, recalling his angry roar at the pond. Figuring a blow-off will be easier to take in print, I swipe the first text, from yesterday afternoon.

It's just one word, along with a little heart symbol: **Sorry ♥**

The second text is from late last night.

T - stopped @ brary to c u but u weren't there that ed dude said ur sick everything ok?–A

Since the voice mails came after the texts, I'm willing to risk listening, assuming he won't lapse into prickdom so shortly after apologizing. I click the icon, and his soft voice joins me at the counter.

"Teddi, I can't blame you if you don't ever want to see me again, but I need you to believe I'm sorry. For everything. I know Willa told you about . . . what happened. And I want to make one thing clear. It wasn't her fault. At all. I was pretty messed up, and—" He's run out of time; robo-lady cuts his soliloquy short.

"Damn, it was just getting good."

Fighting a wave of guilt, I decide to listen to the next message. Yes, it makes me selfish, caring about relationship stuff post-Corey, but I can't help it. I kind of really do.

Corey, I wonder how he'd weigh in. If he'd be on Team Aidan or Team Ed. If he'd remember our long-ago promise to get married one day like Croc Hunter and Terri.

I press the v-mail button.

This message is a continuation of the last.

"I was angry, yes. But . . . hurt, really. And I wanted to hurt you back. I'm not sure why. I had no right to assume you'd say it back to me. 'I love you,' I mean. Anyway, if . . . if you want, call me. When you feel better. If you think we're worth another chance."

A tear splats the screen as I contemplate second chances, realizing how rarely they happen. Blotting the phone with my thumb, I listen to message number seven.

"Morning, Teddi. So, I stayed in last night. Contemplating us, and hoping I haven't managed to commit the biggest mistake of my life. Because it would be, losing you. And believe me, I've made some real freakin' whoppers. Teddi . . . Please call. If you want." Then after a thought-filled silence, he ends with "Love you."

The final message, another text, is time-stamped just a couple minutes ago. I'm puzzled at the brief contents, two seemingly random words: **front door.**

As I glance in that direction, Binks suddenly leaps from his couch spot. Growling, he hurls himself at the blinds, as though he's deflecting a zombie assault, or defending our turf from a member of the Jehovah Squad that roams the neighborhood.

Ignoring the impulse to duck behind the couch, instead, I attempt to meld, unnoticed, into the refrigerator door. Then I hear a brief tap on the glass.

Approaching the front door, I can see through near the bottom where Binks has savaged the venetians, but I can't make out any movement. Crouching closer, I see it.

On the blacktop, just outside our door, someone has drawn a chalk heart. Inside it, speckled with condensation from the day's heat, is a container of Marini's Lemon Ice. Balanced atop it are two paper-wrapped spoons.

Taking Binks by the collar, I herd him into the bathroom. Kicking Cinnamon Girl through the crack, I slam the door, sealing them in.

Returning to the front door, I rest my fingers on the metal bar and peer through the crack in the blinds at the offering outside. As I watch, a small disk of moisture spreads. It's joined by a pair of bare feet, one on either side of the ice cup. I'd recognize those bronzy calves anywhere, even without the large, Aidan-shaped shadow.

The blacktop must be scorching. I can tell not just because of the melt spot from the Italian ice, but because of the way those handsome feet sizzle-dance, seeking shade.

My heart melting as fast as the Marini's, I swing open the

door, catching Aidan off guard, almost causing him to fall into the apartment. Gaining balance, he grins and goes down on one knee to retrieve the lemon ice. Eyes downcast, penitent, he steps inside.

Before I can say anything, Aidan puts one finger to my lips. Peeling back the cup lid, scraping a spoonful, he deposits a scoop of sugar-tart chill on my tongue. Then he presses his lips to mine.

My eyes close. I'm savoring the surprise, when he steps back and says, "Oh! Are you up to this? From the sound of your message, you've practically been on your deathbed."

"I'm better."

He trains those berry eyes on me with sincerest concern, kissing me again. Something in the back of my throat dislodges. It's like when Prince Charming kissed Snow White, loosening the apple, bringing her back. Awake. Only for me, Aidan's kiss looses a torrent.

I can barely speak, and I know I'm freaking him out, mostly because he says, "Okay, Teddi. You're freaking me out here. Do you . . . do you want me to go?"

Beating back panic, I shake my head and manage a loud "No!" that has Binks protesting from behind the bathroom door.

Arms encircling me, Aidan pulls me close. Resting his chin on top of my head, he says, "You're safe, Teddi. I'm here. You're safe."

When no other words will come, I blurt, "Corey is dead!

My best friend, Corey. Eli. He ki-killed him. Corey's dead. Oh God, he's really dead."

Several incoherent minutes later, my rant finally ceases. We're on the couch. Aidan must have led me here or—God, not again—carried me. I'm astonished to see Binks occupying a cushion, one furry elbow resting on Aidan's knee.

Mopping my forehead with a damp cloth, Aidan says, "Hope you don't mind me letting the little guy out. I was afraid he'd hurt himself trying to bite his way through the door."

Voice quivery, I say, "Binks likes you? Wow, he hardly likes anybody."

Aidan replies, "Nope. Binks likes these," as he pulls a fortune cookie from the pocket of his cargo shorts. Cracking the cookie open, he puts the fortune aside and says, "Watch this." Then, standing, he holds the cookie aloft and asks, "Do you like cookies?"

Going bipedal, Binks launches into this viral video–worthy dance. Laughing, Aidan palms him a cookie. The little mooch runs to his bed and lies down, crunching.

Joining me on the couch, Aidan says, "So."

I echo, "So."

Clearing his throat, he grasps for the right word. Then, wearing this lightbulb–moment expression, he raises his hand as he says, "Fortune time!"

I stop him. Taking the slim paper strip from his hand, I squash it into a tiny ball, and cross to the sink. Opening the cabinet, I drop the fortune in the trash.

Aidan says, "You're pretty brave, tossing destiny aside."

To myself more than to him, I answer, "I wish I could."

Joining me at the counter, Aidan puts his hands on my shoulders and repeats, "So." Then he kisses my lips once, briefly. Serious again, he cups my face with his palms before saying, "Teddi, I'm really worried about you. You were . . . um . . . out of it for quite a while there."

"Out of it?"

"Yeah, it's almost four o'clock. I've been here for over an hour, just . . ."—he blushes—"holding you and . . . listening to you talk and, sort of . . . moan. And of course, cry." He's close to crying as he says, "So, are you? Okay?"

I take a moment before answering, "Not really."

"Teddi, who's Eli? And what did you mean he 'bashed Corey'?"

"We'd better sit down again."

We cross to the couch, and Binks appears at Aidan's side, pressing an insistent chin against his knee. When Aid says, "Sorry, bud. No more," Binks mopes his way upstairs. Watching him go, Aidan says, "Guess he figures we could use some privacy." When he looks back at me, his smile disappears.

Studying Aidan's face, I'm unable to speak. Of course, I don't want to burden him, but it's more than that. It's about not wanting to voice Corey's death into truth. The more people who hear it, the more real it will become.

"Tell me, Teddi. Trust me."

And I do. I start by apologizing. "I'm just warning you. Some of the details are soggy, because I was real little when it happened. I can't quite remember it all. And parts of it are going to sound impossible"—I look away—"even crazy to you. But I need you to believe, Aidan. If I'm going to tell, I need you to believe."

"I promise."

I expect his face to go hard when I say, "Even if Pool Girl is part of it?"

And his expression does change. His eyes fill, and those beautiful lips quiver.

I ask, "What is it?"

Wiping his eyes, Aidan says, "I was a shit, Teddi. A total prick when you kept insisting you saw her. I'm sorry. You needed me then, too, and I blew it."

Pressing his hand to my heart, I say, "That's done now. And I learned some things about her these past few days."

He can't help looking nervous as he asks, "So you've seen her again?"

In the interest of putting it all out there, I reply, "Aidan, I am her."

"Wait, what?" His look of confusion would be comical in any other context.

Picturing my toes slipping from the high board, I say, "It seems she was me at seven. That's when the bad thing happened, when my friend was killed. Somehow, a part of me got sort of stuck there."

"But that's—" He stops himself.

"Impossible? Yes, it is. But it happened. I'm not sure whether my visions of her were for real. If she was actually here. Or if they were some kind of . . . visible ripples of memory. Either way, she—I—needed to show me. To lead me back to Corey. Back to truth."

For the next forty minutes, Aidan barely says a word beyond "whoa" or "shit" as I tell my story. At several points, especially when I describe the pond, I'm unable to continue. Aidan calms my quaking with kisses, his soothing voice.

When I talk about Corey's murder, I'm all eerie calm, focused on my upturned palms. As I finish, our eyes meet. Aidan's face is slopped with tears, his eyes puffy.

In that moment, I realize I'm ready. Pressing against him, I kiss his neck. Then, holding his gaze, I say, "I love you, Aidan Robert Graham. I love you."

He says, "I love you, too, Teddi Middle-Name-Unknown Alder. And if I thought you were amazing before, I'm more convinced now. I can't believe what you went through and . . ." He breaks down again. Catching his breath, he says, "Poor Corey . . . and his family." Stroking my cheek, he says, "We've got to tell someone."

Smile overwhelmed by shaking, I say, "We?"

Aidan says, "I'll go with you, Teddi, to the police, wherever." Pulling me close, he continues, "I've screwed up all along the way with you, but that's over. You can count on me from now on." Then, his brow creasing, he breaks our embrace and sighs.

"What's wrong?"

"You probably don't want to talk about this right now, and after what you just told me . . ."

"What, Aidan?"

"Willa, the kiss."

"Oh, God. We really don't have to—"

"Yeah, Teddi. We do. I need to apologize for real."

"You already did, Aid."

"Not face to face."

"Your text and your message were really sweet."

"That's not enough. If we're going to make this work, I've got to be totally honest. I need to warn you."

"Warn me?"

"I already told you about the anger stuff, and well," he looks embarrassed, "I've sort of gone out of my way to demonstrate it, haven't I?"

"Aidan, nobody's perfect. I, for example, am lactose intolerant and prone toward sarcasm."

"Please don't joke. I . . . I need to say this. I do this thing, Teddi. I can't tell you why, but I do. When a relationship is going well, I just can't seem to keep from wrecking it. I ruin things. And I don't want to anymore. I don't want to ruin us."

"Well. Then don't."

He pauses, searching. Finally, he says, "Good advice."

We kiss again and, though I try hard not to imagine Corey alongside us on the couch, I can't help sensing him there. Smashed skull resting against the back cushion, he swings his sneakered feet.

29

B elow the clip-art megaphone, the flyer screams YOU'RE INVITED! in ginormous cursive. Enthusiasm continues with JOIN A HARDWORKING CREATIVE GROUP OF SUMMERTEENS WRITERS FOR THIS SPECIAL READING OF THEIR WORK! All the pertinent details follow.

WHEN: FRIDAY, JULY 26, 6:30–8:30 P.M.

WHERE: L718, THE LIBRARY'S SPECIAL EVENTS ROOM

In bold italics, it promises:

FRESH FICTION! GREAT CONVERSATION! REFRESH-MENTS! FREE! FREE! FREE!

Willa says, "So, what's the admission fee?"

Standing between her and Aidan in front of JJ's Town Happenings board, I manage a laugh. It's my first outing, following three straight days of visits from Aidan, and Willa and Nic. They even came to see me together yesterday.

The kiss thing has totally blown over, and we're seemingly back to status quo, Willa faux-flirting with Aid, Nic feigning outrage. They've made no mention of Nic's expulsion from the play, and I don't intend to bring it up. I'm content saving that drama for another day.

I have no expectation of life ever being quite normal again. Still, when I'm with them, I feel a bit less like I'm being squeezed to death and digested by some giant boa constrictor of grief.

Willa's been her best possible self where Corey's concerned, totally fierce and supportive since I told my story. It was hard getting through it, and even though she knows my humor better than anybody, she said I was horrible for ending with "So, Wills, it's official. You no longer have competition for the position of best friend."

It was a stab at lightening the moment, badly aimed. Might have been more successful if we weren't both sob-wracked. Willa just kept blowing her nose and repeating, "I wish I'd had a chance to know him."

I'm working hard to approximate a new ordinary, with limited success. When I try to be respectful of Corey, to own what happened as the worst sort of tragedy, I fear I'll blow into pieces.

And there's no chance I can re-forget it, much as I want to. So I'm hoping it's okay to approach it as I do most things, head-on, with a double shot of humor.

But people—and by people I mostly mean Brenda—just don't get it when I make some "inappropriate" remark. For instance, the other day, I said, "If it was me, I wouldn't be caught dead in a Gordy the Cereal Frog T-shirt."

Brenda just gawked as if I'd told her Binks and I had eloped. Then she said, "I'll never understand it, Teddi, how you can be so cold."

Of course, she's never exactly known how to take me. Never really known me at all, I guess. Yeah, I'm being a tad melodramatic, but I'm entitled. This whole discovery has sort of magnified all the ways Brenda's failed me as a parent. All the ways she continues to fail. I'd never say it to her, but I don't really need to. Her lockbox overflows with evidence.

In her defense, when I told her what I'd remembered, she managed to hold it together. She even asked if there was anything she could do. And she waited 'til I'd left the room to run to the fridge.

She also offered to take me to Massachusetts to meet Micah and his mom. If that's something I want. I haven't figured out how to tell her I'm horrified just imagining that reunion.

Aidan runs his thumb down the nape of my neck, bringing me back to JJ's, back to right now. "So, you're reading at this thing?"

I don't even need to scan the list of SUMMERTEENS writers because, as is often the case, Alder occupies the alphabetical top spot. I answer, "News to me."

I assume the flyer was printed before the world imploded. I've missed the last four workshop sessions; really doubt I have anything to offer. Plus, the prospect of seeing them all again literally makes me ill.

Each time I've recounted what happened at the pond—
including in a rambling e-mail to Eleanor yesterday—not my
best work; hope she resists her critique impulse—it's gotten a
little easier. And that's just wrong. I'm afraid if I have to tell it
to the workshop group, all those faces drinking in details, it'll
lose its power, become meaningless.

I know this sounds nuts, but the story is mine. Mine and
Corey's. That last moment together something we alone
shared.

Terrible, but solely ours.

The Precious Dreadful.

It's all I have left of him. And I'm afraid if I share it too
freely, it won't belong to us anymore. That would mean losing
him all over again.

Willa says, "Teddi, you need to do this. Don't you think
Corey would want you to read? Would want you to go on with
life?"

"That's very Hallmark of you, Wills, but Corey was a seven-
year-old boy. If it was a monster truck show, he might be into
it. But I doubt his ghost is all that invested in me making my
SUMMERTEENS open mic debut."

Aidan risks a laugh, shakes his head.

From behind us, I hear, "So do it for you."

It's Ed, looking awful earnest as he says, "It might help you
to jump back in, do something to take your mind off it." When I
raise an eyebrow, he adds, "Eleanor showed me your message."

Touching my shoulder, he asks, "How you holding up?"

The usual spark of tension leaps from Aidan to him, but then Aid smiles at me and says, "She'll get through it. She's amazing."

Ed and Willa say, "Agreed," one after another.

Kissing my forehead, Aidan says, "I'd better get back to the beans before Norah gets bent."

As he heads behind the counter, Willa and Ed reintroduce themselves—a lifetime's gone by since July 4th—and I go back to studying the flyer, considering whether they could be right about giving the reading a shot. I guess there are worse ways to spend my birthday. Yep, it's in two days, July 26. Some sweet sixteen.

"I'll do it."

They seem surprised at my decision—but pleased. Willa says, "You can count on me and Nic being right up front, T Bear. Wouldn't miss it!"

Ed adds, "That's great. Eleanor wants those seats filled. Of course, that means I'll need to set them up. Do you feel like coming by later to give me a hand?"

"Um, I guess, but remember, you have a girlfriend. And the big guy in the apron is the jealous type."

"I'll take my chances."

When Willa says, "Nope, this isn't uncomfortable in the least," Ed and I both laugh. It feels good—a sip of carbonation—before a guilt dart swoops to burst the bubble.

We text Nic, and he meets us at the library. Fist-bumping
Ed, he claims he's always been a "natural chair setter-upper."

Willa says, "More of a natural chair sitter-in-er," and Nic
does his patented sad walk.

Ed smirks, enjoying their back-and-forth. I'm not sure why
it matters to me that he gets along with my friends, but I savor
watching him watching them.

Standing in L718 feels right, like I belong here. And the
reading won't be such a big deal. Might even be nice to have
some plan for my sixteenth birthday beyond sequestering
myself in blankets and memory, sobbing on my bed.

But two nights later, peering from the podium at the eager
faces of friends and family—my own and those here for the rest
of the group—reality is different. Awash somehow, I'm nause-
ated. Part of it's natural, nerves. I've never been cool as center
of attention. And the assortment filling the seats doesn't help.

It was weird seeing everyone from group, knowing they
knew about Corey. I asked Ed to fill them in on the details, to
save me having to tell it all over again. I also said to be sure to
let them know I'm fine, to please act normal around me.

Ken's idea of acting normal was to pump my hand and say,
"Welcome back, Teddi. I'm very sorry for your loss. It sounds
cataclysmic."

Todd surprised me with a plastic Boba Fett figure, no
explanation. I pocketed it with a heartfelt "Wow."

Jeanine hung back with the other three kids, while Petra gave me an extended hug. Handing me a card everyone had signed, she said, "Teddi, I know a little what you're going through. I lost somebody special, too. I mean, not this way, but . . . every death is its own kind of bottomless pit, you know?" Looking embarrassed, she continued, "If you ever need to talk—"

"Thanks."

Marisol warned me her tia Adaluz was eager to see me. That brought a pang, this slice of anger. Did she want to gloat about the fact that she was right, that it wasn't a girl, but a dead boy with a message? But when she arrived, she just took me in her arms. Eyes drowned in tears, she said, "Oh, Teddi. *Mi corazón esta roto.*"

Trying not to cry, I whispered in her ear, "Mine too, Tia Luz, mine too."

Eleanor let her formal demeanor slip when she saw me. Pooh-poohing my initial resistance, she, too, draped me in an embrace.

Upon release, I hesitated, wishing I could stay there, enveloped in her serene essence, forever. As she broke the connection, straightening my shoulders, she said, "Don't move."

After a brief expedition into her tapestry bag, she returned, holding out a small object, tissue-wrapped. Opening it, I discovered an intricately carved pin, a Celtic cross.

As she fastened it to my collar, she said, "It's alder wood, seemed appropriate. You truly do have the strength of an alder. Use it well."

I sort of stammered, "Um, I . . . I'll try."

She looked away then, scanning the room. Dabbing the corner of her eye with her pinky, she said, "Your telling—even in e-mail form—was masterful, Teddi. You have a writer's soul. Nurture it." Then, extending her hand past me, she asked, "And whom have you brought to our little fete?"

"Mom, this is Eleanor, our teacher. Eleanor, this is my mom, Brenda."

They did the whole "pleased to meet you" thing, and then Eleanor stepped away to greet other arrivals.

I always have mixed emotions about public appearances with Brenda. Well, not so much mixed, I guess. Purely negative. It's just nerve-racking, the possibility she'll show up sloshed. But at least tonight, she's behaved. She opted for the mock colada at my birthday dinner. I insisted Nic and Willa come with, to sort of deflect Brenda's attention.

They definitely deflected attention here at the reading. Nic left during the break, after they got in one of their fights. So I have a grand total of two in attendance—three, if I count Ed, which I sort of do—as I take my place at the lectern.

Aidan's a no-show.

I'm not disappointed, though. I'm trying not to dwell on his warning: "I ruin things."

This is different. He texted this afternoon to say he couldn't make dinner, had to cover last-minute at JJ's. Honestly, I was relieved he'd be spared Brenda's tableside manner. But he promised he'd make it to the library in time to hear me read.

Seriously, though, he's not missing much.

Actually, the first few readers were solid. After Eleanor's official welcome and intro, Marisol started the evening with the piece she wrote about Adaluz. It was touching, her cousin and Tia Luz all misty, holding hands as Mari read.

Acting as MC, Eleanor presented Todd next. He read a story about a futuristic society where sweat's the sole form of currency, but ironically, average worldwide temps have plummeted to twelve degrees, so sweat is in short supply. Odd, but interesting, similar to the writer himself.

And Eleanor must be some kind of miracle worker, because Ken's condor piece turned out sort of brilliant. She got him to work past strict, scientific description to create what she called "a unique melding of prose, poetry, reportage, and surrealist observation."

I'm not quite sure what that meant, but I don't think I'll ever forget the line "Fidelity swathed in black, the master bird delivers life through death, rancid carrion his bride prize."

Though his story elicited only a smatter of polite applause, Ken blazed when Eleanor commented, "So unique, Kenneth. Bravo!" She followed that with "Well, I'm sure you're all ready for refreshments, so let's take a fifteen-minute intermission."

I'm guessing the audience had "rancid carrion" on the brain because nobody exactly dashed to the snack table.

Now it's my turn. Ed stands alongside my chair as Eleanor

returns to the pedestal to announce me. Hand on my shoulder, he says, "You got this?"

I nod, even as my stomach begins crawling up my esophagus.

Eleanor says, "As an intensive, SUMMERTEENS demands much of its participants. The writing process can be challenging, leaving us bruised, but if we take our craft seriously, stay attuned to our muse, we can reap great benefits of mind and spirit."

I glance at Ed, with an *Any clue what she's talking about?* expression. He returns a *No freakin' idea* smirk.

She continues. "Our next writer has shown enormous gifts of creativity and natural ability." Brenda squeezes my hand as Eleanor finishes. "However, I am most impressed that she lives up to her name, showing us all what it means to possess the strength of trees. Please give a special birthday welcome to our next reader, Teddi Alder."

I can't help flashing back to one of those long-ago Alateen meetings, especially when the audience responds in unison, "Happy birthday, Teddi."

Stepping to the podium, I mutter a self-conscious "Thanks." Then, summoning power from the two seven-year-olds I imagine crouched by the tag-sale toys in the corner, I open my journal and slide out the pages I typed this morning.

Inhaling a heavy breath, I begin.

"There once was a pair unlike any before or since, a lonely giraffe and her one true friend, a small, brown frog."

30

Joy—I can't help it, I do prefer that to *Ed*—and I wander away from the crit clique. No one seems to care, or even notice our slow retreat across the parking lot. Petra's preoccupied, sharing a pink cotton cloud with Ken and Todd. Jeanine bailed on her, saying she needed to get home. And Willa made an excuse; I think she just felt out of place, celebrating my sixteenth with my new writing group friends.

Brenda took the night bus to the college right after the reading. Standing at the stop, she held my hands, told me for at least the hundredth time how proud she is. I felt strangely parental, as if I was sending her off to camp, when she boarded.

The scent of popcorn mingles with zoo straw and that unmistakable goaty smell. Calliope tunes blare from the temporary midway. Somehow, even though this wonderland sprang up overnight, Pelletier Bros.' Pet Zoo Extreme has the appearance of long-term dilapidation. The rides look ultra-rickety, and the ponies circling the fenced-in ring remind me of minimum wage workers, longing to punch out and hit the bar.

Joy smiles, his cheeks lit with what seems to be heightened anticipation. Or else it's the fluorescent beams of the Ferris wheel. "So, what do you think?"

Shrugging, I answer, "I haven't come here since I was little."

"Your folks bring you?"

"My mom. And Peter. We brought Corey once, too."

It's a happy memory, one I haven't thought of in far too long—the two of us sharing a camel ride—but it feels sharp against my ribs, as if it might tear a hole there. The ache must show on my face, because when I finally look back at him, Joy's wearing this super concerned expression. And holding out a dime.

"What's that for?"

"Your thoughts. I'm betting they're worth more than a penny."

"Cute."

"So?"

"Nothing, guess I was feeling sort of nostalgic. But for something that never really was."

"Ah, the most powerful brand of nostalgia." He takes my hand, which is strange, since he knows about Aidan and me. I meet his serious hazel gaze.

"Um . . . what's with the hand-holding?"

He seems to contemplate letting go; instead, he squeezes gently. "Is there some rule against friends holding hands?"

"Are we?"

"Are we what, Teddi?"

"Friends."

"What do you think?"

"That you're this sweet, sort of odd dude I've gotten way too comfortable flirting with." He drops my hand, and I immediately regret the *odd dude* remark. "But we both know nothing can happen between us, Ed. I—"

Shushing me, he leans closer. Fingers tracing the curve of my cheek, he says, "Why not?"

"Well, for one thing, I'm in a relationship."

"Really? Now *that's* odd." He stops, stares above my head at the flashing Ferris bulbs.

"Odd how?"

"Oh, I don't know, I just think it's a little sad you calling it a relationship. Must be sort of a challenge having one with an empty chair."

"Wow, Ed, why don't you tell me how you really feel about Aidan?"

"Sorry, I know it's none of my business."

"No, it's really not."

"I just can't believe he didn't show up, Teddi. He had to know what tonight meant to you."

"I told you, he had to work."

"Right. Well, JJ's closes at, what, seven o'clock? It's past nine now."

"God! Would you just leave it alone? You want me to admit

I feel shitty about him not showing up? That I'm wondering where he is, why he hasn't even bothered to text me. On my freaking birthday! Fine! I feel shitty! Happy?"

"It's . . . of course it doesn't make me happy." He fumbles in his pocket, looks away. Then he says, "Look, Teddi, you're going to think I'm a total prick for telling you this, but . . . I saw Aidan the other night at the library."

"I know. He told me he talked to you after class, that you said I hadn't been there. Ed, I really think I should—"

"No, I mean, before he came looking for you. He was in the park, with these two guys and . . . some girl. They looked pretty, um,"—he pinkens—"'skeezy' is the word I'm looking for."

"Look, I don't monitor all his social interactions, okay? And apparently Glade doesn't have to give you permission to talk to another girl."

At the mention of Glade's name, he backs off for a moment; then he says, "Aidan wasn't just talking, Teddi. That would've been difficult with this girl's tongue wrapped around his tonsil."

I try not to react as if someone's dumped a steaming bucket of heartbreak over my head. Taking a deep breath, I say, "So you expect me to cry or some shit like that."

"If you need to, it's okay with me."

"Well, aren't you the perfect confidant."

Cheeks darkening, Ed swipes his forehead with the back of his hand. Then, attempting a comforting smile, he says, "I wouldn't go that far."

"No? Well, you sure seem awfully interested in my relation-ship status. Why is that, Ed?"

"I just don't want to see you get hurt."

I avoid looking him in the eye as I say, "I wish you'd stop saying that! What makes you think I can't take care of myself? Or that Aidan has any plans to hurt me? I told you we've been having some problems. So he was hanging out with another girl while we were broken up. So what!"

He takes this scuba-worthy gulp of air. I can tell he's wind-ing up for something big. "Teddi, there are things you don't know about him."

"Wait. And you do? How do you *know things* about him, Ed? I'm the one who introduced you!"

"That's not exactly . . ." He fumbles; then, fingers tracing his wrist tattoo, he says, "All I can say is I knew him a while back. We were friends."

"You were *friends?*"

"Yes. And he was into some stuff you wouldn't like."

"What kind of stuff?"

"I'd rather not say."

"All right, now you're pissing me off. You can't half say something and then get all freaking cryptic. It's not fair." I grab his wrist. "What are you talking about?"

Pulling free, he refuses to meet my eyes. Worrying the hem of his T-shirt, he twists it into a knot at his waist. Finally, his voice a rush of air, he says, "We used to get high together,

Aidan and me, this whole group of friends. We'd meet in the park mostly. By the pond."

I can barely process what he's saying, but somewhere in the back of my head, gears start to click into place. How could I have overlooked the clues? The way Aidan acted that night in the store, and at play rehearsal. His anger when I asked about the park. And Willa's worries about Nic and Aidan. What was it she said? He's different, *since he's been hanging with Aidan*. It can't be true.

"Why are you telling me this?"

"It was a long time ago. I gave all that up, didn't recognize the person I was turning into. January fourth I'll be two years clean."

"Congratulations." I turn to go.

He stops me with "But Aidan—"

"What?" It comes out a little girl whisper.

"Maybe this isn't fair. Maybe he's changed, too. Maybe he really does care about you. But the Aidan I knew only cared about getting high."

"He told me he loves me."

"Teddi, wait. You're upset. I'm sorry; I didn't mean to upset you. I just . . . I couldn't keep his secret anymore."

"Why not?"

He pauses, just briefly. Then, in a library-style hush, he answers, "Because I have feelings for you, Teddi."

"Really? And what about your girlfriend?"

Looking hopeful, he says, "It hasn't been right with Glade

for a while. Since way before I met you. But I sort of figured it would run its course. That we'd end things when I left for school this fall."

"Very practical."

Seeking momentary distraction, I look past him, drawn by squeals. Following the revolutions of the Rotor, I feel my stomach drop as if I'm spinning along with the screaming occupants. I refuse to give in to queasiness; instead, I allow anger to take over. Without looking back at him, I say, "Now I get it. You figure since your relationship is in the shit, you'll bust up Aidan and me. Thanks a lot!"

"It's not like that, Teddi."

"Well, it sure seems like that. Why else would you be trying to turn me against him?"

Ed snorts, a *You're ridiculous* laugh that seriously makes me want to hit him. "I'm hardly trying to turn you against him!"

"What exactly are you trying to do?"

He tilts his head upward, seems to study the night sky. For a second, I think he's going to bless himself. When he looks back at me, there's no mistaking the sincerity on his face. He says, "I'm trying to save you from getting hurt, Teddi. Because," he shrugs, "because I care about you."

As the Rotor screeches to a stop, he continues, "Anyway, for what it's worth, it's officially over between Glade and me. I broke up with her yesterday, Teddi. Told her I'd developed feelings for someone else."

I look down, studying the daisy pendant. "Does she know it's me?"

He takes my chin in his hands.

I wait for him to continue, but he only stands in front of me, for what stretches beyond reasonable awkward pause length. Just as I'm beginning to think nervous thoughts—of cleavage-fumbled corsage applications, Jumbotron marriage proposals—Ed clears his throat. Thankfully, he does not produce a jewelry box from his back pocket.

"I need to show you something."

"I really think we should get back to the group."

"Please, Teddi. Give me a chance. I know you'll want to see this."

I wait just long enough for him to put his arm around me. Bringing his other hand up, whispering, "It's a surprise," he gently covers my eyes.

I tense; a mix of fear and expectation makes me tremble, and I touch his hand with mine. As I move to uncover my eyes, he says, "Trust me."

"I do."

Leading me across the parking lot, Ed guides me carefully around cables snaking the ground. The carousel music fades slightly, and I sense the air thickening, closing in, as he leads me beneath the awning of the large, blue-and-yellow-striped tent.

The animal smell is dense in here; somehow, it feels even more humid than outside. I hear the bleat of goats, children giggling. Ed places my right hand atop the enclosure fence and says, "Wait right here. And no peeking. I'll be two seconds."

He steps away, and I hear the clunk of coins, the grind and spill as he cranks the feed dispenser handle.

"Ready?" Lifting my hand from the fence, he upturns my palm, depositing a fistful of grain pellets.

I hear the quick rustle of hooved feet, and Ed says, "Whoa! Watch out, Teddi! It's a stampede!" Laughing, he turns me quickly, raising my cupped hand shoulder-high.

"Can I look now?"

"Not yet. Don't move."

Supporting my right hand with his own, he leans into me, places his left against the small of my back. Again, I feel a shiver of excitement as Ed, murmuring, "Closer, closer," stretches my arm skyward.

"Ed—"

"Shhh." He lets go of my hand, just as I feel it, soft pressure on my palm, at once damp and somehow rough.

I fight my reflex to pull away as Ed says, "Teddi, meet Teddy."

The moment they open, my eyes spill tears. Locked on me, enormous brown orbs peer from above, as Teddy the Giraffe continues to probe my palm with his sinewy tongue. Once my hand is empty of grain, he lowers his head slightly, resting his chin for the briefest moment on my open palm.

An electric warmth blazes through me, this moment filling me completely, washing away the discoveries of these last weeks, the news about Aidan. For these few seconds, transfixed in the gaze of a giraffe, I am utterly happy. At peace.

Lightly brushing his velvet nose, I study the creature's paisley hide, his immense neck arching in a tawny, spattered rainbow. Teddy grants my palm a last nuzzle. Then, lashes fluttering, his head lifts slowly upward, bristled horns just kissing the fabric ceiling.

"That was unbelievable."

Leaning forward, Ed whispers in my ear, "*You* are unbelievable, Teddi Alder. Truly unbelievable."

Before I even realize it, I've stretched onto tiptoe. Twining my fingers behind Ed's head, I pull his lips to mine. We linger mid-kiss, a chorus of pygmy goats serenading us.

Opening my eyes, I'm met with a Joy-drunk grin. "So, I guess you've reconsidered."

All I can say in return is "That was nice."

"But?"

Pulling away, I reply, "But I told you. I'm with Aidan."

"And you didn't feel anything just now?"

"I didn't say that."

"Then, don't you owe it to yourself, to me—in a weird way even to Aidan—to see what's there?"

"NO!" I bang my fist against the enclosure fence, scattering goats.

"Teddi, can't you see—"

"Can't *you* see? It's not about what I feel for you right this minute. Or what I feel for Aidan. Or even what I feel about me right now. My brain, my heart, they're all scrambled, in an all-out tug of war or something, and I don't even know which side to root for. My head tells me you're the better choice. And if what you said about him is true—" His eyes glisten, hopeful. "But Aidan has a stranglehold on my heart."

Looking fresh-slapped, Ed says, "Well, we both know heart trumps head."

As usual, I can't shut up, can't leave things alone. Especially with him looking so hurt. "It's not just up here." I tap my temple. "I do have feelings for you, Ed. There, I've said it."

He smiles.

"But that doesn't mean we have a future. I'm in this pretty deep with Aidan, and I owe it to him—to us—to work on it. I believe he loves me, despite his chronic bullshit behavior. And if what you told me is true, then he really needs me. I can't just throw that away for a what-if with you. Don't you get that?"

He hesitates, some argument on his tongue. Then he says, "Yeah, unfortunately, I do."

"I'm sorry."

"Are you?"

"Yes. I really like you, Joy." He bristles at the name. "Sorry, Ed."

"No, it's okay. You call me Joy. It can be our thing."

"I'm not so sure it's a good idea for us to have a thing."

"Well, I'm afraid it's too late."

Briefly, something clouds his eyes, and he reaches for me.

"Ed," I punctuate the name with a single step backward, "I really need to go. Aidan could be at my place right now, wondering where I am. I've got to see him, to try and make sense of all this."

"Promise me something, Teddi."

"What?" I anticipate some sort of demand.

"Promise me you'll decide what's best for you."

"What do you mean?"

"Not for me. Not for Aidan. Think only of you."

31

Binks's hackles stand on end. A deep rumble escaping him, he strains at his leash. The yelling from the woods wedges beneath my skin, too. I feel this impulse to race for the house, 'til I realize laughter's mingled with the hollering.

"Relax, boy. It's just some party at Stone Loop."

Binks sinks into a defensive hunker. I squat, too; on one knee, I steady for whatever's about to happen.

Tugging, he slips his collar, darts toward chaos, into the woods.

As someone shouts "SKUNK!" the smell assaults me.

It's followed by a crashing through the brush. A jumble of shadows in shorts and tanks. Bouncing flashlight beams. The smoke haze is drenched with skunk, the voices an equal mix of laughter and swear words. Some girl stumbles onto the open hill. Falling drunk—or high—she can't stop cackling.

When she strays into my flashlight beam, I recognize Jeanine. I'm about to raise my hand, to call, when she turns back to the woods. Folding at the waist, she sprays puke into the grass, lands on her knees. A guy appears. Laughing, he weaves along the tree line, collapses beside her.

"Shit, it's Nic."

Rolling onto his back, he howls at the cloud-rimmed moon, shaking with laughter. Jeanine laughs, too, for just a moment, before retching again.

Gulping breath, Nic sits up. Grabbing Jeanine, he shakes her. Then, looking around, he says, "Where is he? Aidan. Have you seen him?"

Jeanine just stares at him, mumbles "Skunk," and falls backward.

I note my shifting reaction to the mention of Aidan's name. Where it used to cause a ratcheting up of my temperature, lately those five letters have brought nothing but undue weight, a hippo roosting on my heart.

But this is different.

Something about Nic's tone—and the absence of skunk-scented heartthrob busting into view—has me in instant panic.

Ditching Binks's leash, I sprint toward the path, flashlight beam ricocheting. Without meaning to, I scream, "Aidan!"

Jeanine and Nic, epically wasted, struggle to sit up, to focus on me.

From the woods, eerie stillness, followed by a low wheeze, from farther in. I know it's him. Tromping through thorn and vine, I focus on breathing evenly.

Inhaling deeply, I catch this fruity chemical scent in the air. Is it weed? Meth? Brenda would know. Fear morphs into fury as it becomes clear exactly how Prince Charming's been spending his nights.

I'm about to turn back, begin a search for Binks, when I hear a garbled moan from my left.

Muttering "Asshole," I take another cleansing breath, hoping to exhale anger. But when I finally find Aidan, faceup in matted fern, I'm pissed.

Stomping toward him, teeth clenched, I shine the beam directly into his face. Puzzled by his lack of reaction, I utter only "Ai—" before noticing the tremoring in his hands and feet, the way his head jerks deeper into the pillow of fern.

Falling to my knees beside him, I clamp my lids shut, just briefly, trying to erase the image burned behind them: *Corey mouths my name. His eyes stare up at me, flat, unseeing.*

Like Aidan's are now.

Leaning close, pressing my cheek to his lips, I confirm the worst. My boyfriend has stopped breathing.

My brain lurches backward to freshman CPR class. Staring down at my dying boyfriend, I attempt to detach, pretend it's just the rubbery practice dummy on the ground. Positioning the flashlight in the grass, I reach for him.

Hands trembling, I turn Aidan's head to the side and brush my fingers across his lips. I tremble, caught in the irony that a few weeks ago, these lips, this guy, seemed unreachable.

Focusing, I sweep his mouth for obstructions. As my index finger brushes Aidan's tongue, he retches violently, a good sign.

Then, his body goes rigid.

Slapping his cheek, I call his name, starting low, then in a frantic chant that threatens to overtake me.

"Aidan. Aidan-Aid-AID-AIDAN!"

His body hitches, and I'm forced to pull back, protect myself as stiff arms beat the air. Finally, he stills, lying flat in the grass, peaceful. But I'm granted only the briefest relief.

I whisper, "Aid," and his gaze fixes on me for the shortest second. His panicked eyes question. Then, as if he's swimming deep in some murky swamp, those blueberry eyes dull, stare past me—flat, black marbles—before rolling up into his head.

He convulses again.

Digging my nails into his bare shoulders, I shout his name. When he doesn't respond, I stand. Facing the open grass, praying Nic or Jeanine will run to our rescue, I scream, "Someone help me!"

Silence.

Fumbling my phone from my pocket, I punch in 911. The screen pulses with a feeble greenish hue, as a message appears.

Low battery.

Shrieking, I drop the phone. It's instantly sucked into Aidan's bed of fern and vine.

Mind going blank, I waste precious seconds, as the world dims around me.

Then I hear my name.

Landing beside Aidan, I stare at his mouth, but his lips are frozen. Even in the weak flashlight beam, I can see they've begun to tinge blue.

Teddi.

The voice throbs. It's inside my head. Doubling on itself, it repeats, escalates.

Teddi, listen.

It's Corey. And Marisol's tia Luz. They speak as one, urging me on.

You can save him, Teddi.

You know what to do.

Leaning over Aidan, gaping at him, I'm struck by how peaceful he looks, how unlike Corey.

The voices silence as a new image blooms inside my head. I see it with the laser pulse of memory.

Corey's head is cracked, blood and thicker stuff sticky on my hands. He tries to talk, a low burble all that escapes his lips. Rocking forward, I scream—

"NO!"

Hands over my ears, I block the memory. Summoning the voices, I focus on their soothing tone. Soft. Comforting.

You can do it.

Believe, Teddi.

We will help you.

Breath slowing, I'm filled with an eerie calm.

As if from above, I watch as a pair of hands move forward. Mine but not my own, they're smaller, darker: Corey's. They brush the spittle from Aidan's face, gently tilting his head back to open his airway.

I sense stubby fingers—Tia's? Lacing behind my neck, they draw me closer to Aidan's ashen face.

Swallowing panic, I cross myself. Then, throwing my head back, I drink in humid midnight air. Clamping my mouth to his, I exhale forcefully. As I do, a familiar tang registers on my tongue.

For the briefest moment, carried on my breath, I taste it, a faint pucker of sour apple candy, Corey's favorite.

As I blow frantic life into my boyfriend's lungs, I force my mind blank. Then, from deep within this black hole of terror, I hear them, actual voices.

"This way, in the woods."

"Hit the ferns with your high beams!"

Pausing, I look over my shoulder, see a pair of cops hustling up the bank. Their cruiser's parked on the grass behind the pool house, headlights blazing toward us. One officer stops to check on Nic and Jeanine. The other parts the ferns that mask Aidan and me.

I barely register his yell to his partner, "Oh shit, we've got a 10-54," before—vision dimming—I slump next to Aidan in the tall grass.

32

The bench cups my spine. Running fingers over the bronze oval, I touch Corey's face, memorizing his sculpted features like Braille. Inspecting the writer's callous that graces my index finger, I trace his name. Then I lift focus to sky. Weak afternoon sun dusts the thinning alder canopy.

I whisper, "Corey, the leaves are rusting, dropping around me."

Same as when I was seven, I feel myself coming fully awake again in October. Mrs. Goulet's long gone. She retired when I was in middle school, moved away—New Hampshire, I think.

I still come here.

After they found him—dented, mud-sunk barrel, weighted with stones; lonesome little bones draped in T-shirt scraps (it was on the news; no need for me to tell it)—I vowed I would never come back to the pond.

But when they held the town meetings to determine whether it should be drained permanently, I knew I had to be there. To stand up for Corey. To beg them not to turn the pond into a spillover parking lot.

I like to imagine I made a difference with my plea for our place, for remembrance. That I had some impact.

It's got a name now: Boatwright Pond. Hence the memorial bench. It's a little hokey, but Corey would love the idea of his face overseeing the change of seasons, the bird rustle, the frog splash.

I'm here a lot—usually alone, when I need to talk with him. Life's quieter now. Mirror Teddi no longer offers advice. I sort of miss her. But sometimes, if I listen real close, I can hear Corey. He's outgrown his little boy rasp, sounds a bit like Micah.

We haven't kept in touch. It must be too painful for Micah and his mom. They probably can't help linking me with the story I told about Corey's last moments. I ended up having to repeat it countless times.

For so many people.

But parts of it I saved. Just for us. The details that couldn't have mattered to anyone else. Croc Hunter, my last "I love you." And when I need to think about that stuff—the way I do today—I come here.

Other times, I might bring Willa. She has whole conversations, about me, of course, with the bronze plaque. Claims it was Corey who convinced her to give Nic one last chance. They're mostly back to normal, equal parts exasperated and enamored with each other. She says she owes it to Corey, that she's so glad they've become friends after all this time.

And I've brought Aidan to visit a few times, too. Now that he's living back at home. It was tough, especially in the beginning when he was at Omni House, seeing him. But I went. I had to. Even though most of our early visits would begin and end with him asking me my name.

He never was good with names.

In the end, he didn't manage to ruin himself entirely. But he came pretty close. His mom is movie-parent strong. His dad moved out, moved on, but not her. She's full of hope. And somehow able to subsist on the "small strides" Aidan's making.

I continue to visit; at first, I told myself it was mostly for her sake. But truthfully, it's for my sake, and Aidan's, too. New Aidan? Old Aidan? Doesn't matter. A corner of my heart will always belong to him.

Ed, my Joy, doesn't seem to mind. He's actually been great. We've taken Aidan to the movies a couple times when Ed's been home from school. I know it might seem bizarre, double-dating with the new boyfriend and the ruined former boyfriend, but they did used to be friends. And I think, for Ed, Aidan's slow road back has been a reminder of how differently he could have turned out. If he hadn't chosen change.

One time I apologized, after a challenging mall trip—Aidan went missing in the comic book store—and Joy said, "Teddi, never apologize for love." Then, he apologized for "being cheesy, going all inspirational bookmark" on me.

Cheesy or not, I'd say the boy's a keeper.

Lifting the pendant from deep within my hoodie, I savor the way faint October rays seem to warm the pewter giraffe. It's the perfect replacement for that faded daisy. Joy gave it to me on our first official date, back in September. I haven't taken it off since.

Little Teddi's daisy has joined the other artifacts in Brenda's lockbox. Actually, it's my box now. But I hardly ever feel the need to look inside. It's on the shelf above the bed in my room at Tia Luz's.

Yep, I made the move mid-August. Brenda grudgingly agreed some time apart might be for the best. She's started attending weekly meetings, even talks about taking a class or two at the college during winter session. I'm cautious, but hopeful.

The transition to Adaluz's house has been smooth overall. It's nice having an actual, closeable bedroom door. Nicer living with someone I don't particularly want to shut out. We can talk to one another without the echoes of past arguments interrupting. And Marisol's down the hall, so it's almost like being part of a family.

Even Binks and Dixie have forged a fragile peace.

Fragile.

Ruined.

These past months have made me realize how fragile applies. To everything. But mostly to the connections we make with one another.

Ruined.

Unfortunately, life has lobbed me too many examples of that one.

But also: beautiful.

Like a giraffe.

Like someone we've lost is beautiful, after we polish the sad edges away.

I guess that's all life is, really, just a series of moments. Some ruined, some beautiful.

And I've learned one thing. There's no escaping any of them.

Like Eleanor says, "A writer's real calling is to notice."

I've taken her advice, have continued to "nurture my writer's spirit." I'm on the staff—Petra and I partnered as co-editors—of Jefferson High's newly revamped literary journal, *Echoes*.

So my snarky prediction came true. We got to be friends. Not that we're best buds or anything, but Petra is an awesome critique partner, always pushing me to go for it in my writing.

Example: I'd been having these dreams about a monster hunting me. All red eyes, jaws slobbering, dragging me to blackness. And Petra insisted, "Teddi, you've got to write every bit of it. Every damn detail. Be page-courageous."

I said, "Eleanor's definitely rubbed off on you," but Petra was right.

I wrote it all. Ended up with sheets and sheets. Poetry. Essays. These terrifying short stories, just a torrent of words.

I wish I could say writing chased the nightmares away. But they continued. Sometimes, even during school, I'd be jolted by a flash, Eli invading my thoughts.

Is he out there?

When will he come for me?

Pleasant.

I got my answer recently. Brenda called last week as I was doing homework, told me to check e-mail. Her voice was all watery, and I immediately knew she'd been drinking.

When I called her on it, she said, "No, but I came close. Honey, brace yourself."

She'd sent a link to this online news report about a factory fire in Taunton, Massachusetts, some abandoned mill turned crack house. Couldn't imagine what it had to do with me, until I saw the photos, captioned BODIES OF THREE MEN FOUND.

As I faced the mug shots on my laptop screen, the world stopped. There, in the center, my demon. A little older, the hair close-cropped, silvering. But the eyes, the nightmare eyes.

Blue ice.

Eli.

Trembling, I said, "Thank God, Corey. Eli's gone."

I watched the video, read the accompanying article two dozen times. There was no mention of Fawn. So I imagine she got away. That she's someplace beautiful. Or even ordinary, but free.

And when I write about her, I always write Fawn happy.

I can't give up on possible.

ACKNOWLEDGMENTS

Writing my debut—ignoring that "Who-do-you-think-you-are?" voice—took audacity. Starting book two, I feared *The Namesake* was a fluke. Sure, I'd written a novel. It got published. Readers eagerly anticipated my next. Gulp.... Fortunately, I have amazing support. Before book one was even published, my wife said, "Your *second* book will be a big success." She knows things, so clearly there would be a second. The challenge: What to write?

When I shared ideas with my friend, poet Edwina Trentham, she asked, "Is writing in a different genre wise, when readers are expecting your next YA?" That perceptive question sent me into a doubt skid; I commenced tinkering with two separate YA ideas that refused to cooperate. One night—July 7, 2013; it was a Sunday—I wrestled insomnia. At 5:20 a.m., a name, "Teddi Alder," lodged in my head. And Teddi had a voice. As I listened, she began her story. Sans bedside pen, I wrote five hundred words on my crappy cell, e-mailing bits to myself. In daylight, I recognized potential. Huzzah!

But as the story took shape, I worried. What qualified me to tell this girl's truth? Then, I figured, growing up with sisters, having incredible female friends, and being husband to Janet and father to Jillian, two brilliant and hilarious women, equipped me to write strong female characters. Doubt evaporated as trusted readers, strong women all, declared Teddi's voice authentic. To the following group of exceptional women, I offer love and gratitude.

It seems right to start by thanking Teddi for choosing me as her spokesman. Dearest Janet, Jillian, and Edwina, your bottomless well of faith sustains me. Cathy and Stacey Mendkya, there was never a more supportive sister or niece. Chelsea Clow, you're high on my strong women list. Bonnie Goulet, your enthusiasm was a sparkler lighting my way. YA hero, Stephanie Kuehn, your willingness to read for blurb consideration, your insight, and your praise are deeply appreciated. Terry Laslo, your belief from the very start was a gift. Patti Pallis, word-lover, your deeming my story "beautiful," fed my spirit. Kate Pelletier, your support—during caffeinated a.m. pep talks—was indispensable. Julia Petitfrere, your writing, which stuns me, is equaled by your extraordinary friendship. Andrea Petrario, during your darkest hours, you found grace to cheer me on. I thank you all, along with friends near and far (Elaine, Joe, Kim, Sister Angeline, lately gone home, and many others) who lent support, story unseen. Special thanks also goes to my two wonderful former students, Jennifer Melissa Gomez and Demesis Negron, for help with my very rusty Spanish.

ACKNOWLEDGMENTS

This book also benefited from my publishing family. To my fellow Uncommon YA authors, I treasure your camaraderie and generosity. Though my agent, Victoria Marini, and I parted midway through *The Precious Dreadful*, her feedback helped hone the work. My editor, Jacquelyn Mitchard, affirmed my faith in this story, and guided it with her experience. To everyone at Merit Press, especially Meredith O'Hayre, and Molly Hansen, for copyedit magic, and Stephanie Hannus, for *two* beautiful covers, thank you for your investment of time and resources in this book that began with my sleepless night. To my new publishing family at Simon Pulse, my heartfelt thanks! My initial conversation with Mara Anastas confirmed I'd made a most fortunate landing at Simon & Schuster. Major gratitude goes to the Pulse team—Mike Rosamilia, Chelsea Morgan, and Stacey Sakal—for wrangling my slippery compound words. And I truly appreciate editor Jessi Smith, who could not have been more welcoming—or insightful in suggesting final tweaks.

The Precious Dreadful is ultimately a story of friendship, struggle, and healing after significant loss, and I experienced such loss while writing it. Fire claimed my childhood home, informing my nostalgia for gone things. Most profoundly, my father's death, during my revision homestretch in July 2016, provided fresh perspective on the ways we're all connected—and how those bonds extend beyond this realm. Finally, thank *you*, reader, for joining me in Teddi's world. I hope her journey moves you.

ABOUT THE AUTHOR

Award-winning author and poet STEVEN PARLATO has had work published in *Freshwater*, *Peregrine*, and other journals. A college English professor (with a giraffe-filled office), illustrator, and actor, Steven has played roles including the Scarecrow, Macbeth, and the Munchie Mania Guy in a Friendly's training film. He lives in Connecticut with his wife, two teens, and a Binks-like cockapoo. Follow Steven online at stevenparlato.com and on Twitter @parlatowrites.